The night was misty, the river lightly covered with fog, the streets apparently floating. Bridget hurried along from Aldgate, glad to see a few people about, people out late. Reaching Commercial Road, she made good progress. But a soft sound intruded after a matter of seconds. Through the mist and by the light of a lamp she glimpsed movement on the other side of the street, the movement of someone walking ahead of her. A solitary man, vaguely seen, he disappeared into the darkness, and she stopped to let him get well in front of her, remembering the silent person who had brushed by her last night.

For the first time, Bridget almost wished she had the company of Constable Fred Billings, her new lodger, as she trod the darkened streets homeward.

THE GHOST OF WHITECHAPEL

Mary Jane Staples

CORGI BOOKS

THE GHOST OF WHITECHAPEL
A CORGI BOOK : 0 552 14548 3

First publication in Great Britain

PRINTING HISTORY
Corgi edition published 1997

Set in 11/12pt Linotype New Baskerville by
Phoenix Typesetting, Ilkley, West Yorkshire.

Corgi Books are published by Transworld Publishers Ltd,
61–63 Uxbridge Road, London W5 5SA,
in Australia by Transworld Publishers (Australia) Pty Ltd,
15–25 Helles Avenue, Moorebank, NSW 2170
and in New Zealand by Transworld Publishers (NZ) Ltd,
3 William Pickering Drive, Albany, Auckland.

Reproduced, printed and bound in Great Britain by
Cox & Wyman Ltd, Reading, Berks.

To Jill, Judith, Carol and
with happy memories of Howard

Prologue

It was in 1888 that Jack the Ripper stalked the dingy streets of Whitechapel, and left behind him not only the corpses of gruesomely murdered women, but also the mystery of his identity.

There had been many guesses, many theories and many conclusions, but none led to his capture and conviction. He remained a dark and elusive spectre, an intangible figure in the eyes of the police and a frightening one in the imagination of the people of Whitechapel.

By 1900, however, after twelve years had elapsed, there was a general assumption that he was as dead as his victims, that the devil had claimed him for his own.

The assumption, of course, could have been born of wishful thinking.

Chapter One

It was the last thing she was expecting, the one thing he had in mind. From behind, his left arm whipped around her and his hand clapped itself hard over her mouth. Her head was jerked back, and his right hand, wielding a razor-sharp knife, came swiftly round to effect the act of execution. The blade sliced her throat deeply from ear to ear. She fell forward, dying, her blood gushing.

Damn the scarlet river, he thought.

But at least he himself had escaped the flood and he knew what to do next.

'Murder! 'Orrible murder in Tooley Street!' So shouted London newsboys and street-corner newsvendors on both sides of the river. It was a day in November, 1900, the last November of the nineteenth century, and first thing that morning an unfortunate woman had been found with her throat gashed in Tooley Street, close to the south side of London Bridge. The early editions of evening newspapers carried reports of the shocking murder.

The day was misty, the mist an aftermath of the thick fog that had blanketed London last night.

Fog had its own ways of behaving. It could

creep, skulk, creep again and take its time to slowly smother living beings and inert buildings. It could also arrive with malicious speed and put traffic into hopeless confusion and people into doubt as to where a kerb was. A clear night could precede a thick yellow morning, and the thick yellow could make the whole day a torment for those who suffered from asthma or bronchitis. And to people of a nervous or imaginative disposition, the eerie pall of a night fog was apt to pervade London's darker alleys in a manner fearful and menacing, muffling the footsteps of warped creatures who dealt in all forms of villainy and deeds most foul.

Such a deed had been committed last night, and Scotland Yard was investigating. The dead woman's identity had been established immediately on discovery of her body. She was Maureen Flanagan, an Irishwoman of thirty, who worked in the calender room of Guy's Hospital laundry, where sheets and towels were dried and pressed. The woman who found her, just as the fog was lifting, knew her because she too worked in the laundry and was on her way there. The time was ten minutes to eight. The examining police surgeon diagnosed she had been dead for about ten hours, which meant the murder had been committed at approximately ten last night, when the fog had been at its densest. The police surgeon, however, pointed out that the woollen scarf wrapped around her neck had absorbed only a relatively small amount of blood, nothing like all she would have shed. It indicated that the murder could not have been committed at the spot where she was found. It was his opinion that she had been carried there

10

sometime after the monstrous deed had been done. The thick fog would have provided a very helpful cloak for the murderer.

Chief Inspector Charlie Dobbs was in charge of the investigation. He had a reputation for being a relentless tracker of criminals devious or blood-thirsty. His most recent success concerned the breaking of what had seemed a husband's perfect alibi in respect of the murder of his wife by poison. The Dalston police had hoped for his assistance in finding a different kind of murderer, a man who had battered a young woman to death late one night in Queensbridge Road. But because of Dobb's commitment to the former case, Scotland Yard sent another senior CID officer to investigate the Dalston crime. That investigation was still going on.

Despite being hardened by experience, Chief Inspector Dobbs was sick with disgust as he regarded the body of the murdered woman in Tooley Street. He could understand the reasons behind some crimes: he could never bring himself to rationalize about vicious murder. He addressed the police surgeon in respect of the conclusion made, that the victim had been dumped in Tooley Street after being murdered elsewhere, her coat thrown over her.

'Carried here, you believe?'

'Undoubtedly. Otherwise, the unfortunate woman would have been soaked in her own blood, Chief Inspector.'

'I can't argue with that,' said Dobbs. 'Not that he'd have risked a long haul.'

'Long haul?' said the medical man.

11

'Say from Soho and all the way over the bridge to Tooley Street, not even in last night's fog. Far too long for that kind of carrying job.'

'Why Soho?'

'You've seen her clothes?' said the Chief Inspector.

'Decent coat and hat, fairly stylish maroon skirt and white blouse.'

'The skirt's short, so's the petticoat,' said Dobbs. 'Tarty. Lace-up boots, black stockings, tarty French garters. And no underpinnings, even on a cold damp night.'

'So I noticed,' said the surgeon.

'Not uncommon with some of the women who stand in doorways around Soho,' said Dobbs. 'Unless the cut-throat took hers as a kind of pervert's souvenir.'

'That's your problem, Chief Inspector,' said the surgeon.

Chief Inspector Dobbs mused in the misty air of the sealed-off street. Five-feet-ten, forty-two, with broad shoulders and a solid chest, he looked the epitome of a Scotland Yard man in his curly-brimmed brown bowler, unbuttoned overcoat and thick-soled polished black boots. His features were pleasantly rugged, his blue eyes clear and keen, his dark brown moustache military in style. He had a cheerful look normally, on or off duty. On duty, it was sometimes deceptive. At the moment, it lacked all cheer. His assistant, Detective-Sergeant Robert Ross, twenty-seven and a fairly handsome man, made himself heard.

'Have you thought, guv,' he said, 'that as she had a job, she didn't need to stand in Soho doorways?'

'Good question, my lad,' said the Chief

Inspector. 'Have you got the answer as well?'

'Not yet, guv,' said Sergeant Ross.

'Nor me,' said Dobbs. 'But cheer up, sunshine, the tarty factor could give us what you might call a helpful lead. Now, if she was on the game, where was her pitch, this side of the water or the north side?'

'Well, we know she lived this side, in lodgings in Tanner Street, off Tower Bridge Road,' said Sergeant Ross.

'Not much custom around Tanner Street,' said Dobbs. 'A lot more in the West End.'

'Listen, guv, she had this job, in the laundry at Guy's, she didn't need to be on the game.'

'Didn't you just say that?'

'Worth repeating, I thought,' said Ross.

'Next time, give me the answer as well,' said Dobbs. 'Anyway, I dare say when her neck was all in one piece, you'd have called her attractive, and I dare say further that laundry wages don't amount to much. And there's no telling what some women'll get up to to put extras in their petticoat pockets. Safe there, y'know, my son, you can't pick a petticoat pocket.'

'Hers was empty,' said Sergeant Ross.

'Hadn't been paid at the time the sod did for her, that's my opinion,' said Dobbs. 'There's no handbag, by the way, is there?'

'He's got that, of course, the bloke who did for her,' said Ross.

'Has he? I suppose so,' said the Chief Inspector, 'except I ask myself, did he need to cut her throat for it? If he did, all we need now is a sight of this presently unknown bloke walking around London with a lady's handbag.'

'I presume that's not a serious observation?' said the surgeon.

'Just a comment in passing,' said the Chief Inspector. 'Had she had intercourse?' he asked.

'No.'

'Ah.'

'Lost a point there, have we, guv?' asked Ross.

'Not necessarily, not if the bugger decided it would give him more satisfaction to cut her throat.'

'Of course, you know what some people in the East End are going to say, don't you?' said Ross.

'Do I know?' asked the Chief Inspector.

'I think you do,' said Sergeant Ross, 'they're going to say the Ripper's come back.'

'That's it, cheer me up, I'd like some of what me forebears in the Yard had to put up with twelve years ago, wouldn't I?' said Dobbs. 'But you're off the mark. This isn't Jack's handiwork. It's a clean staightforward slash with a sharp knife. No disembowelling or suchlike. Nothing nasty.'

'Don't know about that, guv. Nasty enough for her, poor cow.'

'Don't answer me back, sunshine,' said the Chief Inspector, 'or I'll have your Scotch grandparents looked into.'

'Scottish, guv, Scottish.'

'Same thing. Now, before we interview some of her workmates, let's take a look at Flanagan's lodgings. By the way, bring the scarf along.'

At the house in Tanner Street, close to Tower Bridge, the landlady, Mrs Pritchard, opened the door to them. A beefy woman with a red face, due to a liking for a frequent drop of port, she had an acquired aversion to representatives of the law on

14

account of their busybody noses. But because they had a lot more legal clout than she did, she let the Scotland Yard men in. Her weighty figure nearly hit the floor of her dingy passage when she learned that one of her lodgers, Maureen Flanagan, had been done to death.

'Oh, me gawd, where's me port?' she gasped, staggering through to her kitchen. The bottle was on the dresser, conveniently to hand, and she drew the cork and swigged. 'Lord 'elp us, that's a bit better,' she said. 'You gents like a drop?'

'Thanks, no,' said Sergeant Ross.

'Well, o' course, you ain't a friend to Flanagan like I was,' said Mrs Pritchard. 'You sure it's 'er?'

'Sure,' said Ross.

'Gawd 'elp us,' said the suffering landlady, and took another swig before replacing the bottle. 'Poor woman, who'd of thought she'd 'ave got 'erself done in so cruel? It don't 'ardly bear thinkin' about. No wonder she didn't come back 'ere last night. I thought she might of been stayin' with one of 'er laundry friends.'

'A man friend?' asked Sergeant Ross.

'Oh, yer bleeder,' breathed the landlady, ''ow can yer talk like that of a poor victimized woman that was as respectable as I am?'

'Sorry, missus,' said Sergeant Ross.

'So yer should be,' said Mrs Pritchard.

'Did she stay out all night sometimes?' asked Dobbs, bowler hat in his right hand. His dark brown hair had a widow's peak.

'Not as I know of,' said Mrs Pritchard. 'I thought it was a bit unusual, 'er not bein' 'ere this morning, but like I just said, I thought she might of put up at a friend's 'ouse. Well, the fog was an 'orrible

15

pea-souper last night. Oh, me palpitations, done in, poor woman.'

'What sort of a lodger was she?' asked the Chief Inspector.

'Oh, cheerful, yer know, cheerful. Irish, she was. Liked 'er job at the laundry, and liked goin' out a bit of an evening.'

'Attractive woman,' said Ross.

'Oh, she 'ad nice looks,' said Mrs Pritchard, taking the weight off her feet by sitting down at her fireside. Her range fire was alight, the coals slowly smouldering, and she leaned, took up the poker and stirred them into life. She pulled out the damper to let the air get at the coals. They glowed.

'She wasn't married,' said the Chief Inspector.

'No, but she 'ad a bloke, she said. Went out a bit to meet 'im sometimes, and brought 'im 'ere once. Good chest, he 'ad, and decent looks. Liked a drop of beer. Well, we 'ad a couple of bottles in the house and we all 'ad a glass or two in me parlour, me old man as well.'

'Did her bloke go up to her room with her?' asked Ross.

'No, we 'ad a sociable evening in me parlour. Bit of a joker, 'e was, about forty, but couldn't of been a marrying man or 'e'd 'ave churched Miss Flanagan, which might of pleased 'er. Well, she acted very nice to him.'

'Do you know where he lives?' asked the Chief Inspector.

'No, course I don't. 'E didn't say, and I didn't ask. 'Ave you gents got chilblains? Mine are killin' me like they always do once winter starts gettin' cold and damp, and the shock ain't doin' them much good, either.'

'Do you know the man's name?' asked Ross.

'I can't remember if I was told 'is full name, but Miss Flanagan called 'im Godfrey.'

'Godfrey?' said the Chief Inspector.

'Fancy name all right,' said Mrs Pritchard, and breathed heavily. 'Oh, that poor woman.'

'Would you say he was an educated man?' asked Ross.

''Ow do I know what school 'e went to? Mind, he spoke quite nice, but I wouldn't say 'e was posh. A lot of laughs, that was 'im, like Miss Flanagan was. You still sure it's 'er that's 'ad 'er throat cut?'

'I'm afraid so,' said Ross. 'One of the laundresses identified her on the spot.'

Mrs Pritchard quivered and put a hand to her agitated bosom.

'Oh, me gawd, I just thought,' she gasped. ''E ain't back, is 'e?'

'Who?' asked Dobbs.

'Him, o'course, bleedin' Jack the Ripper.'

Chief Inspector Dobbs growled under his breath. Any mention of the Ripper pained his soul and put his ruggedly cheerful front under strain.

'Be an obliging lady, Mrs Pritchard, and put him out of your mind,' he said.

'But was Flanagan all cut up 'orrible?' asked Mrs Pritchard. 'If she was, I ain't expected to put that out of me mind, am I?'

'She wasn't,' said Dobbs. 'And Jack the Ripper's in his grave.'

'Is 'e?' Mrs Pritchard looked dubious. 'Nobody's told me.'

'The man Miss Flanagan called Godfrey,' said the Chief Inspector, 'I'd be glad if you'd fully describe him.'

17

'As I remember— 'ere, wait a bit, it wasn't 'im that done 'er in, was it?'

'We don't know who did it yet,' said Ross, 'we're making enquiries and we need all the information we can get about the people Miss Flanagan knew. It helps to eliminate the innocent, Mrs Pritchard.'

'Never 'eard of it,' said Mrs Pritchard, 'except we're all innocent round 'ere, includin' me old man that ain't let a drop of the 'ard stuff pass 'is lips since 'e got a job as a lamp-lighter. The Gas Company ain't partial to lamplighters that can't see for lookin'. They sacked one bloke for not seein' where 'e was doin' a Jimmy. Up against one of their lampposts, it was, and 'e got reported by someone as ought to of known better. As for Flanagan's bloke, 'e was about your 'ight and build,' she said to the Chief Inspector. 'Yes, and he 'ad dark 'air and a moustache which he kept out of 'is glass of beer very tidy, like. Mind, I only saw 'im that once, which must of been all of four months ago.'

'But you can say Miss Flanagan still went out to see him some evenings?' said Dobbs.

'Well, now and again when I saw 'er on 'er way out, she'd say she was goin' to meet Godfrey.'

'How did she dress on those occasions?' asked Ross.

''Ow did she what?'

'Dress.'

'Like she usually did, in her 'at and coat,' said Mrs Pritchard.

'In a coat summer and winter?'

'A thin coat in the summer.'

'What time did she usually get back?' asked the Chief Inspector, deciding that the coats were worn to hide short tarty skirts.

18

'Usually, about eleven. I told yer she was cheerful, like most Irish, and I expect she liked the pubs where she could join in a cockney knees-up or an Irish reel. Mind, I don't go in pubs a lot meself, bein' an 'ard-workin' and respectable woman. I just enjoy a little drop of port occasional in me own 'ome.'

'Do you know which pubs she used?' asked Dobbs.

'No, she never said and I never asked.'

'Did she ever come back here drunk?' asked Ross.

''Ere, d'you mind?' said Mrs Pritchard. 'It's bad enough 'earing she's 'ad 'er throat cut without 'aving to listen to them kind of insinuations. I wasn't always up when she got back of an evening, but when I was I never 'eard 'er actin' like she was drunk, and me old man never 'ad to 'elp 'er up the stairs. And she only 'ad one small glass of beer that time 'er bloke spent the evening in me parlour. And she didn't go out ev'ry evening, more like two or three times a week.'

The Scotland Yard officers glanced at each other. There was a suggestion in what Mrs Pritchard had said that Maureen Flanagan hadn't spent too much time in pubs on her evenings out.

'The scarf, laddie,' said Dobbs to his sergeant, and Ross took the brown woollen scarf out of a carrier-bag. It was neatly folded, hiding the fact that it was partially bloodstained. 'Mrs Pritchard, d'you know if this belonged to Miss Flanagan?'

'Yes, that's 'ers,' said Mrs Pritchard, 'she wore it a lot to 'er work in the winter.'

'And when she went out in the evenings?'

'Well, I didn't see 'er every time she went out, but

19

I think I saw 'er wearin' it now and again.'

'Obliged to you, Mrs Pritchard,' said Dobbs, 'and now we'd like to take a look at her room.'

Mrs Pritchard fidgeted and muttered, then said, 'All right, 'elp yerselves.' What with one thing and another, and the loss of Flanagan's rent, she felt in need of a further drop of port. 'The upstairs back,' she said. With a touch of morose wit, she added, 'Yer won't need to knock.'

Chief Inspector Dobbs and his sergeant climbed the stairs and let themselves into the back room of the upper floor. Its small amount of furniture was tidily disposed, the bed nicely made. Dobbs opened up the standing wardrobe, while Sergeant Ross searched for a suitcase. Suitcases were often used for storing a lodger's personal items, such as letters.

The wardrobe disclosed a limited number of clothes. There were a couple of commonplace frocks that the dead woman probably wore to work, alternating with a couple of cheap blouses and dark blue skirts. There was also, however, a very attractive black velvet dress, remarkably short. Maureen Flanagan had trimmed the hemline herself, I'll bet on that, he thought. And she would have had to wear the dress under a coat, unless she intended to stop the traffic. A coat was there, a thin summer one, along with a cheap mackintosh. Dobbs noted two empty hangers. In the wide drawer at the bottom of the wardrobe was underwear, among which were two short waist petticoats with frilly lace hems, similar to the one the unfortunate woman had been wearing last night.

Sergeant Ross had found a suitcase, under the bed. It was on the bed now, and he'd opened it. There were letters, which he quickly found were from her mother in Cork, Ireland. He read one. It was a normal family letter, hoping her daughter was well and describing family happenings at home. Mrs Flanagan did include, however, a message of thanks for the money regularly sent in pound notes.

'Guv?'

'Well,' said Dobbs.

'She sent money home, regularly, and in pound notes.'

'She also owned a tarty velvet dress and tarty petticoats, sunshine. I might have enjoyed the last waltz with her at a police ball if I hadn't been married. Happily, I might say. Anything there about the bloke Godfrey?'

'Nothing, just letters from her mother in Cork.'

'Wake up, I meant in the letters. She was thirty years old, my lad, so if she'd got hopes they'd have been of the kind she'd have mentioned in the letters she wrote herself, and her mother might have asked her questions about him.'

'Would a part-time pro have hopes, guv?'

'Now now, my son, you can do better than that. Use your imagination. Put yourself in her place.'

'In a Soho doorway, guv?'

'If you've got an imagination that stretches that far, my lad, you should be writing for a saucy French magazine. Let me have a turn at repeating myself. If she did mention the bloke Godfrey to her Irish mother, then her mother might have referred to him in her own letters. How many you read?'

'Just this one, guv,' said Sergeant Ross.

'Well, bring them with you when we leave. Now, what else is here, I wonder?'

They searched for other things that might help

the investigation, but found nothing until they stripped the bed and lifted the mattress. There, beneath it, was a brown envelope, and in the envelope were eight white pound notes.

'Savings out of laundry wages or what?' said Ross.

'I'll plump for "or what",' said Dobbs. 'Well, it's my considered opinion that anyone who can save out of laundry wages ought to be Chancellor of the Exchequer. Put that envelope with the letters.'

He was satisfied for the moment, confident they'd established that Maureen Flanagan was a part-time pro who was able, from her night-time earnings, to send money home to her family in Cork. He could have said at this stage that the bloke Godfrey was a good lead, and if not, that they were going to have to track down one of the woman's pick-ups. But before the morning was quite over, he wanted to talk to the laundry workers at Guy's.

He and Sergeant Ross left, after thanking Mrs Pritchard for her co-operation.

'Very public-spirited, missus,' said Ross.

'I ain't 'appy about the sound of that, so keep it under yer bowler 'ats, or someone might break me winders,' said the upset landlady. 'Mind, murder's a bit different to a bit of 'armless smash-and-grab. Poor old Flanagan, don't it show yer it ain't clever to go out in the fog?'

On the way to Guy's Hospital, Sergeant Ross said it wouldn't have done to suggest to Mrs Pritchard that her lodger was on the game some evenings.

'I hope I'll like what you're going to say next,' said Dobbs.

'She might have remembered all the Ripper's

victims were on the game,' said Ross, 'and done her bottle of port serious injury.'

'Are you trying to give me worries I can do without?' asked the Chief Inspector.

'Not me, guv. Just thought I'd mention the point.'

'Well, don't mention it again. Try cheering me up instead with a Scotch joke.'

'Scottish, guv,' said Ross, 'and here goes. When he was asked for a donation to a Glasgow orphanage, Rabbie Burns sent two orphans.'

The Chief Inspector grinned.

'I heard that one when I was ten,' he said.

'Still good for a laugh, though,' said Ross.

'Not today,' said Dobbs. It might have consoled him, however, to know that at this early stage, those people in the East End who did suspect the Ripper was back were convincing themselves he was operating south of the river this time.

As a uniformed sergeant stationed in the East End, he had known the condemnation and abuse suffered by the Metropolitan and City police forces during the frantic and frustrating months in 1888 when Jack the Ripper had eluded all efforts to catch him.

In 1889, Charlie Dobbs had been admitted into the Metropolitan Criminal Investigation Department, where he made a name for himself in helping to put several unpleasant characters in the dock at the Old Bailey, and worked his way up to his present rank by dint of a natural talent for detection.

He was married, with two children, a boy and a girl, and the family occupied a house that overlooked Victoria Park. His wife put up with her married name of Daphne Dobbs, with her husband's erratic hours, and with his suspicions of anything she placed on the supper table that he didn't immediately recognize. What's that, Daphne? It's marrow stuffed with the best minced beef, Charlie, with a light cheese sauce covering. It looks like something that ought to be arrested, Daphne. It's a recipe of Mrs Beeton's, Charlie. She could get arrested too. Well, if you don't like it, Charlie, you can arrest me.

His kids liked him because he played football in the garden with his twelve-year-old son, and lashed out on pretty frocks for his ten-year-old daughter.

What he didn't want at this fairly enjoyable stage of his life was a murder case that the press and the public might associate with Jack the Ripper.

Chapter Two

About midday, Bridget Cummings entered a house in Ellen Street on the south side of Whitechapel, and away from the worst of the neighbourhood's slum-afflicted centre. It was a typical flat-fronted East End dwelling of two storeys, three rooms up, three down, but with an upstairs lav, and also one in the back yard. Just as typically, out of school hours the street was full of ragged kids, although not quite as ragged as the kids of the central slums, nor as starving. But no-one could have said they were alive with health.

Bridget lived here with her sister Daisy, nineteen, and her brother Billy, seventeen. They'd lost their parents. Their mother had died of consumption four years ago, and their father of suffocation a year later, when the side of a gravel pit collapsed and buried him. The company employing him reimbursed his children for his loss by handing Bridget fifty pounds. That was a godsend to Bridget and a relief to the conscience of the company when she accepted the amount and signed the paper.

The fifty pounds kept them going, and when Billy left school he secured a job as an errand boy for the grocers in Whitechapel Road, while Bridget found evening work washing-up in the kitchen of a well-patronized West End restaurant. Daisy was in and out of jobs, and presently unemployed, which meant they were only just scraping along, especially as Bridget had to fork out nine bob a week for the rent. She earned three bob a night at the restaurant, and four bob on Saturday nights. Billy earned five bob a week as an errand boy, but he did get penny tips from some customers to whom he delivered.

Bridget had decided to take a lodger, so there was a card in their parlour window, announcing,

ROOM TO LET FOUR SHILLINGS A WEEK

HOT SUPPER SIXPENCE.

She'd been out shopping. She placed the bag on the deal top of the kitchen table.

'I'm just goin' to fry some left-over taters with some bacon scraps,' said Daisy.

'Never mind that,' said Bridget, ''op off to Guy's Hospital and ask for a job in their laundry.'

'Eh?' said Daisy. She was pretty but with the paleness common to inhabitants of the East End, her body slender. Her black hair was a smooth cap that built up into a bun at the back of her neck. Her dress was an old brown one, with a button-up bodice, her boots worn but clean. Her sister Bridget was full-bodied, and handsome rather than pretty. There was an old brown straw hat sitting on her mop of black hair, and her brown eyes were so dark they looked like polished coals at times.

'Yes, 'op off quick,' she said, and took a folded evening paper from her shopping bag. She'd picked it up out of a dustbin. It smelled a bit fishy, but it did contain the news that a Guy's Hospital laundry worker had been found murdered in Tooley Street. 'There,' she said, opening up the paper, 'see that?'

'Oh, 'elp, that's 'orrible,' gasped Daisy.

'It ain't exactly nice,' said Bridget, the family stalwart, 'but save yer sorrowing for later, Daisy. The laundry's a worker short, and there'll be a queue for the job a mile long tomorrer morning. You 'op off now, ask to see the laundry superintendent and tell 'er you're a friend of the misfortunate Maureen Flanagan. Well, say you were while she was alive. She lodged in Tanner Street, not far from Tooley Street. It's all there, in the report, and it says she was Irish. Tell the superintendent that Maureen would've liked you to 'ave 'er job if she ever left it, and don't forget you did laundry work once in the Whitechapel bagwash.'

'Bridget, I can't go and say I was a friend.'

'Yes, you can.'

'But it ain't true,' breathed Daisy.

'Well, cross yer fingers when you mention it,' said Bridget. 'Don't let religiousness come between you and a job.'

'But won't it seem a bit – well, sort of a bit cold-blooded tryin' to step into that poor woman's shoes so soon after 'er dyin' such a shockin' death?' said Daisy.

'Someone's goin' to,' said Bridget, 'so it might as well be you. Tell yer what, 'ere's thruppence. Buy a bunch of violets from old Ma Perkins in Commercial Road on yer way, and give 'em to the superintendent for 'er to put in the laundry room in memory of Maureen, your unfortunate dead friend. She'll like yer for that, she'll be 'eart-warmed. Daisy, you got a chance to get yerself a real steady job, so go after it with your 'ead screwed on right – Daisy, you listening?'

'Course I am,' breathed Daisy, picturing herself

in clouds of warm steam instead of traipsing cold streets looking for any kind of work. 'But I'll 'ave to do what you said, I'll 'ave to keep me fingers crossed about bein' a friend of the poor woman's.'

'Time you forgot you once went to Sunday school,' said Bridget, 'but all right, keep yer fingers crossed, then. Now put yer 'at and coat on and get goin'. Me, I'll be busy this afternoon, lining up with the strikin' workers that's goin' to march on the fact'ries, but when I get back later I want to 'ear you've got the job.'

'I'll do me best,' said Daisy, 'but, Bridget, don't you get too mixed up with a load of trouble.'

''Oppit,' said Bridget.

Daisy was out of the house a minute later, and hurrying, a shawl over the shoulders of her shabby coat, the skirt of her long dress rushing around her ankles, a worn boater on her head.

Chief Inspector Dobbs managed, without difficulty, to look like a fatherly figure amid the white-aproned workers in the calender room of Guy's Hospital laundry. He could do that, he could take on a fatherly air, his blue eyes becoming mild, his expression paternal, his gravelly voice mellow. As for Sergeant Ross, he stood by with his bowler hat placed over his heart, his ears in tune with the guv'nor's questions and comments. The calender room forelady was present, and so was the superintendent, a matronly-looking woman in uniform.

'I'm highly appreciative, ladies, of all you've told me,' said Dobbs, 'which was, speaking gen'rally, a commendable character reference for the – um – late Miss Flanagan. Unfortunately, yes, very unfortunately, someone with the sort of mind none of us like thinking about, didn't take as kindly to her as her friends and workmates.'

'Bleedin' villain, that's what 'e was,' said one of the workmates.

'Language, Smithers,' said the forelady, frowning.

'I'll give 'im language if I ever get me 'ands on 'im,' said the laundress. Work was at a stop for the moment, the whole contingent in a state of shock. 'I'll cut 'is odd-jobbers off to start with.'

'That's enough,' said the Superintendent.

'I suppose none of you ladies ever saw Miss Flanagan out with her favourite gent, did you?' enquired Dobbs.

'What favourite gent?'

''Ad she got one, then?'

'Her landlady mentioned one,' said Dobbs.

A young laundress said, 'Oh, she did say to me once she'd met a quite nice bloke, but I never saw her with him. I did ask if he was serious about her. Well, Maureen wasn't young any more, and at her age she had to have someone serious about her if she was ever goin' to get married. She didn't say who the man was or his name, she just laughed and said she'd got hopes.'

'Haven't we all,' said Sergeant Ross, and the Chief Inspector looked at him in a way that suggested he was slightly out of order. 'No offence, ladies,' said Ross.

'Oh, none taken, I'm sure,' said a cuddly-looking laundress.

'I'd like to ask, if I might, if any of you ever happened to meet Miss Flanagan in a pub,' said Dobbs.

'Us?' said a middle-aged woman. 'We don't 'ave

money to go to pubs. What some of us do 'ave is a broom 'andle to keep our 'usbands out of them. And I don't know I ever 'eard poor Maureen mention any pubs.'

'Mind, if she did 'ave a bloke,' said another woman, ''e might 'ave treated 'er now and again.'

'She told me once she was savin' up to go back to Ireland one day,' said the young laundress.

'Yes, she mentioned that to me not long ago,' said the Superintendent.

'Tragic, ladies, tragic,' said Dobbs, shaking his head, 'but many thanks for assisting us with our enquiries.'

'You 'opeful of catchin' the beast that done it?' asked the middle-aged woman.

'Ah, that's the word, hopeful,' said the Chief Inspector, and allowed a touch of reassuring cheerfulness to break through. 'I'm always hopeful in my work, and whenever I'm able to add assistance from the public to hope, a bit of welcome optimism creeps in. Good day, ladies, good day, Superintendent, sorry to have interrupted your work. I know how you all feel, and I share that feeling. Sergeant Ross?'

'I'm here, guv.'

'Thought you'd gone home.'

They left together.

'Superintendent?' The calender room forelady put her head into the office. 'Someone wants to see you.'

'Who?'

'A friend of Miss Flanagan's.'

'Oh? Show her in.'

Daisy entered and the forelady left.

'Good afternoon, mum,' said Daisy, bracing herself, and the superintendent regarded her kindly. The girl had a wrapped bunch of violets clasped in her left hand. Her shabby handbag was under her arm, her right hand just out of sight behind her hip. Daisy was crossing her fingers.

'You knew Maureen Flanagan?' said the Superintendent.

'Yes, mum. Ain't it 'eart-breakin'? Maureen that wouldn't 'arm a fly 'erself. Oh, me name's Daisy Cummings, by the way, and I brought just a few flowers that you might like to put in a vase in mem'ry of Maureen workin' 'ere and bein' looked after very kind by ev'ryone.' She placed the bunch of violets on the desk.

'Well, thank you, Miss Cummings, I'm sure her workmates will be very touched,' said the Superintendent.

'Oh, I felt I 'ad to show me grief,' said Daisy, not a bad young performer when her mind was made up and need was the incentive. Further, her fingers were tightly crossed. Well, she'd been a regular attender at Sunday school when growing up. 'And me sympathy to them as'll miss her 'ere now she's passed on. I just can't believe anyone could send 'er to 'er death so frightful.' Daisy made that remark in complete sincerity. She felt for the tragic woman. But, like Bridget said, more or less, life for the living had to go on, and someone was going to have that vacant job.

'You knew Miss Flanagan well and went out with her a lot?' said the Superintendent, instinctively doing a little work on behalf of that fatherly Chief Inspector.

'Oh, yes,' said Daisy. 'Well, fairly frequent, like.'

31

'You met young men, I suppose.'

'Oh, only in passin', like,' said Daisy. Help me, Lord, I ain't a bad girl really, just terrible poor.

'Did you meet Miss Flanagan's young man?'

'Well, I might 'ave mum.' Daisy's nerves twitched. 'But only in passin', you might say.'

The Superintendent noted what she thought was the girl's distress. This probably wasn't the right moment to ask too many questions of her. But Chief Inspector Dobbs might like to talk to her. He obviously had a man acquaintance of Miss Flanagan's in mind as a possible suspect, and would know exactly how to extract the right kind of information from this nervously sad girl.

'Well, I'm sure Miss Flanagan's workmates would want to send you a little note to thank you for coming in and leaving these flowers. Could I have your address, Miss Cummings?'

'Oh, that reminds me, mum,' said Daisy, gulping a little, 'but could I 'elp you out with your inconvenience?'

'Pardon?'

'Well, it's the inconvenience to your laundry of losin' Maureen, mum,' said Daisy valiantly.

'Oh, that's a very small thing at the moment,' said the Superintendent.

'Still, while I'm 'ere, I feel I ought to offer me 'elp,' said Daisy. Silently asking the Lord to forgive her, she went on. 'Maureen always said that if she left 'er job, she'd ask you to consider me for it if I didn't 'ave a job meself, but I never thought it would 'appen like this.'

'Oh, I see,' said the Superintendent, a firm and competent commander of the laundry staff, but nevertheless not without a heart. At the moment, her heart was in as much distress as she imagined this girl's was. 'Yes, I see.'

'Oh, I 'ope you don't think I come 'ere just for that, mum,' said Daisy, her tightly crossed fingers beginning to feel they might suffer cramp. 'But being 'ere, as I am, it occurred to me just a bit ago that I could offer me services. I've had experience, I worked for the Whitechapel bagwash for a year, mum, then I got tonsillitis, and they 'ad to give me job to someone else. But they'll give me a reference, and I'm a strong girl, mum, I've chopped wood in our backyard and lifted baskets in the markets to earn a bit of money.'

The Superintendent made up her mind.

'I'll give you a trial,' she said. 'Report to the fore-lady of the calender room first thing Monday morning at eight.'

Daisy wanted to do a bit of a dance. She checked the impulse and made do with uncrossing her fingers instead. Her fingers were grateful for the relief, but she didn't know how the Lord felt. She drew a breath.

'Oh, thank you, mum, thanks ever so. I'll be that 'appy takin' poor Maureen's place, and doin' the work as good as she ever did, really I will.'

'A month's trial,' said the Superintendent. 'Let me have your full name, your age and your address.'

'Yes, mum,' said Daisy, and gave the required details. Her nerves righted themselves, and exultation took over.

'Seven-and-six a week to begin with,' said the Superintendent.

Crikey, thought Daisy, we might be able to have meat and two veg nearly every day now, and I might

33

be able to treat meself to a frock down Petticoat Lane.

'Thank you, mum,' she said.

'Very well, Miss Cummings, we'll see you on Monday,' said the Superintendent, and Daisy did a little bob and left, feeling vital enough to run all the way home.

Chief Inspector Dobbs was required to talk to newspaper reporters that afternoon, to give them the kind of details they were hungering for, while leaving out what he preferred to keep to himself, such as the probability that the murdered woman had practised the ancient art of street-walking. He knew what they would make of that, and the one thing he didn't want was to find himself at the centre of an investigation into the supposed return of Jack the Ripper and his vicious liking for cutting up prostitutes. He'd be hounded, badgered and near to crucified, just as the investigating officers had been in 1888, unless he laid quick hands on the guilty man. Noting the faces of the reporters, he was quite aware of what they were hungry for. It was as plain on their faces as suet pudding. He gave them an outline of police progress which, although sounding meaty, didn't fool anyone, least of all himself. However, it managed to keep their pencils and notebooks occupied for a good fifteen minutes. Charlie Dobbs was a dab hand at giving out large helpings of police porridge. He sugared it by asking these Fleet Street scribblers to get their papers to print a description of a man known at the moment only as Godfrey and as a friend of Maureen Flanagan. He was required to come forward to be eliminated from enquiries. Dobbs gave the description. Mrs Pritchard had said the man was about thirty-five. He quoted a little over thirty, thus more definitely dissociating him from the Ripper of twelve years ago. There was no great response from the reporters. Dobbs knew why. They didn't want a suspect who failed to relate to the Ripper.

The *Westminster Gazette*, full up with porridge, cut in.

'Apart from this man Godfrey, a friend of Miss Flanagan's, what you're telling us, Inspector—'

'Chief Inspector,' said Sergeant Ross.

'What you're telling us, Chief Inspector,' said the *Westminster Gazette*, 'is that you're struggling.'

'What I mean,' said Dobbs, lighting his pipe, 'is that it's early days yet. Early hours, in fact.'

'Nothing came out of the hospital laundry?' asked the *Daily Mail*.

'Well, the usual amount of washing, you might say,' said Dobbs, 'and it's probably all being ironed now.'

Journalistic titters ran around the room. Dobbs looked blandly gratified at this response. Sergeant Ross passed his hand over his mouth.

'I'm assuming you've no real leads, sir?' said *The Times* politely.

'That's a good question,' said the Chief Inspector. 'Very good. Or is it? Let me see. There's leads, of course, but I don't know yet how real they are. They're all real to some extent. Come to that, gents, so's a blank wall or a blind alley, if you could see your way through them. If you can't, and I can't, I suppose you start again somewhere else. You live and learn about blank walls and blind alleys, and how you can end up at a full stop. That's real enough, but disappointing. Well, that's all, gents, for the time being.'

Sergeant Ross, knowing his guv'nor was handing out more porridge, kept his face straight.

'Will it hurt you, Chief Inspector, to suggest you've just given us a large amount of nothing?' said the *Daily Chronicle*.

'It'll pain me considerably,' said Dobbs, 'and won't do my self-respect much good. But thanks for coming, gents, see you again sometime next week.'

'Next week?' said the *Morning Post*.

'If you're not too busy,' said Dobbs.

'You're out of order, Chief Inspector,' said the *Daily Mail*.

'You're thinking of coming back tomorrow?' said Dobbs, looking slightly put out at the prospect.

'That's the usual way of things,' said the *Westminster Gazette*. 'Hope you'll have something for us by then. Meanwhile, is there a thought in your mind that—'

'Good afternoon, gents,' said the Chief Inspector, having seen the danger signals. He rose to his feet.

'A moment, sir,' said *The Times*.

'Yes,' pursued the *Westminster Gazette*, 'is there a thought in your mind that this murder heralds the return of Jack the Ripper?'

'Don't print that,' growled Dobbs.

'Don't print what?' asked the *Daily News*.

'That question.'

'It's the answer we're interested in.'

'Don't print that, either,' said Dobbs.

'We haven't had an answer,' said the *Evening News*.

'Now I ask you, is there one?' said the Chief

Inspector, putting his growls away and appealing for a reasonable attitude.

'We'd like your opinion,' said the *Daily Mail*.

'It's a plot to make a monkey of me, and to keep the public in at night,' said Dobbs. 'It's seriously inadvisable as well. So I must inform you that, if any papers intend to mention Jack the Ripper, I'll have to put my official hat on and apply to the Chief Justice for an injunction to stop all presses rolling on the grounds that they're making a deliberate attempt to put the fear of God into the people of London.'

'The Commissioner won't sanction that kind of censorship, Chief Inspector,' said *The Times*.

'I consider that a sad remark,' said Dobbs. 'Now I put it to you fair and square, lads, is it going to make sense bringing the Ripper in? Ask yourselves, could you accept the responsibility of making seven million Londoners spend all day tomorrow wetting themselves? All week, probably. And that could include your mothers and grandmothers. Think about it. You all love your mothers, don't you? Leave it. Leave it for a day or two at least. I promise to give you the go-ahead then, if my suspicions coincide with yours and we can all believe the Ripper's climbed out of his grave.'

'What makes you think he's dead, Chief Inspector?' asked the *Morning Post*.

'Certain facts I'm not permitted to disclose,' said Dobbs, 'as well as the fact that an aunt of mine read it in her tea leaves. And that's definitely all.'

'Definitely all is pretty close to nothing,' said the *Daily News*.

'It's not a good day for me, either,' said Dobbs, 'but there's a silver lining somewhere.'

*   *   *

'I've never had a look at the Ripper's file,' said Sergeant Ross when the press representatives had departed.

Back in his office, Dobbs said, 'File? There's a hundred, my son, and they're all dead.'

'Dead?'

'As a hundred dodos.'

'Closed to staff?' said Ross.

'Buried,' said Dobbs.

'Why?'

'Orders,' said Dobbs.

'Too many names?' suggested Ross, who had heard there was an embarrassment of well-known monickers hidden in inaccessible files.

'And too much bloody shame,' said Dobbs. 'Have you asked questions about the Ripper's case since you've been at the Yard?'

'Now and again,' said Ross. 'What copper wouldn't be interested?'

'And what answers have you had?' asked Dobbs.

'All negative, guv. No-one can get at the files without the permission of the Assistant Commissioner.'

'Officially, the Ripper's dead and so are the files,' said Dobbs. 'D'you know Whitechapel and its stew-pots?'

'I know it, but have never covered a case there.'

'You don't know it, then,' said Dobbs. 'Robinson!' he bawled.

In came Detective-Constable Robinson, double-quick.

'Sir?'

'Been down in the dungeons lately, Robinson?' said Dobbs.

'No, can't say I 'ave, guv,' said Robinson.

'Well, go down there now and fetch me this file,' said Dobbs, handing over a slip of paper.

'This one?' blinked Robinson.

'That's it, one of the dead 'uns,' said Dobbs.

'Well, guv, the Chief Superintendent—'

'Fetch it,' said Dobbs.

'Right, sir,' said Robinson, deciding that where Chief Inspector Charlie Dobbs was concerned, his wasn't to reason why. He disappeared. It took him twenty minutes to return. ''Ad a bit of a barney down there with Constable Ward, sir, but he's staying mum for 'alf an hour and here's the file.' He placed it on the Chief Inspector's desk. Dobbs looked up from the letter he was reading, one of those Mrs Flanagan of Cork, Ireland, had written to her daughter Maureen.

'You took your time,' he said.

'The filing system down there, guv, ain't what I'd call the best, specially not concernin' these forbidden files.'

'Feel sort of put-upon, do you, sunshine?' said Dobbs.

'Not by you, guv,' said Robinson, and departed with a grin and at a nod from the Chief Inspector, who opened the file, leafed through its browning contents and extracted a clipping from *The Times*. 'Read that, Ross,' he said, handing it over.

The clipping was of a published letter from an anonymous resident of Whitechapel. Sergeant Ross perused it with interest.

We are Sur, as it may be, livin in a Wilderness, so far as the rest of London knows anything of us, or as the rich and great people care about. We live in muck and filthe. We aint got no privvies, no dust bins, no drains, no water splies. We all of us suffer, and numbers are ill, and if the colera comes Lord help us.

'Christ,' said Ross.
'Perfect conditions,' said Dobbs.
'Pardon, guv?'
'For selling your body, your soul and your sister,' said Dobbs, 'and for murder. Now read this.' He handed over a sheet of notepaper, which contained an excerpt from the writings of a physician by the name of William Acton.

Subject matter: The cruel, biting poverty that forces women to become prostitutes.
   Unable to obtain by their labour the means of procuring the bare necessities of life, they gain, by surrendering their bodies to evil uses, food to sustain and clothes to cover them. Many thousand young women in the metropolis are unable by drudgery that lasts from early morning till late into the night to earn more than 3s. to 5s. weekly. Many have to eke out their living as best they may on a miserable pittance less than the least of the sums above-mentioned. Urged on by want and toil, encouraged by evil advisors, and exposed to selfish tempters, a large proportion of these girls fall from the path of virtue.

Sergeant Ross looked at the Chief Inspector.
'When was this written, guv?'
'Years before the Ripper made such women his victims,' said Dobbs. 'Finally, my lad, finally, cop this.' He handed his sergeant another clipping

from *The Times*, dated 27 September 1888, and Ross read it. It concerned Annie Chapman, one of the Ripper's victims.

> *She had evidently lived an immoral life for some time, and her habits and surroundings had become worse since her means had failed. She no longer visited her relations, and her brother had not seen her for five months, when she borrowed a small sum from him. She lived principally in the common lodging houses in the neighbourhood of Spitalfields, where such as she were herded like cattle. She showed signs of great deprivation, as if she had been badly fed.*
>
>   *The glimpse of life in those dens which the evidence in this case disclosed was sufficient to make the authorities feel there was much in the 19th-century civilisation of which they had small reason to be proud.'*

'Can't say it gets better, guv,' said Ross, handing back the clipping.

'There's none of it that's a credit to anyone, Ross, nor to Her Majesty herself, poor old lady,' said Dobbs. 'You see now, don't you, why certain persons wanted it all wrapped up and buried.'

'Certain Westminster persons?' said Ross.

'You're a bright lad, Ross. At times. You've forgotten the Church and our lords and ladies. What you've just read would shame a digger of ditches, let alone our archbishops, our gentry, our Houses of Parliament and our Prime Minister. The Ripper files contain facts, sunshine, facts, on the living conditions of the poor sods in the slums, conditions which the high and mighty did nothing about, and which were unknown to most people outside of London. I'll grant people knew there was pathetic poverty around, but not that men, women and kids in places like Whitechapel were dying in their own filth. You'll ask, of course, why the Government didn't do something for them. Are you asking?'

'I'm listening,' said Ross.

'So you should be. Listen some more. Many MPs don't bother with people who don't have a vote. Haven't you heard the story of the MP who came across a man lying in the gutter, close to mortal starvation? He asked what he could do for him. Help him, said a bystander. So he asked the dying man which party he voted for, and the dying man croaked he hadn't even registered. The MP said he was busy at the moment, but would try to come back later. Which he didn't, of course. My lad, there's a country's horrible shame written down in black and white in the Ripper's files.'

'I believe you, guv,' said Ross.

'Sensible of you,' said Dobbs. 'The Ripper, my lad, would never have come out of his hole if conditions in those stewpots of the living dead hadn't made butchery easy for him. Better for the country if he'd used his knives on the Lords and Commons. Can you Adam-and-Eve it, that on top of all their daily misery, the suffering people of Whitechapel had to put up with the Ripper dissecting their women? And can we put up with the newspapers bringing back the fear of God to them? Not if I can help it.'

'Scotland Yard buried the Ripper along with the files, guv?' asked Ross.

'What have you heard?' asked Dobbs.

'That he's dead,' said Ross.

'As I told you a little while ago, consider that official,' said Dobbs.

'But what do you think, guv?'

'That I'm not going to like it if the newspapers raise him up from the dead,' said Dobbs. 'They'll land him on my back.'

'Those reporters are sniffing about in search of his live bones,' said Ross, 'and they can't wait to get gnawing.'

'There's one way, laddie, of burying the bones.'

'What way?' asked Ross.

'Handing them a story about a prime suspect who could never be the Ripper.'

'You've got one in mind, guv? The bloke Godfrey?'

'I've already chucked him at them,' said Dobbs. 'That reminds me, if Godfrey shows himself, he's probably not our man. If he doesn't, he's probably a prime case for investigation. Meanwhile, I'll think of a suspect that'll do Fleet Street in the eye, the kind they can't turn into the Ripper. Say a mad female.'

'Christ, guv, would you flannel 'em to that extent?'

'All's fair in law and war, my son,' said Dobbs. 'Now give this file back to Robinson and tell him to re-bury it as soon as possible. That means immediately. Then find out if our artist has finished the sketch of Maureen Flanagan. He should have, he was back from the mortuary some time ago. I want to hawk it around the West End this evening and find out if any of the tarts can tell us where Flanagan's – um – business pitch was. I've got a feeling it was somewhere in the West End.'

43

'You've got an idea, have you, guv, that that's where the villain might be hanging about, looking for another throat?'

'You worked that out on your own, sunshine?' said Dobbs. 'Well done. Yes, if we go looking we might run into Godfrey.'

Chapter Three

Bridget had been out when Daisy returned from her triumphant sally into the den of the laundry superintendent. Daisy was a bit disappointed she hadn't been able to communicate her good news immediately to her stalwart sister. Still, never mind, it didn't affect the happy outcome. She just hoped Bridget wouldn't do anything silly out there. It was like her, to go and help the starving workers in their fight against the bosses, but she could get very aggressive on behalf of the downtrodden, and if the police turned up in force, there was no telling what she'd do. Nothing aggravated her more than a police uniform. The police, she often said, were traitors to the poor because they were always on the side of the bosses.

Mr Pritchard had been home for his midday meal, but hardly touched his food. His wife's agitated description of how the police had talked to her about the murder of Maureen Flanagan had taken the stuffing out of him. He needed a drop of the hard stuff to pull himself together. Seeing there was none in the house he finished off what was left of his wife's port. That fortified him a bit, although more details of the visit by the men from Scotland

Yard hardly made him happy. What with one thing and another, it was the kind of day neither he nor his shaken missus liked at all.

At three-twenty, Mrs Pritchard, ignoring shocked and whispering neighbours out on their doorsteps, set off for the Jug and Bottle of the local pub. The afternoon was bleak with rising grey mist that threatened to turn into fog, but that was a small handicap to a woman in need of a new bottle of port. On her way she met Mr Oxberry, a newcomer to the neighbourhood, a gent down on his luck who had managed to get a part-time job with a shop in the Strand, a gentlemen's outfitters. He worked there from nine till three.

'Oh, 'ello, Mr Oxberry, 'ave you 'eard the 'orrible news?'

'What news, Mrs Pritchard?'

'It's Miss Flanagan,' said Mrs Pritchard heavily, 'she was found murdered in Tooley Street this mornin' with 'er throat cut, poor woman.'

'Good God,' said Mr Oxberry, a dignified-looking man in his early forties, 'can this be true?'

'She didn't come back to 'er room last night, yer know, and no wonder she didn't,' said Mrs Pritchard. 'The police 'ave been round about it, and what with them and all me neighbours comin' round as well, I've suffered the kind of palpitations I wouldn't wish on me worst enemy.'

'I'm appalled,' said Mr Oxberry, 'such news is ghastly.'

'I never felt more ill meself,' said Mrs Pritchard, 'I'm still shakin' all over. Me own lady lodger, would yer believe, Mr Oxberry, comin' to an 'orrible end like that, it don't bear thinkin' about.'

'It's terrible,' said Mr Oxberry. 'I'm truly

appalled. Poor Miss Flanagan. I've had very little to do with her, but I've sighted her from time to time and said good morning to her.'

'I don't know I'll be able to see the day through,' said Mrs Pritchard, her face burdened with gloom, its redness of a paler shade that usual. 'She was such a cheerful woman and all. I told the police that I just 'ope Jack the Ripper ain't turned up again.'

'I'm sure he hasn't, Mrs Pritchard. Calm yourself on that score.'

'I'm goin' to get a bit of refreshment to cure me shakes,' said Mrs Pritchard. 'Just a small bottle of port.'

'Yes, do that, Mrs Pritchard, and if I can help in any way, just let me know.'

'You got a kind and sympathetic 'eart, Mr Oxberry,' said Mrs Pritchard, and went worriedly on her recuperative journey to the pub.

The afternoon had only been a little misty when, at one o'clock, striking workers of the East End began their preparations to march and demonstrate. By four o'clock, however, fog had arrived as a shifting mass that curled thickly around the street lamps of London and all but hid their light. At four-thirty, a woman was crossing Tower Bridge, peering into the murk. Not far behind her walked a tall gentleman in an overcoat and bowler hat, a Gladstone bag depending from his left hand, a walking-stick in his right. The woman was making hurried progress because of the fog and despite the fog. His own progress was measured and careful. She was a flitting figure, and she increased the distance between them, so that when she turned to make her way towards Cable Street and her home, the fog had swallowed her up. Her disappearance was of no consequence to the gentleman, although he turned towards the streets of Whitechapel himself in a little while.

The old were already by their firesides, such as firesides were in the slums of Whitechapel, the fires themselves fed by anything but coke or coal. Ragged kids foraged for fuel by night as well as by day, laying eager hands on anything that would burn and keep a kitchen fire going. In some kitchens at night the kids slept on the floor, feet to the fireplace. Thin, peaky and near to starvation, any kind of warmth at night secured them a little comfort.

Old Queen Victoria, ailing and frail though she was in the sixty-fourth year of her reign, nevertheless demanded action from her Prime Minister to alleviate the lot of subjects suffering abject poverty. Her Prime Minister assured her, not for the first time, that her Government was determined to take the necessary measures to improve conditions.

Some hopes. There were always strong factions in Westminster convinced that to improve the lot of the poor would make them get above themselves.

At this moment, hordes of the poor of the East End were creating bedlam. A continuous muffled roar issued from the area of battle. The fog, shifting and restless, hadn't yet affected the determination of striking workers to make war on the factories and sweatshops of the East End, nor the efforts of the police to resist them.

What a battle it had been and still was, fought between the starving men and women of Whitechapel, Spitalfields and Shoreditch and the uniformed forces of law and order. Since early afternoon, the dingy streets of Whitechapel had been swarming with people desperate for a living wage, their ragged kids hovering on the fringes of the mobs. The factories and the sweatshops of the East End had been grinding their workers deeper into the gutters of abysmal poverty for years, and the workers had finally taken to the streets, threatening to close the factories down and to set fire to them unless conditions and wages were improved.

Destruction of the factories will mean there'll be no work at all for you, said the bosses, and you'll starve. You bleedin' capitalists, we're starving already on what you pay us, said the workers. Give us a decent wage. Make do with what you get, said the bosses, instead of spending it on drink. That's done it, said the workers, we'll burn you down if you don't cough up out of your profits. Our profits are meagre, lied the bosses, and we can't afford any rises.

After an hour of this angry but vain dialogue, the workers went into action, and the bosses called on the police to protect their property. Things turned nasty then. The strikers swarmed, the police produced truncheons, and pitched battles began. The forces of law and order, defending the factories, wielded their truncheons vigorously, but were outnumbered and hard-pressed. The noise was an uproar of angry people close to the kind of starvation that meant early death.

Queen Victoria, hearing of the riot, called on her Ministers to put right that which had driven the strikers to resort to civil warfare. Her Ministers, however, chose to support the right of employers to fix wages, and to back the police in whatever

49

measures were necessary to protect property and to ensure the re-establishment of law and order.

The workers, unlike the bosses, had to fight their own battles and did so with fists, boots, sticks, bottles, clubs and fire-raising methods.

Near Wentworth Street, Whitechapel, one factory was alight and burning furiously, while the mobs impeded the progress of fire engines. Close to Brick Lane, the police were defending other buildings against a surging mob of people led by a popular local advocate of fair wages, Bridget Cummings. Bridget, with her strong and buxom figure that no amount of hunger had ever been able to reduce, was well-equipped to be in the fore-front of the fighting. Even though she didn't sweat in a factory herself, she was heart and soul with those who did. The mob she was leading included fire-raisers, men and women who were carrying pails of hot coals or burning rags or bottles of paraffin. Backing them up were workers wielding clubs and sticks. And some men and women carried bricks for the smashing of windows.

Police whistles were blowing in attempts to summon up reinforcements, and some such had arrived at the north end of Brick Lane, where they were trying to fight their way through the fog and the rioters in an effort to help defend threatened factories. The restless fog swirled, hampering the workers as much as it was hampering the police, but Bridget and her followers were determined to get at the largest factory, an engineering works that as good as sucked the blood from the men who worked there. Her great mop of black hair had lost its pins and was tossing about, her straw hat hanging by its pin at the back of her head, her face flushed with righteous anger and effort.

'Charge, will yer, charge!' she shouted at men and women behind her, shaking a laundry copper stick to encourage them on. They pushed forward, although the fog and encroaching darkness were curtailing vision and shielding targets. The factory itself had disappeared in the murk, and one could only distinguish the enemy by catching a glimpse of helmets. Bridget made herself heard again. 'Come on, shove, the lot of yer, and bury the rozzers. You're fightin' for your right to live.'

'Meself, I can't see for lookin',' panted a frustrated striker, 'not in this perishin' fog, I can't.'

'Get bashin', d'you 'ear me?' shouted Bridget.

The workers shoved and surged, the police shoved back, and a whirling mêlée developed. It broke into individual groups of struggling rioters and truncheon-smiting police, all amid the swirling yellow. One constable downed another. One striker felled a fellow-striker and trod on him.

'Oh, gawd bleedin' blimey,' gasped the fallen man, 'ain't I got troubles enough?'

The fog, buffeted and assaulted, eddied violently about. Two merchant seamen, caught up accidentally in the riot, tried to manoeuvre free. Bridget, glimpsing a peaked cap and instinctively associating it with authority, rushed forward and vanished in the fog as far as the workers at her back were concerned. She smote with her copper stick. One of the merchant seamen took the blow between his shoulder blades. It might have staggered him if he hadn't been as solidly built as he was. Instead, it made him whip round, bringing his right arm with him in a swinging counter. Bridget, alas, paid for her unfortunate mistake as his fist struck her temple. Down she went, out for the count, and her copper stick rolled away. Shifting feet trampled her, and the merchant seamen were sucked clear of her by eddying bodies.

A constable spilled out of a mêlée. His foot connected with Bridget's prone body. A man swore and leapt at him, aiming a blow with a broom handle. Constable Fred Billings parried it with his truncheon, then knocked it from the man's grip and discouraged further aggression by digging him in his stomach and robbing him of breath. The man reeled away and the fog gathered him. Fred peered down at the fallen woman. Police re-inforcements, having fought their way through, arrived at that moment, and the individual mobs besieging the factory were pushed back. With the fog so hampering, and the police reinforced, discouragement set in among the workers, and there was a general melting away of the men and women before conditions and the swelling police ranks turned the battle into disaster for them.

Bridget came to with some fighting still going on elsewhere. In the cloud of yellow fog, palely illuminated by one forlorn street lamp, she saw a rozzer looking down on her, and she saw a police sergeant moving away from him. She heard the sergeant say, 'All right, so it's Bridget Cummings. If you're sure she wasn't tryin' to commit assault, get 'er on her feet, get 'er home and give 'er a stiff warning.' Then he was gone, marshalling other constables and ordering them to help clear the streets.

'You hit me, you bleeder,' said Bridget from the pavement. 'I'll 'ave the law on you for battery and bodily 'arm.'

'Not guilty,' said Constable Fred Billings, 'but given the chance, I'd 'ave tanned your bottom, Bridget Cummings.'

'Oh, ruddy 'ell, it's you, Fred Billings,' said Bridget, her head aching. 'That's like you, that is, downing an innocent woman.'

'Leave off, you minx,' said Fred. 'Get up and I'll see you 'ome.'

'Just go away, will yer?' said Bridget.

'Get up,' said Fred.

'I ain't gettin' up till you've taken yerself off to a dog's 'ome,' said Bridget, 'you'll only knock me down again. Anyway, I can't get up, me 'ead's on fire.'

'Can I help?' A shadow moved within the swirling uneasy yellow to emerge and resolve itself into a figure that Bridget, still on her back and propped on her elbows, saw as dark and looming. By the pale glimmer of the lamp she also saw a Gladstone bag and a black ebony stick, wicked-looking. An image of last night's murder most foul leapt into her dizzy mind, and in a moment of near hysteria, she gasped, 'Oh, Lord 'elp us, the Ripper!'

The gentleman stared down at her, then laughed aloud. It was the first laughter Bridget had heard since the demonstration had begun and battle had commenced. It had not been a time for laughter, or even the smallest smile.

'The Ripper? Old Jack?' said the gentleman, and laughed again.

'It's not as funny as that, sir,' said Constable Fred Billings.

'No, not when things are as bad as they are for the people of Whitechapel, I agree, constable.

I'm a doctor. Is this young lady hurt?'

'Course I'm 'urt,' said Bridget. 'It's me 'ead. A brick fell on it. Or something,' she said accusingly to Fred Billings.

'Do you have a lamp, constable?' asked the gentleman. Fred unhooked his lamp and turned it on. The area was clearing, his colleagues exercising a variety of persuasive methods to get the people off the streets. The gentleman went down on one knee beside Bridget, placed his bag and stick aside, and examined her eyes by the light of the lamp, gently pushing each upper lid back. Then he ran a light hand over her bruised temple. Bridget winced. 'Painful?' he said.

'More like mortification,' said Bridget. 'Me gettin' downed, that's mortification all right, and it's that what 'urts. Lordy,' she breathed, 'you give me a turn, you did, doctor, when I looked up and first saw yer.'

'Look at me now, please,' said the gentleman, and Bridget looked, still a bit suspicious of him. He sensed it, and a faint little smile parted his mouth. 'Any double vision, miss?'

'What d'you mean, double vision?' she asked.

'Can you see double, that's what he means,' said Fred.

'Crikey, one of 'im's enough,' said Bridget. 'I can't see two, thank gawd.'

'No concussion, then, just a slight headache, I fancy,' said the gentleman. 'It won't last long. But be careful of any other falling bricks.' The little smile showed again as he straightened up. 'If you've a headache powder at home, take it when you get there. If not, I've one in my bag.'

Bridget sat up.

'I ain't 'aving that, you'll charge me,' she said.

'Not today,' he said, and opened his Gladstone bag.

'No, it's all right, I've got some at 'ome,' said Bridget. 'Oh, and thanks, doctor, sorry I miscalled yer like I did, but I was a bit dizzy at the time.'

'I'll tell that story to my patients,' he said. 'I've a call to make on one now. Goodbye. Goodbye, constable.' He left, and the fog took him into its restless embrace.

'Well, Bridget Cummings?' said Fred.

'I 'ope you noticed, Fred Billings, 'ow that doctor treated me like a lady,' said Bridget. Reluctantly, she took Fred's hand and let him help her to her feet. 'That uniform don't give you the right to knock me about, yer know, just because I'm on the side of the workers.'

'Will you leave off?' said Fred. 'Of all the cussed females, you're the limit. I suppose you've spent the afternoon goin' it 'ammer and tongs. Come on, I've got to get you 'ome and then report back. Start walkin'.'

'Where's me copper stick?' asked Bridget.

'Shame on you if you were usin' one,' said Fred, 'and lucky if you dropped it. If my sergeant had caught you with it, he'd 'ave made me arrest you.'

'Leave off, will yer?' said Bridget. 'Where's me hat?'

'Lost in the ruddy fog,' said Fred.

'Look at that, it's liftin',' said Bridget. The pall of yellow, which had been shifting and moving all afternoon, as if it hadn't been able to make up its mind whether or not to settle down for the night, was drifting and breaking. Buildings were re-appearing in the thinning murk of the dark

55

evening. 'All right, I'm off 'ome, but I don't need you.'

'Your 'eadache does,' said Fred. 'I don't want you fallin' over on account of gettin' dizzy. Give us your arm.'

'You got a hope,' said Bridget, beginning to walk. 'D'you think I want to be seen arm in arm with a copper, and one that's just been beatin' starvin' men and women unconscious?'

'Not yours truly,' said Fred. 'Fair fight, I'd say, and no quarter.'

'Don't you get ashamed of yerself sometimes the way you and all the other 'eavy clumpin' blue-bottles 'elp the bosses to keep men and women and their kids down in the gutter?' said Bridget.

'You know ruddy well where me sympathies are,' said Fred, 'but I took this job on for better or worse, which means that most of the time I've got to obey orders. I can't always turn a blind eye.'

Bridget ignored the fact that Constable Fred Billings was well-known for his blind eye. As far as she was concerned, he'd put himself on the side of the enemy the day he first appeared in uniform.

'I watched you grow up from a boy to a man, that I did, Fred Billings,' she said, as they crossed the Whitechapel Road into Union Street, with the fog now reverting to no more than mist again, and a litter of broken bottles and discarded weapons of offence adding to ever-present garbage. 'Let you kiss me under me 'ome-made mistletoe ev'ry Christmas, and walk me up Victoria Park some Sundays. I couldn't believe it when near to me seventeenth birthday you went and joined the bruisin' arm of the law. I ain't 'ardly ever spoken to you since, and gawd knows why I am now. It must be that me head ain't normal at the moment.'

'Know how you feel, Bridget, but I was lucky to get into the Force, and it wasn't done to put meself on the side of the bosses.'

'But it did, didn't it? Well, you was always a bit too good for the likes of yer own kind,' said Bridget, 'and I don't suppose it cost you even a small drop of blood to turn traitor.'

'I think you're tryin' to get my goat,' said Fred, 'but I'm dead set on not lettin' it 'appen. I can't afford to give in to me darker side. I'll get dismissed from the Force if I'm caught smackin' yer bottom in Union Street.'

'Don't make me spit,' said Bridget, 'I could eat two bluebottles like you for me supper, and bake yer 'elmets for me afters, with custard. I 'ate coppers, Fred Billings, and I 'ate you worser for 'elping the law to tread on yer own kind.'

'Thanks for the compliments,' said Fred. They crossed Commercial Road into Back Church Lane, leaving the central slums behind, although they were still within the grey citadel of poverty. 'As it 'appens, I was comin' to see you this evening.'

'I don't remember invitin' you,' said Bridget, 'which I wouldn't, anyway. If I did, me neighbours would burn me 'ouse down, and I'd deserve it.'

'Bridget, don't you think I know how bloody bad things are for people round here?' said Fred.

'They ain't bad for you, not with a copper's steady wage and free uniforms and decent lodgings up by Stepney Green,' said Bridget.

'I was comin' to that,' said Fred, a typical law and order type with his firm gait and his straight back. He was twenty-seven, and as he ate three times a day he'd built up a fine framework of hard muscles.

'I'm havin' to move out of me lodgings. Me widowed landlady is marrying again, a widower, and as she's got three kids and he's got two, they want my two rooms. I noticed on me beat yesterday that you've got a room to let, so I thought to meself—'

'Oh, yer bugger,' said Bridget, as they turned into Ellen Street, 'you've got the nerve to think we'd let the room to a copper, and you of all coppers? I'd sooner let it to another Jack the Ripper.'

'That wouldn't do you much good,' said Fred. 'Anyway, I'd like to proposition you—'

'I'll chop yer mucky 'ead off if you try propositioning me,' said Bridget. 'Blimey, what a day, nearly the worst of me life, what with gettin' beaten up by the police and 'aving to listen to you.'

'If you don't leave off,' said Fred, 'I'll run you in.'

'What for?'

'I'll think of something,' said Fred. They arrived at Bridget's door, and as they did so her brother Billy came riding up out of the mist on his errand boy's bike with its large grocery carrier.

'Oh, 'ello Fred, 'ow's yerself?' he said. He was a lean, vigorous and cheerful lad, counting himself lucky that he was earning, Bridget was earning and that Daisy did the cooking. Daisy could put together a tasty meal out of scraps and potatoes. 'Ain't seen much of yer lately, Fred,' he went on. 'Nor 'as Bridget.'

''Ere, you,' said Bridget, 'what's the idea? Ain't I told you never to talk to a copper? Pertic'larly, ain't I told you never to talk to Fred Billings?'

''Ave yer?' said Billy. 'Was I listening at the pertic'lar time in question?'

'Don't show off,' said Bridget, 'or I'll fetch you a clout. What you doin' 'ere?'

'I was just on me way back to the shop when I saw yer with Fred,' said Billy. He didn't finish his rounds until six, and there was still half an hour to go. 'It ain't illegal, seein' yer and stoppin', is it?'

'It's illegal talkin' to coppers, specially this one,' said Bridget.

'Well, I'm blowed,' said Billy, ''oo made that pertic'lar law?'

'I did, yer saucy fleabox,' said Bridget, and aimed a blow at him. Billy ducked and dodged it while keeping hold of his bike. He had to keep hold. If he let go for longer than a few seconds, street kids would appear like magic and cart it off under his nose. 'Stand still, will yer?' said Bridget, then turned. Street kids had indeed appeared like magic to run their hungry glittering eyes over the bike.

Fred stepped forward. At the sight of his uniform, the kids disappeared. Like magic.

'Well, now you're 'ome, Bridget, I'll report back,' he said. 'Nice to see yer, Billy. I'm 'oping to take up lodgings with you and yer sisters.'

'That's a good idea, Fred, be glad to 'ave yer instead of another petticoat,' said Billy.

'He'll get 'imself into our house only over me dead body,' said Bridget.

'Me proposition is five bob a week, Billy, which Bridget didn't give me a chance to mention,' said Fred, 'and which is a bob more than what you're askin', and I'll take supper at a tanner a time.'

'There y'ar, Bridget,' said Billy, 'ain't that a welcome proposition?'

'You Billy,' said Bridget, grinding her teeth, 'go and take that card out of the parlour winder.'

'You mean Fred's got the room?' said Billy.

'No, I don't mean that,' said Bridget, 'I mean we ain't got a room to let while 'e's standin' 'ere in 'is 'obnailed copper's boots. You can put the card back in soon as 'e's gone.'

'Much as it 'urts me, I ain't got time to muck about like that,' said Billy, a bit of an independent young cockney.

The door opened then, and Daisy showed herself. She was wearing her apron, and the apron gave off a slight smell of fish.

'I thought I 'eard talkin' goin' on,' she said. 'I – oh, 'ello, Fred, you're a nice surprise.'

'Considerin' what I've been hearing about me good self this last half hour,' said Fred, 'I'm obliged to you for them kind words, Daisy, and might I mention I like yer domesticated look?'

'Complimented, I'm sure,' said Daisy. 'I'm gettin' some nice plaice ready for fryin', with some fried taters. Fred, you 'ere knockin' for Bridget again after all these years?'

'No, he ain't,' said Bridget, ''e's been sidin' with the bosses again and breakin' the bones of suffering workers.'

'There's broken bones and bleedin' heads on both sides,' said Fred, 'but if I'm sorry for anyone it's for the workers and the starvin'.'

'Fred wants that room we been tryin' to let,' said Billy.

'Crikey,' said Daisy, 'this is our lucky day.'

'No, it ain't,' said Bridget, 'and Fred Billings ain't lodgin' in our house.'

'We've all got a say, yer know, Bridget,' said Billy, 'and before I get back to the shop, I'm sayin' yes. And so's Daisy.'

'Am I?' said Daisy.

'Yes, you just said,' grinned Billy.

'Oh, all right,' said Daisy, thinking of the extra income that would come from Fred's rent and her laundry wages. 'Well, we couldn't 'ave a more respectable lodger, Bridget.'

'I'll leave you to sort it out and call again tomorrer, when Bridget's head is feelin' better.' said Fred. 'So long till then, and keep Bridget behavin' 'erself, Daisy.' Off he went. Billy mounted his bike, and away he went too. Daisy and Bridget walked through to the kitchen.

'Daisy, we're not 'aving a copper as a lodger,' said Bridget.

'No, course not,' said Daisy, slipping plaice from a dish into the frying-pan that was warming on the range hob. The closed hob cooked slowly. 'Still, Fred's different, and the kids don't chuck fish 'eads at him like they do at the other coppers. Oh, Bridget, what d'you think, I got that job at Guy's laundry.'

'You did?' said Bridget, looking at the old tin clock on the mantelpiece. The time was twenty-five minutes to six. She had to be at work at six-thirty and wouldn't finish until eleven. Billy would be in from the shop by five past six, when he and Daisy would sit down to supper. She herself would be offered something in the restaurant kitchen, and she always accepted the option. It meant a little saving on housekeeping money. She listened while Daisy gave her a bubbling account of her interview with the superintendent. 'Well, I'm proud of yer, Daisy, you spoke your piece very clever. Seven-and-six a week wages is goin' to be a real 'elp. We don't need a lodger now.'

'Yes, we do, if we want things to get really comf'table for us,' said Daisy, 'and if we want to 'ave some decent clothes for a change. You can't get good-payin' and well-behaved lodgers easy. Look, I treated me and Billy to plaice tonight to celebrate me laundry job, I took a bit of money out of the cocoa tin. We ought to celebrate, Bridget – crikey, I just noticed, your clothes are all messed up, and where's yer 'at?'

'Lost it, and the copper stick,' said Bridget tersely. 'We got beat by the fog and a million blue-bottles. Now I'm goin' to wash and get changed, and I'll talk to you and Billy in the morning about that room. I ain't 'aving Fred Billings in this 'ouse. If 'e gets just one of 'is copper's flat feet over the doorstep, I'll only 'ave to chop 'is bleedin' 'ead off.'

'Bridget, that ain't a bit nice,' said Daisy. 'You don't 'ave to talk like you was brought up in a workhouse.'

'Can I 'elp it if Fred Billings makes me forget I'm a lady?' said Bridget, and disappeared to put herself to rights before she went to her job.

A young woman, arrested by the police for helping to set the blazing factory alight, slipped them before a Black Maria arrived to cart her and other suspects off to the lock-up. She was in Commercial Street now, not far from where Mary Kelly, the Ripper's last victim, had been murdered. The foggy mist was dogging her, drifting at her back, rising in front, the dark street haunted by the transient nature of the atmospheric phenomenon. She passed the entrance to an alley. A shadow moved. Her back turned icy, and she looked over her shoulder. The misty darkness seemed to break apart to admit a figure. For a moment she stood rooted. Then she screamed and ran, taking herself through the rising mist in a frantic dash for her home in Lamb Street.

There was no pursuit, nor did her scream arouse any attention. Since early afternoon the mobs of workers had flung screams, shrieks and yells in every direction.

The figure was that of the tall gentleman. The young woman's hysterical flight had aroused a smile in him. She had been in no danger, for he had felt no urge to repeat his performance of last night, especially as he had not known whether the young woman now running was a prostitute or not. What he did know was that Chief Inspector Dobbs of Scotland Yard was investigating the murder of Maureen Flanagan. That was sufficient unto itself, since he was sure Dobbs would certainly fail with this case. He would never know who to look for.

For the time being, the gentleman was content to indulge his morbid interest in walking in the footsteps of the Ripper. The latent atmosphere of evil in the misty darkness of Whitechapel, with its ever-present echoes of gruesome murder, was so much to his liking as to fascinate him. Even the danger to himself as a target for Whitechapel's creeping villains was an excitement.

Chapter Four

The fog was back again by seven as a thick blanket, which caused Chief Inspector Dobbs to cancel his foray with Sergeant Ross into the back streets of the West End. At eight o'clock, having had supper, he was in his living-room with his wife, a cheerful fire burning brightly, his son and daughter next door with their neighbours' children. On the mantel-piece the clock, set in a walnut case, ticked gently. On the wall above it hung a large photographic portrait in sepia of his wife's parents. On the op-posite wall hung a massive colourful picture, bought in the Caledonian market, of a magnificent Highland stag. Chief Inspector Dobbs liked that stag, he like its proud defiant look, and he liked the aggressive nature of its antlers. It did not bother him in the least that there were thousands of homes owning similar pictures, including Balmoral. Not that he had ever been to Balmoral, and in any event he'd think twice about going if the old Queen went off her ageing head and invited him. He under-stood male guests had to wear kilts. An invitation would mean he'd have to break a leg in order to escape Balmoral and a kilt.

Patterned curtains draped the windows, hiding the foggy nature of the night. On a small table beside his armchair were a number of letters. Carpet slippers on his feet, his jacket off, he settled into his fireside chair and picked up one of the letters. He drew the missive from its envelope.

Mrs Daphne Dobbs, seated in the opposite armchair, glanced at him. Thirty-six, fair-haired, she wore a high-necked brown velvet dress, its collar fastened by a cameo brooch, a birthday present from Charlie. She favoured velvet in winter. Its warmth was a protection against the draughty nature of Victorian houses. Her features were pleasant, her disposition equable, her background lower middle class, her father a schoolteacher soon to retire. She had married Charlie when she was twenty-two and he was a uniformed police sergeant, not yet in the CID. It had been a case of choosing between a policeman and a stores floorwalker. She opted for Charlie because Edward, the floorwalker, was so pleasant and courteous of demeanour and speech that she always felt he was never outside his esteemed working self on the first floor of the Stamford Hill stores. Charlie, on the other hand, was a breezy suitor, and always good for a laugh or two. So, because he appealed to her sense of humour, he was the one she elected to marry, and after a few years she was really quite pleased with herself for having chosen to take an extrovert presence into her life instead of a merely courteous and pleasant one, especially as Edward proved neither courteous nor pleasant on the day he discovered he was an also-ran.

She said now, 'Don't mind me.'

'Well, I won't, Daffie, and I like you excusing me,' said Charlie. 'I see you've got your knitting.'

Daphne Dobbs was a compulsive knitter.

'And I see that you've got some old love letters that aren't mine,' said Daphne.

'They're letters from a Mrs Flanagan in Ireland to her unfortunate daughter Maureen.'

'Ghastly,' said Daphne. They'd discussed the murder on his arrival home.

'Ghastly letters?' said Charlie.

'No, ghastly crime,' said Daphne. 'You promised me once you'd never bring work home with you.'

'I consider it lucky to have a wife who understands there's some promises I can't always keep,' said Charlie.

'Some luck goes a long way,' said Daphne, 'but might not always last for ever. Can I ask what you're looking for in the letters?'

'Mention of a bloke called Godfrey, a friend of the murdered woman, and accordingly suspect,' said Charlie, perusing the letter and thinking it odd that Mrs Flanagan had neighbours who let their domestic animals, like chickens, share their cottage with them at night.

'Godfrey Who?' asked Daphne.

'That's it, Daphne, Godfrey Who? I haven't got his surname. I'm hoping I'll find it in these letters. I read a dozen or so in the office without any luck. Now I've got a dozen more to read. In keeping these letters from her mother, Maureen Flanagan kept hold of her family links. Decent woman on the whole, I'd say. Yes, on the whole.'

'You're definitely suspicious of this Godfrey man?' asked Daphne.

'I'm not unsuspicious, not yet I'm not,' said Charlie, 'and I could get very suspicious if, when the newspapers publish his details, he doesn't come forward to clear himself.'

'Is that all you've got so far, Charlie, suspicions of a man who was the woman's friend?'

'That's all,' said Charlie, reading a second letter.

'She could have had other men friends,' said Daphne.

'You sound like Sergeant Ross,' said Charlie.

'I quite like Sergeant Ross,' said Daphne, knitting away.

'That's fair, seeing you're two of a kind,' said Charlie. 'I mean, he has bright moments too. Not all the time. Say frequently. Well, now and again, say.'

Mrs Daphne Dobbs smiled.

'Thank you, Charlie,' she said.

Not until he reached the final letter in date order did the Chief Inspector come across a relevant reference, when Mrs Flanagan wrote that it was the first time her daughter had mentioned she had a special man friend. 'Tell us more about him,' she wrote, 'we all thought you'd never have someone special now you're just gone thirty.'

The Chief Inspector sat up. According to the dates on the missives, Mrs Flanagan and Maureen wrote to each other once a month. He checked the date of this final letter, the only one that referred to a special man friend. 2nd of November. November. That would have been the last Maureen Flanagan received. In Ireland by tomorrow morning at the latest, the Cork police would have advised Mrs Flanagan of her daughter's death. Today was the 15th of November. Was there a chance that Maureen Flanagan had replied to that last letter, that she'd given her family the full name and some informative details about Godfrey Who?

He looked up, musing.

'Should I think about going to Ireland?' he said.

'Well, I shan't stop you, Charlie,' said Daphne, 'but I've heard the Irish Sea can be very rough. Weren't you a little seasick when we did a boat trip from Hastings to the Isle of Wight one summer?'

'Something I ate,' said Charlie, 'but I won't say I didn't congratulate myself on joining the Force instead of the Navy. In any case, what would be the point of sailing the Irish Sea if Maureen Flanagan hadn't replied to her mother's last letter before she came to her sudden end?'

'What was in her mother's last letter, then?' asked Daphne.

'A request for her daughter to tell the family more about a special man friend,' said Charlie.

'You mean Godfrey Who?' said Daphne.

'What do you think, Daffie?'

'The same as you, Charlie. The scuttle's your side, so would you put some more coal on the fire? Then I'll make us a pot of tea before Jane and William come in from next door for their bed-time cocoa.'

'One thing I'm sure of,' said Charlie, building up the fire.

'What's that?' asked Daphne.

'I'm a lot better off at home than sailing the Irish Sea,' said Charlie.

'Well, of course you are, and we'd all be surprised if you weren't,' said Daphne. 'After all, you've never been seasick in your armchair.'

Whitechapel on a foggy winter night offered shifting pictures and images very little different from those of twelve years ago. Such images were of sleazy lodging houses, moistly grimy bricks and

68

cobblestones, dark depressing alleyways, and the unlovely façades of deteriorating houses, all shrouded in ghostly fashion by the fog. Here and there, homeless people without a penny huddled together in what shelter they could find. In the doorways of ill-lit pubs, unkempt sluts, painted doxies and down-and-out women, most of whom were the worse for drink, exchanged obscenities and sexual ribaldry with the roughs, the toughs and the slick-haired pimps of the neighbourhood. What if there had been a murder last night? It wasn't keeping such women off the streets or out of the pubs. It had happened on the other side of the river, which was another world to them.

The dark shadow of the gentleman who had ministered to Bridget late in the afternoon seemed to precede him as he walked through Bucks Row, the scene of the Ripper's gruesome murder of Mary Ann Nichols, his first victim. If the eerie nature of the place disturbed the fainthearted, it did not intimidate the gentleman. His steps were firm and measured, his Gladstone bag in his left hand, his walking-stick in his right. His appearance was that of a professional gentleman. A doctor, say.

He turned into New Road, and from the shelter of a doorway a voice floated, a soft feminine voice not yet coarse or metallic.

''Ello, dearie, like some nice company, would yer?'

He stopped.

'Who is that?'

She came out of the doorway, shawled and hatted, her bright red skirt whispering. She exuded scent.

'Poppy, that's me, ducky, and—'

'What do you want of me, Poppy?'

'Now, yer honour, ain't it what you want of me? My, yer a gent, I can see that, even in this fog. And I'm fresh. Well, I ain't twenty yet. Would three bob suit yer as a fair price, seein' I ain't in the shilling class like most?'

He smiled. He'd enjoyed a very interesting evening, lingering in the areas that had been the hunting grounds of the Ripper.

'Here's sixpence,' he said.

'Now now, dearie, is that fair? A tanner for a fresh gal?'

'Take the sixpence,' he said. 'I want nothing from you for it.'

She took the silver coin, saying, 'Well, you're a kind one, you are, mister, and when you're feelin' a bit perky I'll only charge yer 'alf a crown. Just knock on the door if I ain't around. Who are yer?'

'A doctor,' he said and resumed his walk, going south. He was smiling. He had been called something else in the late afternoon of the day.

Poppy Simpson bit the sixpence, decided it was genuine, lifted her skirt and put the coin into her petticoat pocket.

At ten o'clock, Billy and Daisy were having a chat before going to bed.

'We've got to outvote Bridget,' said Billy.

'She'll pull the roof off the 'ouse if we let Fred 'ave that room,' said Daisy.

'No, she won't,' said Billy, 'she might smash a few plates, but she'll leave the roof alone. I got a fondness for Bridget, and you too, Daisy, but I ain't sure it's the wisdom of the ages to let our sister chuck 'er weight about more'n she does already.'

'Wisdom of the ages?' Daisy giggled. 'Where'd yer get that from?'

'Oh, from listening to customers,' said Billy, 'the kind that read books. I admire people that read books, and I might read one meself one day. Anyway, about our Bridget, it ain't our blame she'd like to take Fred up to the top of Nelson's Column and drop 'im all the way down into Trafalgar Square.'

'Oh, she wouldn't do anything like that,' said Daisy.

'I 'ope not, for Fred's sake,' said Billy. 'It wouldn't 'alf muck 'is loaf of bread up, and 'e probably wouldn't ever be able to talk again. Bridget might like that, Daisy, but I ain't approvin' of it meself, it 'ud be 'ard on a decent copper like Fred. Me, I'm votin' we let 'im rent the room. I mean, if Bridget starts layin' down the law to us tomorrer mornin', we've got to stand up to 'er. So you goin' to vote for Fred, same as me, and same as we did when we was arguin' the toss with 'er on the doorstep?'

'I'm goin' to vote for 'aving five bob a week rent off 'im,' said Daisy, 'and sixpence ev'ry day for 'is 'ot suppers. 'Ere, Billy, d'you realize that when I start me laundry job, Briget'll 'ave to do the cookin'?'

'Well, we won't mention that yet, not on top of outvotin' 'er,' said Billy.

'Why not?' asked Daisy.

'Well, it would 'ardly be the wisdom of the ages, would it?' said Billy.

'Oh, I get it,' said Bridget over their usual skimpy breakfast the following morning, 'it's mutiny, is it?

71

Well, it won't work. We ain't lettin' that room to Fred Billings, and that's final.'

'Unfortunately,' said Billy, 'me and Daisy—'

'Unfortunately my eye,' said Bridget, 'you ain't old enough yet to talk like that.'

''E gets it from customers that read books,' said Daisy.

'Yes, I told Daisy I've got a mind to read one meself one day,' said Billy. 'Anyway, Bridget, me and Daisy is votin' Fred in.'

'Well, I'm votin' 'im out,' said Bridget.

'Unfortunately—'

'Never mind unfortunately,' said Bridget.

'You can't vote Fred out,' said Billy, ''e ain't in yet.'

'Is that supposed to be funny?' asked Bridget, her mop of hair piled and pinned, the lace collar of an ancient blouse thankful for the starch that kept it upright around her neck. 'I'm gettin' an aggravated feeling about the way you're growin' up, Billy Cummings. If I 'ave any more of yer sauce about lettin' a certain copper into this 'ouse, something you won't like is goin' to drop on yer head, like our flat iron.'

'But, Bridget,' said Daisy, 'we—'

'I can't believe the trouble I'm suffering lately,' said Bridget. 'I've 'ad to watch starvin' strikers gettin' murdered by the police, I've 'ad the 'orrible misfortune to run into Fred Billings, and now I'm 'aving to listen to me own brother and sister tryin' to rent 'im that room. Talk about trials and tribulations.'

'But, Bridget,' said Daisy, 'think of the rent.'

'Yes,' said Bridget, 'and think of that copper's clod'oppers treadin' all over ev'rywhere. And might I ask what you two are goin' to say to our neighbours when they find out we've got a blue-bottle for a lodger?'

'Oh, they won't mind Fred,' said Daisy.

'Well, I will,' said Bridget.

'I dunno why you get aggravated about 'im,' said Billy. 'Tell yer what, did yer know garlic's got healing properties?'

'Garlic's got what?' said Bridget.

''Ave I 'eard of garlic?' asked Daisy.

'The shop sells it to foreign immigrants,' said Billy, a born receptacle for bits of knowledge and educated words that came out of the mouths of customers. 'A lady—'

'Ladies don't shop in Whitechapel Road,' said Bridget.

'Some do at our grocers,' said Billy. 'I 'eard this one say, while I was loadin' me bike, that a bit of crushed garlic mixed with mashed pertato is good for people that get aggravated.'

'Bridget, you could try that if it ain't too expensive,' said Daisy.

'Well, she's got to try something to stop 'erself climbin' up the ruddy wall ev'ry time Fred gets a mention or she sees 'im on 'is beat,' said Billy.

'The Lord give me patience,' said Bridget, breathing heavily, 'I'll go off bang in a minute.'

'A bit of garlic might easy cool yer down,' said Billy. He got up. 'Time I went,' he said. Bridget chucked a saucer at him. It struck his jerseyed chest and bounced off. He caught it and put it back on the table. 'I could bring some 'ome,' he said.

Bridget sprang up. Billy ran, grabbing his old coat and large-peaked cap on his fast way out of the house.

'Don't come back!' Bridget yelled from the open door.

'Well, I won't, not till later,' called Billy, heading with a rush into safety, the morning damp and misty, Ellen Street grey and moist.

'Robinson,' said Chief Inspector Dobbs, arriving at his desk, 'where's Sergeant Ross?'

'Gone for a Jimmy, sir,' said Robinson.

'Already?' said Dobbs. 'Is he short of a private convenience at home, might I ask?'

'You could pop the question to 'im, sir,' said Robinson.

'I don't need him as a fiancé,' said Dobbs, 'I had one years ago. She's now my wife.'

Sergeant Ross appeared.

'Morning, guv,' he said.

'Feeling better, sergeant?' asked Dobbs.

'Yes, a bit like Mafeking,' said Ross. The Boer War was still a conflict of surging ups and downs, but Mafeking had been joyfully relieved in May.

'Is this your day for making jokes?' asked Dobbs.

'Just a comment, guv,' said Ross.

'Don't let's have too many like that,' said the Chief Inspector. 'Try arranging for a cable to be sent to the Cork police.'

'Eh?' said Sergeant Ross.

'Listen,' said Dobbs, and explained why he needed the cable to be sent. Mrs Flanagan had mentioned a special man friend in her last letter to her daughter, and asked to be told more about him. It was possible that Maureen Flanagan had replied before meeting her unfortunate end. Perhaps the Cork police would do Scotland Yard the favour of finding out by contacting Mrs

74

Flanagan again. It was to be supposed they'd already called on her to inform her of her daughter's death, following yesterday's cable from the Yard. If she was in possession of her daughter's reply to her last letter, and it contained details of Maureen's special man friend, perhaps Cork would do the Yard a further favour by cabling the relevant extract. And if Mrs Flanagan still had the letter from her daughter that contained the original mention of the man, the Yard would like those details too. 'Got that, my lad? Or would you like to sail the Irish Sea and find out in person?'

'Take a lot of time, guv,' said Ross. 'A cable would be far quicker.'

'So it would,' said Dobbs. 'Glad you agree. Right, sharpen your pencil, lick the point and put the cable together. Let me see the draft before you get it sent. Then think about the hospital laundry.'

'Why?' asked Ross.

'Did you see any men working in the calender room, where they've got those ruddy great mangles?' asked Dobbs.

'They're calenders, guv, not mangles,' said Ross, and the look he received was one that befitted a Chief Inspector silently growling. 'Sorry, guv, they're like mangles, of course.'

'The point is, clever Dick, what kind of men work in other sections of the laundry? Fat men, bald men, skinny men, or men an Irishwoman of thirty might fancy for what they've got in their pockets as well as in their trousers?'

'That's a fair question,' said Ross.

'Did you notice if the superintendent had a telephone in her office?' asked Dobbs.

'I didn't get into her office, guv. She came out to us.'

'Careless oversight of yours, my lad. All right, start drafting that cable.'

'Right,' said Ross. 'Oh, by the way, did you know the *Daily Mail*'s done it on us?'

'I stopped reading newspapers from yesterday,' said the Chief Inspector.

'I've got the *Daily Mail* on my desk,' said Sergeant Ross, and fetched it. He opened it up and placed it on the Chief Inspector's desk. Dobbs examined it. A growl rumbled. The headline above the article was all too threatening to his peace of mind.

IS JACK BACK?

He looked up.

'You've read this, Sergeant?'

'Yes, guv.'

'It's hair-raising, is it?'

'Witches' brew,' said Ross.

'Who wrote it?' asked Dobbs, not caring to look at the credit himself.

'Bloke called Harold Wilkins, guv.'

'Well, find out where his mother lives, go round there and burn her house down. That'll upset him even more than he's just upset me.'

'I assume, guv, that's an order I can refuse?'

'D'you take the *Daily Mail*, Ross?'

'I happen to have it delivered,' said Ross.

'Well, cancel it and have a comic delivered instead,' said Dobbs. 'Take this copy away and set fire to it. Then draft that cable.'

'Very good, sir,' said Ross, and as he left, Inspector George Davis came in. That is, he half came in by showing his head and shoulders.

'Might I henquire if you've got a nasty problem, Chief Inspector?' he said.

'Might, I enquire in turn if you think I have?' said Dobbs.

'Just this awkward business about "Is Jack Back?"'

'Stop reading fairy stories,' growled Dobbs, and Inspector Davis took himself away.

A minute later, with the Chief Inspector about to ask the switchboard to telephone Guy's Hospital laundry, his instrument rang. The call was from the laundry superintendent, and he took it.

'Good morning, Chief Inspector.'

'Good morning, marm. I was about to get through to you.'

'Two minds with but a single thought?' said the Superintendent. 'Well, I wanted to let you know that a close friend of Miss Flanagan's came in yesterday after you'd gone. She brought some flowers and also asked if she could have that unfortunate woman's job. Miss Flanagan had promised that if she left us sometime, she'd ask me if her friend could take her place.'

'You're speaking of a female friend?'

'A young lady friend,' said the Superintendent, objecting politely to the use of the word 'female'. 'I asked her one or two questions about her relationship with Miss Flanagan, thinking men friends might be mentioned, but she seemed so distressed about the murder – as we all were – that I decided to leave it until this morning to inform you the girl may possibly be able to help you. She and Miss Flanagan did apparently meet men in passing when they were out together. She should be feeling a little better today, and more able to answer questions, which of course you'll want to ask.'

'Very sensible of you, marm, and very obliging,' said Dobbs.

'Shall I give you her name and address?'

'That would be even more obliging,' said Dobbs, and took down the details that came over the line. That done, he said, 'Many thanks, marm, we'll interview her. Meanwhile, you've men working in the laundry as well as women, haven't you?'

'Yes, indeed, for heavier work,' said the Superintendent. 'For delivering and collecting, for packing and so on. Laundry is very weighty.'

'Do the men come into contact with the ladies working in the calender room?' asked the Chief Inspector.

'Constantly.'

'I'd like to come and take a look at them, marm.'

'I can't quarrel with that,' said the Superintendent, 'I understand your need to take a look at all men known by Miss Flanagan. I'd dislike it very much, however, if any man here proved to be capable of murdering the poor woman.'

'I've got a fixed dislike, marm, of the capabilities of a certain type of wrong-doer.'

'I can understand that, Chief Inspector. You'll be coming here sometime this morning?'

'I'd like to, with Sergeant Ross.'

'Of course. What a nice man he is. Goodbye for the moment.'

I suppose, thought the Chief Inspector, as he put the receiver back on its hook, that that leaves me out of the nice ones. Let's see, about Miss Whatsername – yes, Daisy Cummings of Ellen Street – the distressed friend. Is she fit to be interviewed?

* * *

Looking over, talking to and asking questions of the men who worked in the laundry proved a waste of time until one man, a burly specimen of thirty-two, refused to say where he was or what he was doing on the evening of the murder.

'That's not very helpful,' said Sergeant Ross. 'Not to us or to you. In fact, it makes things awkward for you.'

'Look, gents, can we talk private, like?'

'It's either that or at the Yard,' said the Chief Inspector, brushing his moustache. Well-trimmed, it could have taken him into the Guards if he'd attended a public school.

The talk in private took place in a room smelling of polluted steam. The launderer, Alfred Cook of Ash Street, Walworth, explained that Mrs Cook, his one and only better half, had requested him to repose in a single bed at night instead of sharing the double bed with her. The double bed, in fact, had disappeared when he got home from his work one evening, and in its place were two single beds. Not new, mind, second-hand, but good condition. Mrs Cook, bless her heart, requested this arrangement on account of not wanting to be put in the family way any more, seeing it had happened four times in the past. He couldn't say it wasn't a reasonable request, but he could say it didn't accord with his natural inclinations, which had a habit of raising Old Harry in him. It was a gloomy night life he suffered in his single bed. Well, he had what anyone might call all his facilities in good working order, and his natural inclinations on top of that. One evening he met a widow woman in the pub, and got friendly with her. They found out they both had the same kind of suffering, and as there was only one way of curing each other, they set about it. In her bed, in her flat in Heywood Street. He didn't inform Mrs Cook that he was in fairly regular accord with the widow woman, as she might have chucked him and the single bed out into the street. It so happened he was with the widow woman on the evening of the murder. Mrs Cook thought he was down at the pub, of course. Would the Chief Inspector kindly not inform her otherwise? Mrs Cook was a good wife and mother, but she had some awkward principles.

'Name and address of the widow lady?' said Sergeant Ross, and George Cook supplied the information. 'Is she a working woman?' asked Ross.

'Eh?' said George Cook.

'A working woman?' said Ross.

'Excuse me, guv, but what woman ain't a workin' one, except the rich?'

'There you are, Sergeant Ross, how'd you like your eggs fried?' said the Chief Inspector.

'Tenderly, guv,' said Ross.

'Mrs Amelia Lambert works in the Penny Bazaar by the Elephant and Castle,' said George Cook. 'Pardon me, guv, but yer'll go easy on 'er, won't yer?'

'Very easy, Mr Cook,' said Ross, and he and the Chief Inspector left.

'I suppose you'd better check, my lad,' said Dobbs. 'Meet me back at the Yard, and then we'll get off to Whitechapel and interview Daisy Bell.'

'Daisy Cummings, guv.'

'I know that, sunshine, I just happened to be thinking about a bicycle made for two. For me and Mrs Dobbs on Sunday afternoons in the summer. By the way, I suppose Fleet Street did us the honour today of publishing details of Godfrey Who, together with a request for him to come forward?'

'Haven't you seen the papers?' asked Ross, as they walked along St Thomas Street.

'Didn't I tell you I'd stopped reading them?'

'So you did, guv, but I didn't know if you were serious or not,' said Ross. 'Anyway, Godfrey Who's got a mention in all of them.'

'Well, perhaps he'll come and acquaint himself with us,' said Dobbs. They parted then, Sergeant Ross turning left into Borough High Street, and the Chief Inspector turning right for London Bridge while looking for a hansom cab to take him back to Scotland Yard.

The widow, thirty-five-year-old Mrs Amelia Lambert, interviewed in the little office of the Penny Bazaar, proved to be plump, affable and likeable. Once she was assured of the confidential nature of the interview, she was also forthcoming, letting Sergeant Ross know she quite understood Mrs Cook's determination not to be put in the family way any more. Of course, it was naturally a bit hard on Mr Cook, poor bloke, but a wife did have a right to keep her better half off her when she'd more than done her duty by presenting him with four children. Being childless herself, for reasons that she didn't discuss with men, she was a highly suitable consolation to a man like George. He'd told her all his facilities were in a highly charged condition, which made his suffering chronic. He was a bit of a rough diamond to talk to and look at, but a really nice feller all in all, and he was right about his facilities. Crikey, not half he wasn't, he made her feel the ceiling was falling on

81

her sometimes. Yes, he was exercising his facilities with her between nine o'clock and ten thirty on the night that poor Irishwoman got done in, so he didn't have any cause, anyway, to go after her. Nor would he. Outside of his natural inclinations, he was as gentle as a lamb. If he hadn't been, he might have forced himself on his wife.

'Good enough, Mrs Lambert, thanks,' said Sergeant Ross.

'Oh, pleasure, sergeant, I'm sure. If you want to talk to me again, come round to me little flat at number twelve, Heywood Street, one evening. It's very comfy, with nice cushions and everything.'

'Well, thanks, Mrs Lambert, I'll remember that if we need any other information from you,' said Sergeant Ross.

'How's your facilities?' asked the affable widow.

'Not on a par with Mr Cook's, I'd say. Good morning, Mrs Lambert.'

Chapter Five

'Murphy!'

'Is it meself you're wanting, Sergeant?' asked Constable Murphy of Cork on the north side.

'Well now, would I be hollering for O'Hara if I wanted you?' said Sergeant Corrigan.

'Sure, and it wouldn't be like you to do that,' said Murphy, 'though me own dear mother was inclined to confusion, so she was, there being seven of us and all with different names.'

'I'm not your mother,' said Sergeant Corrigan.

'Jasus, Sergeant, will Mrs Corrigan be thanking the Lord for that?' said Murphy.

'Button your collar,' said Sergeant Corrigan. 'Now, we called at Killarney Cottages up by the high road yesterday afternoon to acquaint the Flanagans with the sad information contained in the cable from Scotland Yard.'

'Ah, that poor Mrs Flanagan and the shawl she put over her head,' said Murphy. He crossed himself. 'A suffering blow to that warm heart of hers, so it was. Murder and all.'

'There's another cable,' said Sergeant Corrigan. 'Read it.'

Murphy read it. It was long but lucid, and it

meant there was another call to make on the Flanagans.

'Hell and the dark devil, Sergeant, is it the murdering swine himself poor Maureen Flanagan fell in with, rest her soul?'

'Hell and the dark devil will have him, Murphy, if he's the man,' said Sergeant Corrigan. 'You've seen what you've got to do?'

'Bless all the saints, Sergeant, is it meself that's got to go?' asked Murphy. 'And them at their wake? And Mrs Flanagan so poor a church mouse would be richer? She's going to miss the regular money Maureen sent.'

'It's you that's got to go, Murphy. Sure, and aren't you a friend to Molly Flanagan, Maureen's younger sister? Where's the bike?'

'In the shed, Sergeant, with Constable O'Toole repairing a puncture of the inner tube.'

'Well now, will you be so good as to hurry him up, Constable Murphy?' said Sergeant Corrigan. 'If there's a letter, and if it's informative, bring it back here, not forgetting the other, if Mrs Flanagan still has it.'

'Ah, it's meself wishing I didn't have to go, Sergeant,' said Murphy.

'Yer spalpeen, is it that kind of wishing that'll help Scotland Yard to lay their hands on the hound of the devil?' said Sergeant Corrigan.

'I'm away, Sergeant, I'm away,' said Murphy, putting his helmet on.

It was lunchtime, and the gentleman was out and about. He did not have his bag with him, or his walking-stick, and his footsteps did not take him to the East End. The East End by day was merely a city slum, sleazy, grimy and dolorous, its wretched people creatures of unloveliness. Only at night, in the fog, did its atmosphere create for him the ghoulish pictures and imaginings that stirred him to his depths.

In the West End, the misty day offered scenes not in the least offensive to the eye. Around Trafalgar Square the traffic, thick with growlers, hansom cabs, carts and horse-drawn omnibuses, moved as slowly as a sluggish river. Closed private carriages looked disdainful of all other vehicles. Women, their long skirts hitched, trod the damp pavements cautiously. Fashionable ladies, accompanied by fashionable gentlemen, alighted gracefully from carriages to enter the gilded portals of the fashionable restaurants in the Strand and in the avenues off Piccadilly Circus.

He strolled around the Circus. A flower girl, shawled, black-skirted, her faded boater tipped, made her play.

'Bokay for yer lady, sir?'

He stopped. Her bright eyes, the brighter because of her pale face, cajoled him.

'Not today,' he said.

'Well, you got a kind face, sir, so buy some for yerself, won't yer?'

'A buttonhole,' he said.

'There we are, sir.' She took a bright red carnation, attached by a little strand of wire to a small fern leaf, and slipped it into the buttonhole of his coat. 'There, makes yer look really swell, sir, and only a tanner.'

He gave her a shilling, and told her to keep the change. She was delighted, and delight made her look pretty. He might have contemplated the pleasure of coming upon her in the fog of Whitechapel one night. But no, his razor-sharp knife was not for any hard-working flower girl. It was for the kind of women who had stirred the mind and hand of the Ripper.

He smiled and went on his way, looking for a pub that would provide him with a drink and a sandwich.

Chief Inspector Dobbs, having received from Sergeant Ross details of his interview with Mrs Amelia Lambert, delayed his visit to Whitechapel until the afternoon. He and Sergeant Ross arrived outside the house in Ellen Street when the mist was floating around the houses, the rooftops, and the ragged kids. Up scampered the kids as the CID officers alighted from a growler.

'Carry yer bags, misters?'

There were no bags.

'Shine yer boots, misters?'

They didn't need shining.

'Want an errand run, misters?'

No errands were required to be run. Just the cabbie needed paying.

''Oo d'yer want, misters? We knows ev'rybody round 'ere. 'Oo d'yer want?'

'We know who we want,' said Sergeant Ross, as the cab moved off.

'Well, that's a bleedin' shame for us, mister, we could've took yer there for a penny. Tell yer what, mister, 'ave yer got a penny on yer for me starvin' sister, 'ave yer, mister?'

It was there, lodged in their eyes behind the cunning born of want, the feverish light of kids who already knew their chances of survival were desperately slim. Most who dwelt in the reeking slums beyond Ellen Street were little old wizened men by the time they were ten, when some would already be coughing themselves to death, and all would be scavenging for scraps. These, the kids of Ellen Street, might be a little better off. Some even had good boots on their feet. But they still knew they had to fight to win themselves a decent existence.

Sergeant Ross detached his gaze from the feverish light. He parted his overcoat, dug into his trouser pocket, fished out three pennies and three ha'pennies, and scattered them. The kids yelled, swooped, pounced and fought. Chief Inspector Dobbs eyed his sergeant thoughtfully.

'One way of getting them from under our feet, guv,' said Ross.

'The mortality rate of kids under twelve is fifty per cent,' said the Chief Inspector, and knocked on the door of the house. The kids had already swarmed back by the time Bridget opened the door.

'Afternoon,' said Dobbs. 'Miss Cummings?'

Bridget's eyes were coal-black as she regarded them in their bowler hats, their overcoats, their polished boots and their well-fed solidity.

'If I ain't mistaken, you're coppers,' she said.

'Chief Inspector Dobbs of the Yard, and Detective-Sergeant Ross. May we come in?'

'Not bloody likely,' said Bridget, certain they were here to question her about her role in yesterday's riot. 'In any case, I'm innocent.'

'Of what, Miss Cummings?' asked Dobbs.

'And I've got an alibi,' said Bridget. 'One of yer own constables'll tell yer I got dragged in accidental and was hit by a brick.'

'You're referring to yesterday's riot?' said Sergeant Ross.

'Good as murder of the workers in the fog,' said Bridget, 'and I'm lucky to be alive.'

'We're not enquiring about the riot, Miss Cummings, but about another matter, and you're not under suspicion,' said Ross. 'We'd just like to talk to you to see if you can help us. Can we come in?'

'I ain't partial to invitin' coppers into my 'ouse,' said Bridget, 'but all right, in yer come, only don't bring those kids in with yer. And wipe yer boots.'

They entered.

A kid yelled, 'Gi's anuvver penny, mister!'

The door closed on him and the others. Bridget led the way into the parlour. The fire was going in the kitchen, but not in the plainly furnished parlour. Bridget objected on principle to making flatties feel comfortable.

'Well?' she said.

'You're Miss Daisy Cummings?' said Sergeant Ross.

'Beg yer pardon?' said Bridget.

'You visited Guy's Hospital laundry yesterday and secured a job?' said the Chief Inspector.

'Not me,' said Bridget, 'that was me sister. She's Daisy. What's goin' on? What d'yer want to talk to 'er about?'

'About a friend of hers, the late Maureen Flanagan,' said Dobbs.

'Eh?' said Bridget, on her guard.

'We'd like to ask her some questions,' said Ross, 'but not to her disadvantage. We think she might be able to help us in respect of a certain man who knew Miss Flanagan.'

'That poor murdered woman?' said Bridget, thinking oh blimey, here's a chicken come home to roost. Daisy hadn't known Maureen Flanagan any more than she knew the King of Siam. 'I'm not sure Daisy's 'ere just yet.'

Daisy, however, came in at that point. She'd heard voices. She saw the callers, two impressive men with their hats off, the older one rugged and fatherly-looking, with a kind of benign expression, the younger quite handsome and sort of sympathetic-looking.

'Oh,' she said.

'Miss Daisy Cummings?' said the Chief Inspector.

'Yes, that's me,' said Daisy.

'Daisy, they're from Scotland Yard and they want to talk to you about that murdered woman, Maureen Flanagan, about you bein' a friend of hers,' said Bridget. Daisy gulped. Bridget gave her time to think by going on. 'Daisy, I didn't know you knew Maureen Flanagan. You sure you didn't mix 'er up with Mary Finnegan that used to live in Whitechapel Road?'

'Oh, lor', I've gone all dizzy, where's a chair?' breathed Daisy. She selected one and sat down.

'You couldn't have mistaken Maureen Flanagan for anyone else under the circumstances, could you?' said Sergeant Ross.

'Oh, me 'ead,' said Daisy.

'Take your time,' said Dobbs, observing the expressive features of the elder sister. Now there's an interesting young woman, he thought. Eyes as brilliant as black diamonds, and as challenging as a cavalryman's going at full gallop. Strong buxom body, even if she is hard-up, and she has to be hard-up living here. A cubic foot of black hair shaped into a beehive was fit for a Gypsy empress straight out of Hungary. A lion tamer would have problems getting the better of this woman. 'Miss Cummings,' he said to Daisy, 'I understand you shared outings with the late and unfortunate Maureen Flanagan.'

'Oh, it's only unfortunate gettin' murdered, is it?' said Bridget. 'I thought unfortunate meant you'd just lost yer purse or fractured yer collarbone.'

'I suppose you could say there are degrees of misfortune,' said Dobbs.

'I suppose Maureen Flanagan could say that as well,' said Bridget.

'Can you answer some questions, miss?' asked Sergeant Ross of Daisy.

'Oh, me 'ead,' said Daisy, getting ready to cross her fingers.

'You're still distressed about your friend's death, is that it?' suggested the Chief Inspector.

'Well, I do feel sort of ill,' said Daisy, hands in her lap, fingers now crossed.

'That's understandable, very,' said Dobbs, 'but I hope you won't mind, Miss Cummings, if I suggest you've got something to tell us that's making you feel uncomfortable, not ill.'

'I wouldn't be surprised if she was ill,' said Bridget. 'seeing most people round 'ere would be paralytic with illness if they 'ad their parlours cluttered up with policemen. Of course, that ain't personal. I mean, I can't say, can I, that you and Sergeant Cross don't honour yer mothers and fathers.'

'Um – it's Sergeant Ross,' said Dobbs.

'Oh, beg 'is pardon, I'm sure,' said Bridget.

'Miss Cummings' Sergeant Ross addressed Daisy again. 'Were you a close friend of Maureen Flanagan's, close enough to know if there was one particular man in her life?'

'If I say no, will I get arrested?' asked Daisy.

'Only over my dead body,' said Bridget.

'Arrested for what, Miss Cummings?' asked Dobbs.

'For saying I was a friend when I wasn't,' said Daisy.

'What?' said Ross. 'What?' he said again, this time in disbelief.

'Hold on, hold on,' said Dobbs, 'you are the young lady who applied to the laundry superintendent for Maureen Flanagan's job, aren't you?'

'Oh, yes, that's me, sir,' gulped Daisy, 'only I wasn't 'er friend. I just said I was so's I 'ad a better chance of gettin' the job.'

'If that's a fact, guv,' said Ross, 'we've been done to a turn by a Whitechapel hen cuckoo.'

''Ere, watch what yer callin' me sister,' said Bridget.

Daisy was pink. Sergeant Ross, the wind taken out of his sails, was temporarily out of action. Chief Inspector Dobbs, on knowing terms with the frailties of human nature far longer, reacted philosophically.

'You mean you didn't know Maureen Flanagan at all?' he said to Daisy.

'Oh, beggin' yer pardon, no, I didn't,' said Daisy. 'You ain't goin' to arrest me, are yer, sir?'

'I'm thinking about it,' said Dobbs. 'I could have you locked up in the Tower of London.'

'And beheaded,' said Ross.

'Oh, yer monsters,' said Bridget.

'Oh, me 'ead,' gasped Daisy at the thought of losing it.

'Daisy, your 'ead's all right,' said Bridget, 'it's theirs that ought to be chopped off.'

'Don't you know it's a chargeable offence to lead the police up the garden?' said Ross.

'Well, it ain't Daisy's garden,' said Bridget. 'All we've got is a back yard.'

Sergeant Ross glanced at the Chief Inspector, who said, 'Miss Cummings, that's positive, is it, that you didn't know Maureen Flanagan in any way at all?'

'Oh, I never saw the poor woman in all me life,' said Daisy.

The Chief Inspector put his hat on. Sergeant Ross put a hand into his coat pocket. Daisy and Bridget both thought he was going to produce handcuffs. Daisy quivered and Bridget bridled. Sergeant Ross drew out a handkerchief and blew his nose.

'Time we left, Sergeant Ross, someone's been wasting our time,' said Dobbs.

Bridget followed the men from the parlour to the street door.

'You ain't goin' to charge Daisy, are yer?' she said.

'Tell her it's her lucky day,' said Dobbs.

'There's no lucky days for Whitechapel people,' said Bridget, 'only some days that ain't as bad as most.'

'You can take it from me, Miss Cummings, I don't disbelieve that,' said Dobbs, and he and Sergeant Ross left. They made progress through the mist with long strides, distancing themselves from the street kids.

'Flammed us, by Christ,' said Ross.

'Not us, my son, the laundry superintendent,' said Dobbs.

'I could say it was the same thing, guv.'

'You could, and you could say it twice over, but it wouldn't be true,' said Dobbs. 'At no time did Daisy Cummings tell us she knew Flanagan. We got that from the superintendent. So you could say she was the one who supplied us with false information. Was it you who told Daisy Cummings we could have her locked up in the Tower of London?'

'Not me, guv. That was you.'

'Who mentioned beheading?' asked Dobbs.

'I did,' said Ross.

'Thought it was you,' said Dobbs. 'How'd you feel about arresting the laundry superintendent and mentioning beheading to her?'

'Give over, guv. You going to inform her that Daisy Cummings told her a fairy story?'

'Well, my lad,' said Dobbs, 'you could say that was none of my business.'

'I'd have thought—'

'Or yours, sunshine.'

'We're going to let Daisy Cummings get away with what you might call fraudulent deception?' said Ross.

'Well, I was guilty of that myself once,' said Dobbs. 'Told a Bethnal Green bloke who'd taken to burglary that his old lady had blown the gaff on him, which made him come clean. Come to think of it, I also told Basher Morris of Stepney, noted while wearing a mask for putting coppers into hospital, that the footprints I'd found on a constable's chest matched his right boot. He swore he'd trod on the constable's chest accidental. I charged him. Fair cop, he said. By the way, I've got an idea that at some time during the progress of this investigation – if you can call it progress – I mentioned blank walls. Can you confirm that?'

'Yes, you mentioned it to the reporters,' said Ross.

'Well, we've just run into one, so I'll be able to mention it again whey they turn up later. Stop that cab.'

Ross stepped off the kerb in Leman Street to hail an approaching hansom. The vehicle took the CID men back to Scotland Yard, where a cable from Cork awaited Dobbs. It informed him that the Flanagan family had not heard from Maureen Flanagan since October, when in her last letter she mentioned, quote, 'By the way, I've met a man who's a bit special.' Just that. No name, no details.

'That's no help,' said Ross.

'Well, I'll say this much,' said the Chief Inspector, 'it's nothing I'd have sailed the Irish Sea for.'

'Crikey,' said Bridget after the CID men had gone, 'you nearly got done for, Daisy, tellin' the laundry superintendent you knew Maureen Flanagan.'

'Me?' said Daisy. 'Well, I like that, it was you that went and suggested it.'

'I wasn't meself at the time,' said Bridget, 'I 'ad the starvin' and strikin' workers on me mind. When I think 'ow we all got bashed and brutalized by the bluebottles, I still go livid. Daisy, 'ow can governments let their own people as good as starve to death, 'ow can they send the police in to break the 'eads of workers fightin' for a livin' wage?'

'They can do it because none of them live in the

94

East End,' said Daisy. 'If they did, they'd soon change their minds about all the 'orribly poor people.'

'No, they wouldn't, they'd just go and live somewhere else,' said Bridget.

'Did that police inspector really say I wasn't goin' to be charged?' asked Daisy.

'Yes, he said this is yer lucky day.'

'I don't know it is,' said Daisy. 'I mean, s'pose 'e tells the laundry superintendent? She'll take me job away before I've even started it.'

'If she's goin' to do that she'll write to you and say so,' said Bridget. 'If she don't write, then go in on Monday mornin' as if nothing's 'appened. If she wants to 'ave a word with you, tell 'er you wasn't yerself at the time, that you'd 'ad 'orrible dreams about a gravel pit fallin' in on our dad and suffocatin' 'im to death, which it did. That's it, Daisy, try and break her 'eart about our dad and 'ow it left us suffering and penniless, and 'ow the dream upset you so much that you wasn't yerself all day and the day after.'

'But I didn't 'ave no dream,' said Daisy.

'Well, say you did and keep yer fingers crossed,' said Bridget. 'You've got to get that job, Daisy.'

'All right,' said Daisy, 'I'll do that, I'll keep me fingers crossed.'

'And if that copper Fred Billings comes round anytime I'm not 'ere,' said Bridget, 'you make sure 'e don't even get 'is big toe over our doorstep. You 'ear, Daisy?'

'Well, Billy says—'

'I'll 'ave a word with Billy,' said Bridget. 'That boy thinks that just because 'e wears trousers, he can come it over you and me.'

The Fleet Street scribes were gathered together like a flock of expectant owls. Chief Inspector Dobbs, addressing them, first made it known he was considerably put out by an article in the *Daily Mail* that suggested a certain notorious villain given to butchery had risen up from his grave to take up where he'd left off. Consequently, the panic-sticken people of Whitechapel had rioted.

'Come off it, Inspector,' said the *Daily Mail,* 'that—'

'Chief Inspector,' corrected Sergeant Ross.

'Yes, I heard you yesterday, sergeant,' said the *Daily Mail.*

'No reason to be forgetful, then,' said Ross.

'Chief Inspector,' said the *Daily Mail,* 'that riot took place before the article appeared.'

'I'm expecting to hear any moment that the East End people are out on the streets again, all due to a misguided piece of newspaper talk putting the wind up them,' said Dobbs. 'If that means another riot's going to develop, I won't like it, nor will the Commissioner, nor the Home Secretary. Your editors will be on the carpet.'

'Can we have a progress report, Chief Inspector?' asked the *Daily Chronicle.*

'It's slow going, I won't deny it,' said Dobbs. 'But you know how some investigations work. Unless the perpetrator gives himself up and obligingly confesses, it's a question of making enquiries, listing the possibles and probables, searching for footprints, looking for a weapon, filling up notebooks, going about the process of elimination—'

'Could you stop there, Chief Inspector, and

simply let us know if you've got any suspects?' asked the *Westminster Gazette*.

'Several,' said Dobbs.

A ripple of interest ran around Fleet Street.

'Several?' said the *Morning Post*.

'Bound to be in a case like this,' said Dobbs. 'I've told you, of course, that it's pretty certain Tooley Street wasn't the actual scene of the crime.'

'No, you haven't told us that, sir,' said *The Times*.

'You sure?'

'We're sure,' said several voices in concert.

'Well, we all suffer from oversight at times,' said Dobbs. Sergeant Ross kept his face straight. He knew his boss liked to feed meat bit by bit to the hungry of Fleet Street. Porridge he ladled out. 'Yes, you can publish that piece of information, that it's pretty certain the unfortunate victim was already dead when she was – um – placed in Tooley Street. The guilty man or woman—'

'Woman?' said Fleet Street almost as one.

'We haven't finished eliminating our several suspects,' said Dobbs.

'There's a woman suspect?' said the *Daily Mail*.

'I hope the possibilty'll teach your editor not to fall over himself concerning his own ideas about who did what and who didn't,' said Dobbs without a single quiver of any eyelash. 'Come to that, gents, don't fall over yourselves about this possible female. Stick to several suspects. I don't want any particular suspect to get the wind up and vanish, and you don't want that, either. It would count as assisting the enemy, which could be a chargeable offence.'

'Balls of fire, you're proscribing the freedom of the Press?' said the *Daily News*.

'Sergeant Ross,' said Dobbs, 'what's proscribing the freedom of the Press?'

'No idea, guv,' said Ross.

'Well, gents, just print what's fair, reasonable and sensible,' said Dobbs. 'Print that we've eliminated all the victim's acquaintances at her place of work, including one who refused to produce an alibi until we talked seriously to this person.'

'Person?' said the *Morning Post*.

'Another woman?' said the *Daily Mail*.

'Did I say so?' said Dobbs. 'Have I said so? Person, I said. You can print that.'

Sergeant Ross hid a grin. The Chief Inspector was giving the reporters the run-around.

'What about this man called Godfrey?' asked *The Times*.

'Ah,' said Dobbs, and brushed his moustache.

'You've got something?' said the *Daily Mail*.

'I've got a duty to ask questions,' said Dobbs.

'Chief Inspector, has he come forward?' asked the *Westminster Gazette*.

'The victim's known friend?' said Dobbs. 'The person known as Godfrey? No, not yet.'

'He must have seen what's been printed about him,' said the *Daily News*.

'On the assumption that he might be illiterate—'

'Illiterate?' said the *Morning Post*.

'To help you, it means, gen'rally, someone who can't read or write,' said Dobbs.

'Thanks for that,' said the *Daily Mail*.

'Pleasure,' said Dobbs. 'Where was I, Sergeant Ross?'

'You were mentioning that the suspect Godfrey might not be able to read or write, guv,' said Ross.

'So I was.' Dobbs brushed his moustache again.

'In that case, anything in a newspaper would be double Dutch to him, which could be the reason why he hasn't shown up. But if he has seen any of the reports and been able to read them, he'll have to come forward or risk being considered a prime case for investigation. There shouldn't be any difficulty in tracing him. Someone who knows him will recognize his description and offer us information about him.'

'You still think it's a straightforward murder?' said the *Westminster Gazette*.

Chief Inspector Dobbs regarded the questioner in mild surprise.

'Myself,' he said, 'I don't see any murder as a straightforward act, but a very nasty one. It's what the Yard terms the ultimate in mortal violence, a capital offence that deprives the victim of his or her life. It's upsetting all round, and every one gives me a headache.'

'I meant you still don't think there's a threat to other women at the hands of another maniac?' said the *Westminster Gazette*.

'Another maniac?' said Dobbs threateningly.

'Another—'

'Don't say it,' said Dobbs. 'If you'll excuse me now, gents, I'll get on with doing something about my headache. Afternoon.'

'What's the weather like?' asked Dobbs at five o'clock.

'Foggy,' said Sergeant Ross.

'How'd you know?'

'Look at your window, guv,' said Ross.

The Chief Inspector turned in his chair. His window showed nothing of the lights of London.

They were hidden by that which frequently fouled the air, a mixture of moist soot and dirt that exuded each winter from the chimneys of the sprawling city's houses and factories.

'That looks like a large amount of fog,' said Dobbs.

'Does that mean our visit to the West End is postponed again?' asked Ross.

'How far would we get, d'you suppose?'

'I think we could get as far as you want, guv. Say as far as Soho.'

'I didn't mean that,' said Dobbs, 'I meant with finding tarts who knew Flanagan and could tell us something about her. And you can forget Soho. So can I. She couldn't have had her throat cut there, too far from where her body was found,'

'Unless he loaded it into a closed cab, guv.'

'Is that a serious assumption?' asked Dobbs.

'Just a quick thought,' said Ross.

'Put a bomb under it and blow it up,' said Dobbs. 'No villain, however clever and crafty, could get away with that dodge. And I think you're on the wrong track about the West End. That's also too far from Tooley Street.'

'Might I correct you, guv? I think you suggested the West End.'

'Did I?' Dobbs eyed his sergeant enquiringly. 'What did you suggest, then?'

'I just went along with you,' said Ross.

'You agreed we'd see if we could spot a likely suspect lurking in the proximity of some suitable tarts in the West End?'

'Yes, guv.'

'Was that because I'm a Chief Inspector?'

'Yes, guv, that and the fact that you're a bit of a thinker,' said Ross.

'Well, my lad, I think I thought wrong. I think, as I said, that the West End wouldn't have been the place, after all. If Flanagan was on the north side of the river that night, and if she had copped it in the West End, he'd have had to carry her body over Waterloo Bridge. From there, would he have gone all the way to Tooley Street? Not on your life, my son. Looking at Tooley Street, he'd have used London Bridge or Tower Bridge to get there – no, wait, a bit, what am I talking about? Once on any bridge, he'd have dropped her into the river, wouldn't he?'

'But we know he didn't,' said Ross. 'Neither of us think she was the type to stand in East End doorways looking for custom. Let's assume she was definitely picked up in the West End, and that the bloke then told her he'd take her to his flat or hotel in a cab. Isn't it possible he cut her throat in the cab, paid the cabbie at a certain point near Tooley Street, told him the lady was one over the eight, and then lifted her out and disappeared with her?'

'Very good, sergeant,' said Dobbs, 'but might I ask what the cabbie later did with all the blood and how he managed to beat the pea-souper? Most traffic was at a standstill.'

'Sod it,' said Ross. 'I think I just committed an oversight.'

'Come to that,' said Dobbs thoughtfully, 'just where is all that blood? There were traces of a small amount on the scarf, a little on her blouse. Where did most of it finish up? Down a drain? Say a drain around Tower Hill? That's a point, sunshine. Tower Hill's not an unoccupied area at night. I think that tomorrow we'll ask a few questions around that area, and yes, around the streets close to her lodgings as well. Flanagan might have decided Tower Hill was as far as she wanted to go north of the river that evening, because of the heavy fog, or alternatively to have risked her own neighbourhood.'

'It's a thought,' said Ross.

'Yes, I – no, hold on, my lad, what're you talking about?' said Dobbs. 'Who the hell around Tower Hill or her own neighbourhood or anywhere else would have spotted anything that mattered to us through that kind of fog?'

'Beg to point out, guv, it wasn't me that suggested making enquiries around—'

'Shake yourself a bit, my lad,' said Dobbs. 'We've got one particular problem we need to take into consideration every time you make – or I make – suggestions concerning possible witnesses.'

'What problem is that?' asked Ross.

'That pea-souper of a fog,' said the Chief Inspector. 'A great help to the villain, but no help at all to us.'

Chapter Six

Coming off duty, Constable Fred Billings braved the fog to make his way to Ellen Street. It was fifteen minutes to six when he knocked on the door of the Cummings' house.

Bridget, suspecting who was using the knocker, answered the summons in quick time.

'Evening, Bridget,' said Fred.

''Oppit,' said Bridget.

'Have a heart,' said Fred.

'I don't 'ave any heart for coppers,' said Bridget.

'Allowin' for that,' said Fred, 'might I come in and discuss rentin' yer spare room?'

'What spare room?' asked Bridget.

'The one you're advertisin',' said Fred, 'the one we discussed previous.'

'I wish you'd get it into your thick 'elmet that it excludes applications from bluebottles,' said Bridget.

'It's cold out 'ere and foggy,' said Fred, 'so could I come in and talk about yer problems?'

'Don't get funny,' said Bridget, 'just 'oppit.'

Daisy appeared, in her apron.

'Oh, 'ello, Fred, come in,' she said. 'I'm cookin' supper for me and Billy, but you can still come in.'

'No, 'e can't,' said Bridget.

103

'Bridget, that ain't nice, keepin' Fred on a cold doorstep,' said Daisy. 'You'd best get ready for goin' to work, it'll take time in this fog. Come on in, Fred.'

Bridget ground her teeth as Fred slipped past her and followed Daisy into the kitchen which, basic though it was was with its plain and cheap furniture, was nevertheless warm from the heat of the range fire. Bridget usually managed to find a bit of money for fuel, and whenever she couldn't, Billy always managed to scrounge some from the yards of local coal merchants. It was done with the aid of a sack, a quick survey of a yard, a fast furtive sortie into that part of the enemy's territory which was littered with nuggets, and an even faster dash for home. Neither Bridget nor Daisy discouraged Billy's acquisitive sorties, an enterprise commonly practised by the quick and active younger residents of Whitechapel. It was miserable enough to be poor, it was even more miserable to be cold as well.

'Now,' said Fred, sniffing at the aroma of cheap bacon pieces slowly frying, 'about me offer to rent the room – no, hold on, kindly accept this first, with me sincere compliments.' He produced a bottle of port and placed it on the table.

'Oh, ain't that nice of Fred?' said Daisy. 'A whole new bottle of port. Just like Christmas.'

'Just like a crafty bribe, you mean,' said Bridget. 'We ain't acceptin' it.'

'Well, I am,' said Daisy, 'it was given with a good 'eart, and me and Billy can enjoy a drop with our supper. Thanks, Fred, you're a gent.'

'Don't make me laugh,' said Bridget, 'it's a bribe, I tell yer, Daisy.'

'Just a friendly gesture,' said Fred, 'and I've only

come to ask if you've decided I can 'ave the room.'

'Well,' said Daisy.

'No,' said Bridget.

'But Billy's agreed,' said Daisy.

'That boy wants 'is head examined,' said Bridget. 'I'm goin' to get ready for me work now, and when I come down I 'ope Constable Fred Billings won't be where he is now, in our kitchen.' She disappeared with an aggressive flounce of her skirts, and a few moments later Billy arrived home. He'd been able to leave work a little early. He said a typically cheerful hello to Fred. Seventeen-year-old Billy was one of the few optimists who dwelt in the East End, and his optimism was invariably visible in his approach to life, people and opportunities.

''Ave yer come about the room, Fred?' he asked.

'That's it, me young cocksparrer,' said Fred.

'And he's give us a bottle of port with 'is kind compliments,' said Daisy, keeping an eye on the frying-pan and its aromatic contents.

'Well, that's pleasin', that is, a bottle of port,' said Billy. 'When d'yer want to move in, Fred?'

'Anytime,' said Fred, 'except Bridget's still a bit contrary.'

'Oh, yer don't want to take too much notice of Bridget and 'er funny ways,' said Billy.

'Her funny ways might include chuckin' her flat iron at me,' said Fred.

'Well, you can take a flat iron or two, can't yer, Fred?' said Billy. 'I've taken saucepans, saucepan lids and enamel meat dishes occasional. I ain't sayin' they didn't 'urt a bit at the time, but there ain't no scars. In fact, Fanny, the grocer's daughter, 'as been 'eard to remark I could go on the stage. That was when I was in the stores at the back of the shop wiv 'er, and she 'ad her mince pies shut.'

''Ow could she 'ave remarked on yer looks when she 'ad 'er eyes shut?' asked Daisy.

'It was in between kisses,' said Billy. 'Mind,' he added thoughtfully, 'she still 'ad her mince pies shut. Still, I daresay she knew what she was talkin' about.'

'You Billy,' said Daisy, turning the pieces, 'you shouldn't kiss girls in a grocer's storeroom.'

'Oh, I wouldn't say that, Daisy,' said Fred. 'A lot more private than a railway station. About the room, do I wait until Bridget's come round to agreein'?'

'Well,' said Daisy. Daisy needed, in a manner of speaking, the strong arm of a supportive voice when she was uncertain of herself.

'I'm wiv yer, Daisy,' said Billy, 'I'm agreein' wiv yer that Fred can rent the available accommerdation.'

Daisy, hearing Bridget on her way down, said, 'Yes, all right, Billy, we'll talk to Bridget tomorrer mornin'.'

Bridget, entering the kitchen in hat and coat, frowned to see that Fred was still present.

'Someone's big feet still crowdin' the floor, are they? Well, I'm goin' now. Billy, you can see Constable Fred Billings out.'

'I'll walk yer down to the Aldgate tube, Bridget,' said Fred.

'Not much you won't,' said Bridget, 'I don't reckon it's safe walkin' anywhere in the fog with a copper.' Off she went. Leaving the house she collided with the fog. It did nothing to improve her temper. But on she went, into the swirling yellow, and towards the Aldgate tube station. She couldn't afford not to be at work, she knew there were plenty of girls ready to step into her place.

In the kitchen, Daisy said, 'Supper's ready, Billy, bacon pieces and mash.'

'Good on yer, Daisy,' said Billy.

'I'll push off,' said Fred.

'Listen, Fred,' said Billy, 'yer best bet is to move in when Bridget ain't 'ere. Once yer in, yer in, and Bridget won't do more than chuck a few plates. The enamel ones. Then she'll accept yer. Like I already said, you don't want to take too much notice of all she says, nor a few enamel plates. You only need to duck if she gets 'old of a saucepan. Bring yer stuff tomorrer evening, when she's at work.'

'Yes, that's a good idea,' said Daisy.

'I might just do that,' said Fred, ready to stand up to enamel plates and to dodge a saucepan. He had a considerable liking for the idea of lodging in Bridget's house, even if the area wasn't quite as salubrious as his present environment. 'Yes, I think I might. So long, Daisy, so long, Billy.'

'Ta-ta, Fred,' said Daisy.

'See yer tomorrer,' said Billy.

'Good on yer, Billy,' said Fred.

On this Thursday evening, the Dobbs family were at supper in their house adjacent to Victoria Park. Not that the park could be seen, not from any of their windows. It was wrapped around by the fog, its lamps shrouded, and was as creepily uninviting as a black pool in the danker reaches of Dartmoor at night. The house, however, was a cosy retreat, globed gas mantles dispensing warm light, and fires burning in the kitchen, the living-room and the dining-room. If Chief Inspector Dobbs did not receive a princely salary from the Metropolitan Police, at least his earnings were on a reasonable level, and his wife had brought to their marriage the interest from an invested monetary bequest made to her by an uncle who had passed away in Canada. This little income enabled her to pay for the services of a daily help, a young woman who came in at eight each morning and finished at four in the afternoon, Mondays to Saturdays inclusive. She saw to the fires among other things. Daphne's husband Charlie saw to the provision of coal, and to all other essentials necessary to a family living in lower-middle-class fashion.

Daphne served a Lancashire hotpot for supper. It contained best end neck of young mutton and two kidneys, neatly cut into pieces, with sliced carrots, onions and turnips, and chopped onions and leeks. It was topped generously with sliced potatoes, browned and steaming when the whole appeared on the table.

'Might I enquire as to the origin of this?' asked Charlie, eyeing the presentation in its large earthenware oven dish.

'It's just Lancashire hotpot,' said Daphne, serving Jane. 'And might I myself enquire as to the reason why we've been having the pleasure of seeing you arrive home in time to eat with us three evenings in unexpected succession, as one might say?'

'It's the fog, it's limited the nature of my present enquiries,' said Charlie. 'Did you say Lancashire hotpot?'

'Yes.'

'It looks like sliced potatoes done to a turn on top

108

of something suspicious,' said Charlie.

'No, it don't, Dad,' said William, 'it looks like one of Mum's Lancashire hotpots.'

'Yes, it's just that the sliced potatoes are a bit browner than usual,' said Jane.

'What's in it?' asked Charlie.

'The usual,' said Daphne. 'Mutton, kidneys, carrots, onions and so on.'

'That's all right, then,' said Charlie, 'I'll have a fairly decent helping.'

'Sure?' said Daphne, serving William. 'Only there's some cold meat and pickle, if you like.'

'On a night like this?' said Charlie.

'Hotpot's best, Dad,' said Jane.

'My feelings exactly, now I know what's in it,' said Charlie. Daphne smiled and Jane and William winked at each other. Charlie received the kind of helping that was generally accepted in most households as the entitlement of the head of the family. And when Daphne had served herself, he said, 'Who's turn to say grace?' That was something Daphne liked, having been brought up in a churchgoing family.

'Jane's turn,' said William.

'Oh, all right,' said Jane. 'For what we're about to receive let's be truly thankful.'

They began the hot and nourishing meal then.

'Anyone going out after supper?' asked Charlie.

'Not me,' said William, 'not even next door.' Next door lived Mr and Mrs Baxter, and their children Eddie, Edith and Johnny, close friends to Jane and William.

'We could get lost just findin' our way to their front door,' said Jane.

'I shouldn't think anyone 'ud want to go out in a

fog like this,' said William. 'Me and Jane could hardly find our way home from next door last night.'

'Wild elephants couldn't drag me,' said Daphne.

'Which tells me', said Charlie, 'that our best bet would be to put the card table up and sit around the fire playing – well, what could we play?'

'"Beat Your Neighbour",' said Jane.

'That'll do,' said Charlie. 'For ha'pennies or buttons?'

'Ha'pennies,' said William.

'Only if I win,' said Jane.

'I'll stake the pair of you,' said Charlie.

'I think dads are sort of useful sometimes,' said Jane.

'Mums are useful all the time,' said William.

'I go along with that deduction,' said Charlie.

Daphne mentally gave him a medal for being the kind of father who, despite the pressures and the time-consuming nature of his work, would always put his worries aside for his children. They liked him to give them some of his spare time. She knew his present case was on his mind, especially as there were snide references in some newspapers to another elusive Jack the Ripper being at large. Also, Charlie had very little so far in the way of leads, except for a certain man called Godfrey, who still hadn't shown up. But as a husband and father, Charlie was willing to sit down to a family evening at the fireside. No wonder Jane and William liked their dad, even though policemen's children were sometimes given a rough ride by other boys and girls.

*   *   *

In bed later, Charlie said he thought the Fleet Street reporters might be in a bit of a confused state.

'Why?' asked Daphne.

'I told them we had several suspects in mind, including a woman,' said Charlie.

'You did what?'

'I mentioned I might have to eliminate a woman suspect.'

'Lord above, is that true?'

'They think it is,' said Charlie.

'But is it?'

'Not as far as I'm concerned.'

'There's not a woman suspect?'

'I haven't found one.'

'Why did you tell the reporters there was, then?'

'To help them take their minds off a second Jack the Ripper.'

'Charlie, you're dreadful.'

'Well, you're not, Daphne, that's one thing I'm certain of,' said Charlie.

'So am I,' murmured Daphne.

The gentleman came this time out of Hanbury Street, where Anne Chapman, the second of Jack the Ripper's victims, had been murdered and butchered. He entered Barkers Row, moving steadily through the fog and taking no notice of sounds that were those associated with people whose only solace was to get drunk on cheap gin. He was alert to the possibility of being waylaid, beaten senseless and robbed, and his grip on his walking-stick was very firm. He continued on and entered New Road. She was not there tonight, the young woman who had offered herself to him for three shillings last night. The bleak, shrouded doorway was empty, but at an upper window of the house faint light struggled in its battle with the fog. She was up there, probably, with a client.

He smiled and went on, out of the grey citadel of abject poverty, desperate women and attendant vice, heading south for the river. In Commercial Street, he slowed in his walk as he heard the sound of a man's voice, husky and muffled. Then a woman groaned. Approaching a shop doorway, he glimpsed shapeless convulsions. Two degenerates, male and female, were lustfully disporting themselves, the female for money, no doubt. As he went by, he lifted his stick and struck the male's back violently, causing a gasping exclamation of pain. He smiled again and kept going, not pausing in his steady stride. Oaths and the sounds of rage issued from the doorway, but he surmised, correctly, that the suffering party was in no condition to come after him.

He continued on through the fog.

Scotland Yard received an anonymous letter the following morning. It was opened and handed to Chief Inspector Dobbs, who had slept soundly apart from a waking interval of ten minutes, when he felt he'd partaken too excessively of Lancashire hotpot and apple pie.

He read the letter.

Deer Sir what about HIM, what about what HE gets up to in pubs with them as is always reddy to go round the back with HIM, what a shame and discrase HIM and them kind of women, what about askin HER where HE was that nite, Mrs Pritchard

112

I mean that's his wife and knows HE had his eye on
Maureen Flanagan that got done in. I'm a friend to
the police.

'Sergeant Ross!' bawled the Chief Inspector, and
in came his helpful assistant. 'Take a look at that,
my lad.'

Sergeant Ross read the unsigned letter.

'Interesting, would you say, guv?' he asked.

'Interesting? Of course it's interesting.'

'Yes, you could say that,' said Ross.

'I am saying it. What's up with you? Had a bad
night?'

'No, a late one, guv. I was with Miss Harriet
Cartright, a friend of mine, a nurse.'

'Walking her around Hyde Park in the fog?' said
the Chief Inspector.

'No, I was with her in her parents' house in
Battersea,' said Ross. 'I live in Battersea myself. It
got very sociable. Well, out of uniform, Nurse
Cartright's a very sociable woman.'

'Out of uniform, I suppose she would be,' said
Dobbs. 'As I can't always mind my own business,
how much out was she?'

'She was nicely dressed in an ivory lace-fronted
blouse, blue skirt with a decorative hem, and a
tortoiseshell comb, guv.'

'I take it you're reminding me of your powers of
observation, Sergeant. Very good. But I won't ask
what you were doing that kept you there late.'

'Playing whist with her and her parents,' said
Ross.

'Playing whist? With her parents? I give up,' said
Dobbs, 'I thought four was a large crowd. Now, this
letter, what does it call for?'

113

'The wastepaper-basket or a knock on Mrs Pritchard's door,' said Ross.

'That answer's a sign you're coming to,' said Dobbs. 'We'll leave here at ten. Is it still foggy?'

'Not according to what's showing through your window, guv. It's misty, that's all.'

'Keep me informed,' said the Chief Inspector.

'Seen the morning papers yet?' asked Ross.

'No.'

'Well, the female suspect isn't mentioned—'

'What female suspect?'

'Come off it, guv. Anyway, she isn't mentioned, but I think they're having their own back on you. After giving you a mention yourself, nearly all the reports suggest that as far as progress in the case is concerned, Scotland Yard doesn't know its arse from its elbow.'

'Are you sure it was the Yard that was mentioned?'

'Not exactly, guv.'

'Well, exactly what, then?' demanded the Chief Inspector.

'Would it be better, guv, if I kept my lips sealed?'

'No, it wouldn't, Sergeant Ross. It was me that got the mention, was it?'

'Which I consider unkindly personal,' said Ross.

'What was it Her Majesty once said when she was a bit younger?' asked Dobbs.

'No idea, guv, she didn't say it to me.'

'I know what it was. She wasn't amused, she said. Well, nor am I, sunshine. And I won't be at home if Fleet Street calls again this afternoon. Inspector Davis can stand in. Right, that's all for the moment. Get your hat and coat on at ten sharp for our visit to Mrs Pritchard.

Chapter Seven

Mrs Pritchard opened her front door. On her step stood two upright manly-looking blokes in bowler hats, overcoats and polished boots. She blinked in recognition.

'Good morning, Mrs Pritchard,' said Chief Inspector Dobbs.

'Beggin' yer pardon, you don't want me again, do yer?' she said.

The Chief Inspector said, 'We only wish to ask you a few more questions, Mrs Pritchard.'

'Well, if that's yer wish, you'd best come in, then,' said Mrs Pritchard reluctantly. 'You can come through to me kitchen, it's warmer there.'

The Scotland Yard men removed their bowlers and stepped in. Ross closed the door for the lady, and followed her and the Chief Inspector into the kitchen. It looked slightly untidy, which didn't detract from its homely atmosphere. The range fire was going, and Mrs Pritchard invited the policemen to sit down. She also said she'd put the kettle on, if they fancied a cup of tea.

'Thanks, but no,' said Ross, as he and Dobbs sat down.

Seating herself, Mrs Pritchard said, 'Is it more

questions about that poor Maureen Flanagan?'

'There are some questions,' said Dobbs.

'Well, all right.' Mrs Pritchard looked cautious.

'Could you tell us something about Mr Pritchard?' asked Dobbs.

'What, me old man?' Mrs Pritchard quivered. 'What's 'e got to do with it?'

'Did he like Miss Flanagan?' asked Ross.

'Eh?'

'Did he like Miss Flanagan?'

'Well, 'e didn't unlike 'er. She was a cheerful woman, like I told yer, and Irish as well.'

'She went out some evenings, you said.' Dobbs looked a kind man, a friendly one. 'Did Mr Pritchard go too?'

'Go where?' Mrs Pritchard was suddenly uneasy.

'Did he go out some evenings with Miss Flanagan? To the pub, say?'

''Ere, 'e didn't go with 'er, 'e went by hisself, and only now and again,' said Mrs Pritchard. 'And only for a small glass of beer. He'd give up the 'ard drink on account of 'is new job as a lamplighter.'

'Would he have met Miss Flanagan on any of these occasions?' asked Dobbs.

''Ere, what d'yer mean?'

'If he liked her, he might have been pleased to treat her and give her a bit of company,' said Ross.

'Me 'usband's a steady-goin' married man, I'll 'ave you know,' said Mrs Pritchard. ''E don't keep company with no woman except me.'

'On some occasions he might have said to Miss Flanagan that he'd go along with her to a pub,' said Dobbs.

'Well, 'e didn't,' said Mrs Pritchard, shifting

116

about on her chair. 'Miss Flanagan didn't ever come down to our kitchen to tell us she was goin' out. She just went straight out and we'd 'ear 'er go most times.'

'Did Mr Pritchard ever follow her out?' asked Ross.

''Ere, what's all these insinuations about?' demanded the nervous landlady.

'Oh, just that someone witnessed Mr Pritchard with Miss Flanagan on occasions,' said Dobbs, 'and we wondered if she ever mentioned a particular man to him, a man we'd like to talk to.'

'Oh, why didn't yer say so?' said Mrs Pritchard. 'I thought you was insinuatin' it was me old man you was after. Well, p'raps 'e did see Miss Flanagan sometimes when 'e was out, 'e was always 'elpful to 'er, 'e'd go up to 'er room on a Sunday to see if there was any little job 'e could do for her. 'E mended a broken strap on 'er shoe once, and one of 'er chairs another time.'

'He liked her a lot, obviously,' said Ross.

'Ted's a friendly man that likes all kinds,' said Mrs Pritchard. 'Mind, I don't know that Flanagan ever told 'im about some partic'ler man she knew. There was that bloke she called Godfrey, is that the one you mean?'

'That's the one,' said Ross, 'and we'd like to get hold of his full name.'

'Well, if she mentioned it to me old man, 'e never mentioned it to me.'

'When does your husband get home?' asked Dobbs.

'You mean you want to talk to 'im?' Mrs Pritchard didn't look overjoyed at the idea.

117

'Only about Miss Flanagan,' said Dobbs.

'Oh, about what she might of told 'im about Godfrey?'

'What she might have told him could be important,' said Dobbs.

'Oh, see what yer mean,' said Mrs Pritchard. 'Well, 'e comes 'ome midday for an hour or so, then goes back to work and later does 'is round lightin' the street lamps.'

'What time at midday?' asked Ross.

'Oh, just a bit after twelve-thirty,' said Mrs Pritchard.

'I see,' said the Chief Inspector. 'We'll call back then, if you and your husband don't mind.'

'Well, you got to ask questions, I suppose,' said Mrs Pritchard grudgingly.

'It's the only way,' said Ross. 'Don't get up, Mrs Pritchard, we'll see ourselves out.'

They left, making their way to London Bridge.

'Any conclusions, sergeant?' asked Dobbs.

'She's jumpy,' said Ross.

'Her old man's got an eye for a skirt and she knows it, would you say?' asked Dobbs.

'Looked like it,' said Ross. 'Wouldn't admit he was friendly with Flanagan until you mentioned a witness. Have we rightly got a witness?'

'Only in the form of an unsigned letter,' said Dobbs. 'Still, beggars can't be choosers, my lad. We'll get back to the house a little before twelve-thirty, and wait at a distance, then follow Mr Pritchard in. That'll make sure his old lady doesn't have time to prime him. Or to wallop him with her iron kettle for making life uncomfortable for her at the moment. Now, d'you want to toddle off to see if Nurse Cartright is on duty?'

'It's against the rules, socializing with a nurse on duty.'

'And while she's in uniform?' said the Chief Inspector.

'I'm sorry I mentioned she was out of it last night,' said Ross.

'Nothing to be sorry about, sunshine. It's natural to prefer them in lace and suchlike. All right, we'll go back to the Yard for a while. There's a chance of some news about Godfrey Who. It's time he got in touch. Well, either Godfrey or someone who knows him.'

'Taking into account that Mrs Pritchard was a bag of nerves, I think I fancy her old man myself,' said Ross.

'As a suspect?' said the Chief Inspector. 'Or in place of Nurse Cartright?'

'Give over, guv. I'm thinking that Mrs Pritchard's twice mentioned her old man's off the hard stuff. What happens to him when he's on it? Goes a bit crazy? If he did for Flanagan at the back of some local pub, say, Tooley Street wasn't very far. Better for him to dump her there than close to his own doorstep.'

'I'm admiring of that theory, my lad,' said Dobbs. 'I'd say you were a promising prospect for promotion sometime in the future. Not yet. Sometime in the future. By the way, in your theory, what happened to the pool of blood?'

'Pardon?' said Ross.

'Well, she'd have dropped dead if she'd been standing up. Bound to have left a pool of blood, noticeable to someone the following morning. That someone would have reported it, wouldn't you say, when news of the murder broke? People don't like murder, not even persistent wrong-doers.'

'I'll admit it, guv,' said Ross, 'there's a weak spot in my theory.'

'Good try, though, sergeant, so don't let it worry you. And Pritchard might still be our man.'

An urchin came running towards them, a second one in yelling pursuit of him.

''Ello, coppers,' panted the first one as he ran past them, 'ain't it an 'ard life?'

On he went, darned socks down, hobnails in his boots. On came the second ragamuffin.

''Ere, you coppers, why didn't yer stop 'im?' he panted. ''E's nicked me bleedin' tanner that I just found.' He continued his yelling pursuit.

'I'm not fond of being instantly recognizable as a copper,' said the Chief Inspector. 'Remind me sometime to recommend to the Assistant Commissioner a change of plainclothes. Say something like a frockcoat, a top hat and a brolly. Now let's pick up a cab on the bridge.'

Bridget and Daisy were enjoying a mid-morning pot of tea. Bridget had slept late after a trying time getting to the restaurant in the fog, an exhausting time washing up mountains of dishes, pans, saucepans, crockery and cutlery, and a nerve-racking time getting home. It might have been even more nerve-racking if an obliging old bloke hadn't given her a lift from Aldgate tube station to Back Church Lane in his horse and cart. He was doing a carrying job, he said, for friends of his. What kind of carrying job? Best not to ask, said the obliging old bloke, except the stuff's in the cart under sacks of onions. He informed her he couldn't see where he was

120

going, but his nag knew the way through the East End blindfold. Sure enough, he was able to drop her off at Back Church Lane, from where Bridget groped her way home. Someone passed her, someone who came looming out of the fog and almost brushed her in going by. Bridget stiffened and went on in haste, trusting to luck that she wouldn't run into a wall. If this fog keeps up all through winter, she thought, I can see meself having to give up this job, which I can't afford to.

Still, she slept well once she was tucked into her bed in the upstairs front. And having woken up late, she was eating a slice of bread and marge with the mid-morning tea.

'Daisy,' she said, 'what 'appened about Fred Billings?'

'Oh, 'e went when Billy and me started our supper,' said Daisy.

'I meant what 'appened about 'im tryin' to get 'imself into that spare room?'

'Oh, it's still spare,' said Daisy, 'but 'e might call again this evenin'.'

'If he does and if I'm at work,' said Bridget, 'chuck the stew saucepan at 'im. If I'm 'ere, I'll chuck it at 'im meself. It's the 'eaviest we've got.'

'I 'eard once that when a woman chucks a saucepan at a bloke and 'alf kills 'im, she's the first to mop up 'is blood,' said Daisy.

'That sort of woman ought to see a doctor,' said Bridget.

'Bridget, Fred ain't a bad bloke,' said Daisy.

'Had a drop of 'is port last night, did you?' said Bridget.

'Yes, me and Billy just 'ad a small glass each,' said Daisy. 'I don't know if Billy sneaked 'imself

121

another glass before 'e went to bed, but when I put the bottle in the cupboard after breakfast, there wasn't as much in it as there should 'ave been.'

'Oh, wasn't there?' said Bridget. She'd had a full glass herself when she finally arrived home. It was what a girl needed after some very trying hours. 'Anyway, I've got to say it again, Daisy, we don't want Fred Billings in this 'ouse. Especially not when we're using the tin bath in the kitchen on Sunday mornings. I 'ope you and Billy understand that.'

'Yes, course we do, Bridget,' said Daisy, and thought about it. 'We'd both be very understandin' if Fred caught you takin' yer Sunday mornin' bath in the altogether.'

Bridget didn't think that a bit funny.

From an advantageous point in Tanner Street, Chief Inspector Dobbs and Sergeant Ross watched the approach of a long-legged man. Clad in a flat cap, thick jacket, hard-wearing trousers and a scarf, his boots made no sound as he walked up to the door of his house.

'Rubber soles,' said Sergeant Ross.

'Interesting,' said Chief Inspector Dobbs.

The man opened the door by its latchcord and went in. The Scotland Yard men crossed the street and advanced with speed on the house. Ross knocked loudly. The door was opened almost at once. The long-legged man, still with his cap on, regarded the callers in curiosity. His face was lean and slightly choleric, his moustache bushy, his eyes dark. He looked near to fifty, but not as if his virility was on the wane.

''Ello, what've we got 'ere, then?' he said. 'Coppers?'

'Good morning,' said the Chief Inspector, 'are you Mr Pritchard?'

'Well, yus, I am, cully, I been that all me life.'

'I'm Chief Inspector Dobbs of Scotland Yard, and this is Sergeant Ross. Might we come in and talk to you, sir?'

Mr Pritchard hardly looked pleased at the prospect. He twitched a bit.

'It ain't what I'd call convenient,' he said. 'I've just come 'ome to 'ave a bite to eat.'

'We shan't keep you long, Mr Pritchard,' said Ross.

'What's it about?' asked the displeased Mr Pritchard.

'We're conducting enquiries into the death of Miss Maureen Flanagan, who lodged here,' said Dobbs.

'Ain't you already conducted some, ain't you already talked to me wife?'

'We have, sir,' said Ross.

'Then what d'yer want to talk to me for?' asked Mr Pritchard, bushy moustache stirring to the aggressive movements of his lips.

'It won't take long, sir,' said Dobbs, offering a smile. The smile made him look as if he was offering friendship as well.

It disarmed Mr Pritchard.

'Well, all right, come in,' he said, and his wife appeared then.

'Oh, yer back already,' she said to Chief Inspector Dobbs, as he and Ross stepped in. 'They come and talked to me earlier Ted,' she said to her husband.

'What for?' asked Mr Pritchard. 'Yus, what for?' he asked the policemen.

'We were hoping to see you, sir,' said Ross.

'What, while I was at work?' said Mr Pritchard.

'Pleased to have found you in now, sir,' said Dobbs in affable fashion. 'Where can we talk?'

'All right, in 'ere,' said Mr Pritchard, and took them into the parlour, which contained a fading aspidistra as well as horsehair-stuffed armchairs and sofa.

'It's a bit warmer in the kitchen,' said Mrs Pritchard, visibly on edge.

'It'll do in 'ere,' said Mr Pritchard, 'the gents don't 'appen to be stayin' long.' He looked at the Chief Inspector. 'Fire away, cully, I ain't got nothing to 'ide.'

'Did we give the impression that we thought you had?' asked Dobbs.

'Yus, you did,' said Mr Pritchard, 'as soon as I saw yer on me doorstep.'

'Sorry about that, sir,' said Dobbs. 'Now, we understand you were fairly friendly with the late Miss Flanagan—'

'What d'yer mean, fairly friendly?'

'Well, we have a witness who says you were seen out with her sometimes.'

Mr Pritchard shifted from one foot to the other.

'Bleedin' Nosy Parker, then,' he said. 'Mind, I ain't goin' to deny I run into Maureen now and again.'

'Attractive woman,' said Dobbs. 'I daresay I'd have enjoyed treating her to a drink myself.'

'As I recollect,' said Mr Pritchard, 'she only ever 'ad a port. No gin. Wise woman, she was, she just stuck to one port. Mind, it was a large one. I asked 'er once why she liked a large one. She laughed, yer know, and said it was to fortify 'erself.'

124

'Against what?' asked Dobbs.

'Bleedin' ups and downs, I suppose,' said Mr Pritchard. 'All that laundry work day in day out, that got 'er down, I'd 'ave thought.'

'Still, I don't know she needed any fortifyin',' said Mrs Pritchard, 'strong and 'ealthy, she was. She didn't need anyone treatin' 'er to anything, and you was daft spendin' money on 'er that you should of spent on me.'

'Only now and again,' said Mr Pritchard, looking irritable, 'only now and again, I've told yer that more'n once. Only when I 'appened to bump into 'er. And she never stayed long in the pub. Soon as she finished 'er port, off she went.'

'Where to?' asked Sergeant Ross.

'Another pub, I suppose,' said Mr Pritchard.

'To get more fortifyin'? said Mrs Pritchard sarcastically. 'To get some other daft man to treat 'er?'

'Mrs Pritchard, didn't you tell us she never came back drunk to her room?' said Ross.

'Well, yes, I can't say she ever did,' said Mrs Pritchard. 'Me 'usband can confirm.'

'That's right, I never saw 'er drunk at any time,' said Mr Pritchard.

Sergeant Ross looked at his guv'nor. Dobbs nodded. They were both of the same mind, that Maureen Flanagan fortified herself not for the purpose of finding another pub and another mug, but for finding an agreeable client or two, and some suitable back street in the West End where she could perform out of sight of people and cops.

'Mr Pritchard,' said Dobbs, 'this friend of Miss Flanagan's, a man called Godfrey. She brought him here once, I believe, when you and your wife entertained them.'

'So she did,' said Mr Pritchard. 'Ugly bit of work, 'e was.'

'What yer talkin' about? asked Mrs Pritchard. ''E was a proper gent.'

'Nasty underneath,' said Mr Pritchard.

'How'd you know?' asked Ross.

'Well, I got instincts, ain't I? said Mr Pritchard.

That, thought Dobbs, could very well be the attempt of an uneasy man to point the investigation away from himself.

'I must say me 'usband does 'ave natural instincts,' said Mrs Pritchard supportively.

'During the evening the man was here, did you get any idea of what his full name was, Mr Pritchard?' asked Dobbs.

'Wish I 'ad,' said Mr Pritchard, 'I'd give it to yer with pleasure. The way 'e looked at Maureen at times, well, now I come to think about it, that look of 'is, I got a feeling 'e was sort of sizing up that nice neck of 'ers.'

'Oh, me gawd,' breathed Mrs Pritchard.

'Mr Pritchard, when we first spoke to your wife,' said Ross, 'she gave us the impression you both thought the man was a friendly and likeable bloke.'

'Yus, well me instincts wasn't workin' correct at the time,' said Mr Pritchard, scowling a bit. 'It was afterwards that I said to meself I wouldn't trust the bloke if I was Maureen.'

'Did Miss Flanagan ever mention him on any of the occasions when you were with her and she was fortifying herself with port?' asked Dobbs.

'She mentioned 'im to me and the missus before 'e came to see 'er that time,' said Mr Pritchard.

'No, did she make a particular mention of him whenever you met her in the pub?' asked Ross.

'Anything that gave you an idea of where he lived, what his full name was, what his work was and so on?'

'Well, now you come to ask,' said Mr Pritchard, 'while I don't recall she ever told me 'is full monicker or what 'is work was, she did say once that he 'ad a bit of a temper.'

Mrs Pritchard fidgeted.

'Miss Flanagan said that, did she?' murmured the Chief Inspector.

'It didn't surprise me,' said Mr Pritchard, 'I'd been 'aving me doubts about him.'

'Due to your instincts, sir?' said Sergeant Ross.

'Yus, that's right,' said Mr Pritchard.

'You mentioned this to your wife, I expect,' said Ross.

'Bound to 'ave done,' said Mr Pritchard. 'Didn't I?' he said to his wife.

'Well, I – well, yes, I believe you did,' said the harassed lady.

'So we've got a certain gent with a bit of a temper, have we?' said Dobbs drily. 'Let's see now, the night Miss Flanagan was murdered—'

'Oh, gawd,' said Mrs Pritchard, and winced. Mr Pritchard chewed at his moustache.

'Painful for you, I know,' said Dobbs, 'but I have to ask. On that night, Mr Pritchard, did she mention to you that she was going to meet this man Godfrey?'

'Mention to me?' said Mr Pritchard.

'Well, you were with her during the evening, weren't you?'

''Ere, who told yer that?' demanded Mr Pritchard.

'Let's see, was it you who told us, Mrs Pritchard?'

127

asked Dobbs, and the poor woman visibly quivered.

'No, I never did,' she gasped.

'But Mr Pritchard was out, wasn't he?'

'Yes, but—'

'Course I wasn't, yer daft cow,' said Mr Pritchard, 'I was 'ere all evening with you, wasn't I?'

Mrs Pritchard sat heavily down on the sofa and put a hand to her forehead.

'I'm that upset I can't think straight,' she said.

'Take your time,' said Dobbs, very friendly, very pleasant.

'Well, thinkin' about it, that evenin', I ought to remember,' said Mrs Pritchard, mentally fumbling. 'Yes, I ought to. Yes, I remember now, me 'usband was 'ome all evenin'.'

'There y'ar,' said Mr Pritchard to the Chief Inspector. 'Mind, I ain't blamin' yer for 'aving suspicions, but I got to say it ain't doin' me old lady much good, you 'aving them about me. I ain't surprised she got confused.'

'With some cases, we get confused ourselves,' said Dobbs. 'By the way, which pub did Miss Flanagan use?'

'Well, the times I run into 'er, which wasn't a lot, yer know, it was the Borough Arms,' said Mr Pritchard.

'Well, perhaps we can find some of the regulars who knew her,' said Dobbs.

'What for?' asked Mr Pritchard.

'Just a question of picking up as much information as we can, sir,' said Ross.

'Well, yer don't want to believe all you 'ear from that lot that uses the Borough Arms,' said Mr Pritchard.

'That's a frequent happening,' said Dobbs.

'Is it?' said Mr Pritchard. 'What is?'

'Coming up against a lot of people we don't want to believe,' said Dobbs, and Mrs Pritchard could hardly credit what a kind smile this police officer had. He was nearly human.

'Me and me 'usband's honest workin' people,' she said.

'It's the other kind that give us trouble,' said Dobbs. 'Thanks for your help, we're obliged to both of you. Good day.'

'I 'ope I've still got time to 'ave a bite to eat,' said Mr Pritchard.

Chapter Eight

The Chief Inspector and his sergeant each ate a thick, well-filled ham sandwich in the Borough Arms, a pub located in Bermondsey Street and midway between Tanner Street and Tooley Street. The Borough Arms, like the Rockingham Pub at the Elephant and Castle, served sandwiches. The CID men chased the food down with some welcome old ale. The Chief Inspector remarked that the sawdust on the floor of the private bar needed changing, and Sergeant Ross remarked that his sandwich could have done with a little more mustard, mustard being a very agreeable condiment.

'I take it, do I, that Nurse Cartright's ham and mustard sandwiches are very agreeable?' said the Chief Inspector, glass in his hand, his eyes on the burning coals of the fire.

'No idea, guv, but her mother served some tasty anchovies on toast at eleven o'clock last night, with a large pot of tea,' said Ross.

'That was probably a reminder to you, as a single man in police lodgings, that you're missing the good things of family life,' said Dobbs.

'I don't think you've met Nurse Cartwright, have you, guv?'

'Not socially.'

'She's admiring of your reputation,' said Ross.

'What reputation?' asked Dobbs.

'Your well-known one,' said Ross.

'Tell her not to believe all she hears,' said Dobbs. 'By the way, what did you think of that bloke Pritchard?'

'That he was out on the night of the murder, and that his old lady knew he was,' said Ross.

'Well, now you've finished your sandwich, go and have a quiet word with the publican. Find out if he saw Pritchard in the public bar on the night of the murder, and if Flanagan was with him. Find out too if he ever saw her leave the pub with men.'

'If I might say so,' said Sergeant Ross, 'I thought we agreed Maureen Flanagan wouldn't have picked men up in her own back yard, on the grounds that she didn't want friends and neighbours to think she was anything but a hard-working laundress. We know that her family in Cork thought this.'

'All the same, best to keep an open mind,' said Dobbs. 'Hop over, sunshine, and talk somewhere private with the publican.'

Sergeant Ross carried out the order in commendable fashion, detaching the publican from his barman, and disappearing with him after a brief few words. He reappeared ten minutes later, when he rejoined the Chief Inspector at the table closest to the fire.

'Well, guv—'

'Not here,' said Dobbs.

They left. The afternoon, wondrously, was clear, and the sun, conscience-stricken about failing the put-upon citizens of London by its prolonged absence, had returned in a penitent attempt to

131

make them feel better. The temperature was mild, and grubby Bermondsey Street was almost basking. Sergeant Ross, walking beside the Chief Inspector, recounted details of his interview with the publican. Yes, the man knew Pritchard, and yes, Pritchard had been in the pub on the night of the murder, in the public bar as usual. Yes, Maureen Flanagan had drunk port from time to time, occasionally in company with Pritchard, but no, the publican couldn't swear she'd been present on that particular night. Certainly, he couldn't remember seeing her with Pritchard, not then. Further, nor could he remember ever having seen her leave the pub in company with a man. She usually took only a short time to drink her port, and once she'd finished it she left almost immediately, and always by herself.

'Well, there you are, guv,' said Ross, 'it looks like we can still stick with your feeling that she went elsewhere on her part-time excursions. The West End's still the best bet.'

'You're upsetting me, my lad,' said Dobbs.

'I'll have to ask why,' said Ross.

They passed a knife-grinder, his barrow stationary beside the kerb, a blade throwing sparks in its frictional contact with his fast-revolving whetstone. He looked up.

'Knives to grind, gents?' he offered.

'I'll ask my wife,' said the Chief Inspector. Walking on with Sergeant Ross, he said, 'When I asked you to talk to the publican, I didn't suggest you should come up with a result that Pritchard would like better than I do. I suppose you realize what you've done? Given him what looks like a clean sheet on the night of the capital crime. I could call that rank carelessness.'

'That's a bit upside-down, guv,' said Ross. 'You've got the publican to blame for these facts, not me. I asked, he replied, and I listened.'

'Between the two of you, you've upset the apple-cart and me as well,' said Dobbs. 'On the other hand, I still see Pritchard as suspect. He was shifting about all over the place during the interview, and his old lady was like a woman having to dance on hot bricks. Now, let's suppose Pritchard fancied Flanagan, shall we?'

'Reasonable,' said Ross. 'Well, I'd say he's given up fancying Mrs Pritchard, and that she prefers port.'

'Further, let's suppose Pritchard made an appointment with Flanagan that night – no, that won't do. There's the knife. I mean, if he fancied her why would he have kept the appointment carrying a knife?'

'Suppose she turned him down on a previous occasion, suppose she laughed at him?' said Ross. 'That might have set him off and made him go looking for her on the night in question.'

'Would she have laughed at him, my lad? More likely to have told him she was a respectable woman, thanks very much. Did the publican tell you what he drank that night?'

'Old ale,' said Ross. 'No hard stuff.'

'What time did he leave?'

'The publican didn't know, didn't notice.'

'More carelessness,' said the Chief Inspector. 'All the same, it's my belief there's something bothering Pritchard, something he's keeping to himself. If he did decide, for one reason or another, that he was going to look for Flanagan and do for her, he'd have had to leave the pub and go

133

back home for a knife. Is that what made Mrs Pritchard twitchy, the fact that she not only knew he'd been out, but had come back and gone out again?'

'And finally, guv, when he got back home for good, did she get landed with the job of washing his bloodstained clothes or getting rid of them?'

'A promising piece of supposition on your part, sunshine,' said Dobbs, 'particularly as he looks capable of the carrying job to Tooley Street. In that fog, he could have done the job outside his own front door, having waited for her, and cleaned up his doorstep afterwards. I think we'll have another word with the Pritchards.'

'Now?' said Ross.

'No, let 'em twitch for a while,' said Dobbs. 'I'd like to get back to the Yard and find out if the other suspect, Godfrey Who, has shown up or made contact. Sergeant, have you noticed something unusual?'

'Such as?' said Ross.

'The sun's out,' said the Chief Inspector.

There was no news of Godfrey. The man was still an invisible factor and accordingly a frustrating disturbance to the Chief Inspector's methodical thought processes. It interfered with his theories concerning Pritchard. One or the other, either Pritchard or Godfrey, had to be eliminated.

Parliament had concerned itself with the riot in Whitechapel, much to the irritation of Her Majesty's senior ministers. The aged Queen herself, increasingly fragile though she was, had sent the Prime Minister a note of disapproval.

134

Liberal-minded MPs favoured justice, decent wages and improved conditions for the people of the East End. MPs of a different mind considered the riot a disgrace, an impudent and insolent challenge to law and order, and a reprehensible attack on private property. It was very irritating to have the poverty of the people of the East End brought to public notice again. It had become public enough during the time of Jack the Ripper, creating embarrassment for the Government. After all, much of the lot of these people was brought about by their own sloth and idleness, and their drunken ways. Yes, it was very irritating, and the several rioters who had been arrested should be punished by the law. It was to be hoped they would. Hard labour should be considered.

The pride of Fleet Street had their notebooks at the ready again. Chief Inspector Dobbs, resisting the temptation to throw a subordinate into the ring, entered it himself.

'Any news, Chief Inspector?' asked the *Daily Chronicle*.

'What kind of news d'you want, gents?' asked Dobbs.

'Come off it, Charlie,' said the *Evening News*.

'Hello, who's being familiar?' asked Dobbs.

'Just an admirer,' said the *Evening News*.

'Concerning the capital crime presently under investigation,' said Dobbs, 'the apprehension of a certain person will take place in the near future.'

'Person?' said the *Manchester Guardian*.

'The woman?' said the *Daily News*.

'Concerning who might have done what and who might not, and police policy gen'rally,' said Dobbs,

'I can say I'm not at liberty to offer you the kind of details the Yard considers unprintable.'

'Is that the right word, unprintable?' asked the *Morning Post*. 'Or do you mean inadvisable?'

'Same thing,' said Dobbs. 'It might seriously affect our chances of apprehending the person in question.'

'Well, between you and us and the gatepost,' said the *Evening News*, 'is this a female person? Do you actually suspect a certain woman of cutting Maureen Flanagan's throat?'

'I appreciate it wouldn't go any further than this room,' said the Chief Inspector, 'but all the same, the requested information isn't disclosable at present.'

Sergeant Ross nodded in a seriously confirmatory way, although he knew the guv'nor was simply having another go at disposing of the spectre of the Ripper.

'Chief Inspector, you're still telling us little or nothing,' said the *Westminster Gazette*.

'Well, sometimes little or nothing is preferable to overdoing it,' said Dobbs. 'Investigations of capital crimes have taught me to proceed with care, caution and not to say anything I'd be sorry for. If I told you all I could tell you, and you printed it, I'd end up in the same condition as the fox that let the rabbit escape. Very sorry for myself.'

'You mean there's not much again for us,' said the *Daily Mail*.

'You know the rules, gents, no disclosure of information beneficial to wrongdoers,' said Dobbs.

'Well, at least tell us if the man called Godfrey has been found and eliminated,' said the *Daily Telegraph*.

'Ah, Godfrey,' said Dobbs, and brushed his moustache. 'How are we on that bloke, Sergeant Ross?'

'Fairly blank, guv,' said Ross.

'Pity,' said Dobbs.

'But you must have eliminated him if the arrest of a certain other person is imminent,' said *The Times*.

'I hope no-one will mind if I don't answer that,' said Dobbs. 'But I can say there's one or two untidy ends floating about, so the Yard would be obliged if you'd print a repeat of the details concerning Godfrey. Give him another chance to come forward.'

'But is he only an untidy end?' asked the *Westminster Gazette*.

'And is there a possibility he doesn't exist?' asked the *Daily News*.

'Would you call that a good question, Sergeant Ross?' asked Dobbs.

'Reasonable, I'd say, reasonable,' said Ross.

'There you are, then, gents, a reasonable question,' said Dobbs.

'But what's the answer?' asked the *Daily Mail*.

'That he's alive and well, but keeping his head down,' said Dobbs. 'That's all for today, gents, I appreciate your help, co-operation and interest.'

'We haven't got much out of it,' said the *Evening News*.

'Have some tea and biscuits,' said the Chief Inspector.

'When are we calling again on Mrs Pritchard?' asked Sergeant Ross later.

'First thing tomorrow morning, sunshine, just

after she's eaten her porridge and seen her old man off, but before she's got her hairpins in place,' said the Chief Inspector. 'Meanwhile, I'm writing up my notes for today. You do the same with yours, then we'll go though all of them from the beginning.'

'What'll we be looking for, guv?'

'We'll be looking to see if you've missed anything, my lad.'

Ross was grinning as he went to his desk.

'I'm off now,' said Bridget that evening.

'Yes, all right, Bridget,' said Daisy. 'It won't be so bad for you gettin' to work this time. It's not a bit foggy outside.'

'It's been a nice day,' said Billy, who had put in an appearance on his way back from a delivery. 'A bit of November sunshine can do wonders, yer know. I was give several tips, one of tuppence, would yer believe, and Fanny, the grocer's daughter, came in and give me a very invitin' smile. But I was too busy loadin' groceries to take 'er into the storeroom and help meself to what she was invitin'.'

'I'll help you to a thump in a minute,' said Bridget. 'Listen, if Constable Fred Billings turns up again, take the front door off its hinges and hit 'im with it. That's all, look after yerselves while I'm at work.'

Constable Fred Billings turned up at seven, just as the hitherto clear evening was turning nasty. Not only did he bring himself, he also brought his modest amount of goods and chattels, packed into a trunk. The trunk was on a barrow pushed by a whippet-like lad.

Fred knocked. Billy answered the door. He saw Fred, and he saw Fred's trunk on the barrow.

'Oh, yer've come to move in, Fred?' he said.

'Yes, now or never, I thought,' said Fred. 'I've got to get out of my present lodgings in a few days, anyway, and I decided I might as well start bein' useful to yer sisters as a protective presence. We all know Whitechapel ain't exactly safe for its lady residents.'

'It's a bit safer 'ere than it is farther up, in the stewpots and dens,' said Billy, 'but I like what yer sayin', Fred. You're goin' to safeguard me sisters.'

Daisy, appearing, said, 'Oh, crikey, are yer movin' in, Fred?'

'Yes, I've brought all me stuff, Daisy,' said Fred.

'Bridget told us to 'it you with the front door if you turned up,' said Daisy.

'Well, all right,' said Fred, a reliable policeman and a fairly affable citizen, 'tell 'er you did and that me helmet took the blow and saved me life.'

'Oh, all right,' said Daisy.

'Come on, Fred,' said Billy, 'let's 'elp yer get yer trunk upstairs.'

The job was done, the heavy trunk manhandled by Fred and Billy. The room for rent was entirely suitable for a single man. Of a comfortable size, it contained a small table, one ancient upright chair, one well-worn armchair, a single bed, a wardrobe with a slightly cracked door, a cupboard, a gas ring, some shelves and a necessary fireplace. The bed had been made up. Fred had no complaints. He paid the lad for his time, his help and the use of his barrow, and sent him back to Stepney with two whole shillings in his pocket. A couple of bob would enable any lad to treat himself to fried fish and chips, a seat in a music hall, a hot faggot with pease

139

pudding after the show, and still leave him with change.

Daisy, to celebrate the arrival of a lodger and five bob rent in advance, made a pot of tea while Billy went out and came back with a hot apple pie, bought from a shop in Commercial Road. Fred sat down with them to share in the treat. Billy pointed out to Daisy that they'd got to talk to Bridget, of course.

'Oh, I'll be in bed when she comes in,' said Daisy. 'Like I usually am.'

'Good idea,' said Billy, 'I'll be in bed too, like I usually am.'

Naturally, brother and sister then looked at Fred. Naturally, someone had to let Bridget know.

'I'll be in bed,' said Constable Billings.

'Bridget won't be in much later than a bit after eleven,' said Billy.

'I'll still be in bed,' said the lodger.

'Swelp me,' said Billy, 'we're all dodgin' it. What's causin' you the problem, Fred, seein' you're a copper?'

'Funk,' said Fred.

'You ain't afraid of Bridget, are yer?' said Billy.

'Yes,' said Fred.

'Why 'ave yer come, then?' asked Daisy.

'Had a brainstorm,' said Fred.

'Oh, lor',' said Daisy, 'Bridget'll take the front door off its 'inges and hit all of us with it.'

'We'll all be in bed,' said Fred.

'That won't stop Bridget,' said Daisy.

'I'll have my door locked,' said Fred.

'Good idea,' said Billy, 'I'll lock mine too.'

'Oh, I don't know if I can find the key to mine,' said Daisy.

140

'Well, I call that 'ard luck,' said Billy, 'you'll get all the wallops. Still, there's a way of makin' Bridget see the light of joy and 'appiness.'

'Crikey, you're pickin' up funny language lately,' said Daisy, 'and I don't know that Bridget's in the mood for joy and 'appiness.'

'It'll be the joy and 'appiness of feelin' safeguarded by Fred,' said Billy.

'Some 'opes,' said Daisy.

'Fred pointed it out to me,' said Billy.

'It was just a thought,' said Fred, 'but I didn't mention joy and 'appiness.'

'That was yer modesty,' said Billy. 'Yes, don't yer see, Daisy, wiv a policeman as good as Fred livin' 'ere, the 'ouse and its valu'bles will all be safeguarded. That includes you and Bridget, you both bein' fearful ladies. No-one's goin' to knock you or Bridget out and nick yer 'andbags when the word gets round that Fred'll be after 'em double-quick.'

'Oh, I never thought of that,' said Daisy. 'Yes, that ought to please Bridget.'

'Billy,' said Fred, 'you sure we can regard Bridget as a fearful lady?'

'Ev'ryone's fearful in them stewpots and dens,' said Billy, 'and we ain't far from 'em, so it wouldn't be a porkie to say Bridget 'as to be a bit fearful at times. Of course, she 'ides it, but it's what makes 'er quick to be aggravated. So when she comes in tonight, Daisy, you can tell 'er why 'avin' Fred as a lodger can give 'er joy and 'appiness.'

'Why can't you tell 'er?' asked Daisy.

'Me door'll be locked,' said Billy.

'You Billy, you're havin' me on,' said Daisy.

'No, tell yer what we'll do, we'll leave 'er a note,' said Billy.

'No, I'll wait up for her and tell her meself,' said Fred.

'Fred, she'll chuck you out, and all yer clobber as well,' said Billy. 'She'll use the stew saucepan first, and when you 'it the pavement you'll be near dead. And near dead can be mortal, yer know. No, you keep yer door locked and let Bridget sleep on 'er problems. She'll come round by mornin', after 'er dreams of bein' safeguarded. She'll see the advantages.'

'Where does Bridget sleep?' asked Fred.

'In the upstairs front,' said Billy. 'Daisy's in the upstairs back, and I'm in the downstairs middle. You got the upstairs middle. Crikey, a banana between two passion fruits.'

''Ere, d'you mind?' said Daisy.

'No, I don't mind,' said Billy, 'do you, Fred?'

'I'm wondering why I've moved in, when it's obvious I'm riskin' my life,' said Fred.

Chapter Nine

The night was misty, the river lightly covered, the streets apparently floating. Bridget hurried along from Aldgate, glad to see a few people about, people out late. Reaching Commercial Road, she made good progress. She turned right into Back Church Lane, seemingly a deserted thoroughfare at this moment. But a soft sound intruded after a matter of seconds. Through the mist by the light of a lamp she glimpsed movement on the other side of the street, the movement of someone walking in advance of her. A solitary man, vaguely seen, he disappeared into the night darkness when he left the light behind. She stopped to let him get well in front of her, remembering a silent person who had brushed by her last night.

She stood quite still for a minute, then went on her way to Ellen Street. The time was eleven-thirty, and she knew the risk she was taking each night was bound to increase. Someone would take note, someone artful enough to lie in wait for her and vicious enough to strike her down, rob her of her handbag and even strip her of her clothes. Everything one had, even the shabbiest garment, was coveted by people poorer than herself.

When she reached Ellen Street, her spine was suddenly attacked by icy fingers. He was there, still across the street, she knew he was. He had stopped to wait for her, listening to her footsteps. Bridget picked up her skirts and ran. Strong though she was, and fearless up to a point, she knew when it was wiser to run. And she ran like the wind, skirts high. Reaching her front door, she opened it by pulling on the latchcord, flung herself in, closed the door and bolted it.

The gentleman left behind hadn't moved. He'd only listened. He smiled and resumed his walk, going south.

Bridget went through to the kitchen. The gas mantle showed a small yellow glimmer. She turned the little tap and light flooded the mantle. The first thing she saw was a note on the bare table. She picked it up and read it.

Dear Bridget,

Fred's come to lodge, which me and Daisy hope you'll be pleased about as we agree a policeman lodger is a safegard for us and will keep you and Daisy sound in yore beds at night and happy by day. Fred will make sure you and Daisy is protekted from all comers and come to meet you at night at Aldgate and see you safe home, it's wot a policeman lodger is for which is good forchune for all of us because of evil-doers being about like they are. You can sleep sound tonight to start with. Fred is safegarding you,
Billy.

Bridget read this homely message a second time before taking the frying-pan off its hook and mounting the stairs at a rush. She thumped on the door of the middle bedroom.

'You in there, Fred Billings, you in there?' She thumped again. 'You in that bed, are yer? Well, get out of it and come out 'ere so's I can knock yer down the stairs. Fred Billings?' No answer. Fred had woken up but was wisely lying low. Bridget turned the handle of the door. It was locked. She kicked it, and it shivered. 'Locked yerself in, 'ave you, you coward? Some copper, I don't think. Get out of that bed and unlock this door, you 'ear me, you sneakin' flatfoot?'

Daisy, woken up, dug herself deeper into her own bed.

'Oh, lor', poor Fred,' she said to herself, 'even if 'e dodges Bridget now, 'e'll get it twice over in the mornin'.'

Her bedroom door opened. Out of the darkness came Bridget's voice.

'Daisy?'

'I ain't 'ere,' breathed Daisy.

'You're 'ere all right, and so's that 'orrible copper.'

'No, 'e ain't, 'ow can yer say such a thing?' said Daisy, voice somewhat muffled since her head was under the blankets. 'I'm by meself.'

'I know that. I'd spank yer for an hour if you weren't,' said Bridget, 'and then sell you for cats' meat. Where's your key?'

'I don't know, I couldn't find it,' gasped Daisy.

'It should be in the little vase on yer mantelpiece,' said Bridget.

'I forgot,' said Daisy, and she heard Bridget moving about. There was a little rattling sound. That was the key in the vase Bridget was shaking. 'Oh, 'elp, what d'yer want it for, Bridget?'

145

'It opens the door of the middle bedroom,' said Bridget.

'Bridget, you can't go in Fred's room, it won't be decent.'

'It won't be peaceful, either,' said Bridget. 'If I don't throw 'im down the stairs, I'll throw 'im out of the winder.'

'Oh, lor',' breathed Daisy, and dug herself deeper.

Back went Bridget to the middle bedroom. She slipped the key into the lock. That is, she made the attempt but it wouldn't go forward. The other key was in. She rattled the handle. She turned it. The door opened. The gas mantle was on, but the bed was empty, the clothes turned back.

'Oh, yer bugger, Fred Billings! Show yerself, you coward.' She looked under the bed. Empty space greeted her. She rushed out of the room. 'Fred Billings!'

'Oh, evenin', Bridget, I'm in here, the lav,' called Fred.

Bridget turned and hit the lav door with the frying-pan.

'What yer doin' in there?' she yelled.

'Just hidin',' said Fred. 'It's a bit late for an argument. How about if I made an appointment to see yer first thing in the mornin'?'

'If you don't come out of there inside a minute,' yelled Bridget, 'you won't live to see the mornin'!'

'Bridget, that would be grievous bodily assault and chargeable,' said Fred.

'No, it wouldn't, it would be aggravated assault committed on an univited intruder, and such aggravation ain't chargeable. D'you 'ear me, Fred Billings?'

'If I come out,' said Fred, 'would yer mind telling me what's goin' to happen?'

'You're goin' to get a piece of me mind,' said Bridget.

'Oh, right. Right. I'll face up to that.' The lav door opened and Fred showed himself. 'Well, 'ere we are, Bridget.'

The gas mantle in the middle bedroom gave light to the landing and to the picture of Bridget in her hat and coat, and Fred in his nightshirt. Bridget looked flushed and fulsome, and Fred looked ready to go back to bed.

'Gotcher, you bugger,' said Bridget, and produced the frying-pan from behind her back.

'Not now, eh, Bridget?' said Fred. 'Like I pointed out, it's a bit late, yer know. Save it till mornin', what d'yer say?'

'You sneaked in behind me back,' said Bridget, 'and now you're standin' on me landing in yer nightshirt.' She went for him then. Fred slipped to one side, stuck out a bare foot and tripped her. Down she went. Wisely, Fred disappeared into his rented room. Just as wisely he locked the door, and even more wisely he left the key in. Bridget, up on her feet, hat and hair lopsided, thought for a second about smashing the door down with the frying-pan, then decided against it.

'I'll get you in the mornin', Fred Billings, see if I don't,' she yelled.

'Right you are, Bridget, see you then,' called Fred. 'Oh, 'ave a good night.'

Bridget had an uneasy first hour, in fact. She kept dreaming about being followed home in the fog by a silent man, she running with all her might but making little or no progress, and finally falling.

Each time the fall woke her up. The recurring dream finally ran itself into oblivion, however, and then she slept undisturbed.

Chief Inspector Dobbs, having gone to bed with his two suspects on his mind, came out of his sleep at three in the morning. He jerked awake and found himself fully conscious, his thoughts quite free of the drowsy patterns of sleep.

The man known only as Godfrey. He hadn't come forward, nor had anyone who knew him offered information about him. Why? Because it wouldn't pay him to show himself, nor pay his friends and acquaintances to give him away? Why, yes, why? Simple. He was a wrong-doer, of course, a wrong-doer of the kind to make informers wish they'd kept their mouths shut. There were London cripples who hadn't been disabled at birth or by accident.

Now what kind of wrong-doer would take up with an attractive Irishwoman who was on the game?

A pimp.

That was it, a pimp, and of the kind who'd go along with Maureen Flanagan's wish to retain an air of respectability out of her regard for her family and her ambition to go back to them sometime. She wouldn't accept the chains of full-time prostitution, and was so determined about that as to keep her job as a laundress.

Pimps were a peculiar and degenerate breed of men, charming to newcomers but vicious if established women cheated or tried to break the chains.

Godfrey, as Flanagan's pimp, would have given her use of a room for the entertainment of clients she either picked up herself or he found for her.

148

Her agreement with him would have allowed her to work only at intervals, say two or three times a week, and only during the evenings. That would be in keeping with what one had discovered so far about her outlook and her character. It was on the cards that she sent most of her part-time earnings to her family, allowing for what she had to pay the pimp.

'That's it, the bugger's a pimp. Did Flanagan try to escape him?'

Daphne turned in the bed.

'Charlie?'

'Woke you up, did I, Daffie? Sorry. I woke up myself and talked out loud. Sorry.'

'Mmm,' murmured Daphne, and curled up and went back to sleep.

Chief Inspector Charlie Dobbs, not unhappy with his assumptions and conclusions, relaxed and let himself fade away.

Bridget, up and dressed by eight the following morning, pounced as Fred emerged from his room. He was now every inch the uniformed constable, helmet on, rolled cape under his arm.

'Mornin', Bridget,' he said.

''Aven't you forgotten something?' asked Bridget.

'Have I?' he said.

'Yes, yer luggage,' said Bridget. 'Get it out of that room and take it with you.'

'Could I leave it till later?' asked Fred 'I'm due at the Commercial Street station in fifteen minutes.'

'I read a note left by Billy last night,' said Bridget, standing in Fred's way. 'What's all this stuff about you safeguardin' me and Daisy?'

'I'll make that me conscientious duty,' said Fred.

149

'If that's a joke, it ain't funny,' said Bridget. 'Where was yer safeguardin' self last night when I 'ad to run from a bloke who stopped to wait for me in Back Church Lane last night?'

'What sort of bloke?' asked Fred.

'Well, as I can't see in the dark, I don't know if 'e was square or round or what. But I know 'e was there, on the other side of the street, waitin' for me, and breathing 'eavy.'

'Bridget, that wouldn't make 'alf a reasonable complaint. Who's goin' to believe you could hear his 'eavy breathing from across the street? Did he follow you?'

'Course 'e did,' said Bridget.

'How'd you know?'

'Me female intuition,' said Bridget. 'Some copper you are, some safeguarder too, lyin' in a bed you wasn't entitled to while I 'ad to run for me life.'

Fred frowned.

'I don't like you havin' a job that keeps you out late,' he said.

'Oh, you don't, don't you?' said Bridget.

'No,' said Fred, 'it shouldn't be 'appening. Around here, there's demented characters on two legs that come up out of holes in the ground at night lookin' for young women like you. Now, this suspicious bloke, you've got some sort of a description, 'ave you?'

'No, course I 'aven't, I told you,' said Bridget. 'I only caught a glimpse of 'im in misty lamplight. And listen, don't make up yer mind that you're lodgin' 'ere. You're movin' out this evening, and just for now you'd better go off to yer job quick before I do you an 'orrible injury.'

Fred wisely departed without more ado, thus

challenging the popular concept of the time that all coppers were brain-dead.

Bridget went down to join Daisy and Billy at the breakfast table. Breakfast was just porridge and tea. Bridget helped herself to what was left of the porridge and put sugar on it.

'I've got something to say to you two,' she said.

'But you saw me note, didn't you? said Billy, who'd slept through last night's racket.

'I saw it all right,' said Bridget, 'and you both ought to 'ave yer heads examined. That copper safeguardin' us? Who thought that up?'

'Fred,' said Billy.

'He ought to be arrested, then, and put away somewhere quiet so's 'e could count buttercups and daisies,' said Bridget.

'But a policeman lodger could be a sort of guardian,' said Daisy.

'Oh, we need a guardian, do we?' said Bridget. 'I 'ope you two didn't connive at gettin' Fred Billings into this 'ouse while my back was turned.'

'Us?' said Daisy.

'Us?' said Billy.

'If you did, you can connive at gettin' 'im out again,' said Bridget.

'We can all 'ave a talk tonight,' said Billy. 'Only could yer refrain from chuckin' saucepans about?'

'And could you get a new copper stick from somewhere, Bridget?' asked Daisy. 'Only you went and lost our old one.' She quivered under Bridget's fierce look. 'No, p'raps not.'

'Come to think of it, I'd like to 'ave a copper stick in me 'and tonight,' said Bridget.

'Thought you would,' said Billy, and winked at Daisy. Daisy smothered a giggle.

151

*   *   *

'You getting anywhere?' asked the Chief Superintendent of Chief Inspector Dobbs.

'Slowly,' said Dobbs.

'Can you hurry it up?'

'Not without falling over my feet,' said Dobbs.

The Chief Superintendent smiled.

'That's a common failing with the Force
according to certain newspapers,' he said. 'Well, in
your own time, Charlie. But how do prospects
look?'

'Not unfavourable,' said Dobbs.

'Leave it to you, then,' said the Chief Superintendent, who was one with Dobbs in the latter's
refusal to make public the possibility that Maureen
Flanagan was a part-time pro. If the press got hold
of that, nothing would stop them from reminding
their readers that the Ripper's victims were women
who sold themselves. The case would take on a
hellishly fanciful aspect.

The Chief Inspector called Sergeant Ross in. He
had an easier relationship with Ross than with
Inspector George Davis, who, in any event, was
currently investigating a case of suspected arson.
Sergeant Ross listened to his guv'nor's new as-
sessment of the bloke known as Godfrey. He
considered it, reflected on it, and decided he
liked it.

'A pimp?' he said. 'I'll go along with that. No
wonder the geezer hasn't come forward. It's odds-
on he was trying to make a full-time pro of
Flanagan, that she wouldn't play and threatened to
break with him. End of Flanagan. Pimps don't
allow desertions. They're smilers carrying knuckle-
dusters in their pockets. Remember Mrs Pritchard

152

telling us what a cheerful character Godfrey was? And when you come to think of it, what she said of Flanagan's attitude to him fits that of a woman who liked her pimp. They all like their pimps to begin with. It's the pimps who seduce the new ones and get them on the game. But why, I wonder, did Flanagan bring hers to the house to meet the Pritchards?'

'Let's suppose he called on her without being asked to,' said Dobbs. 'It would've been in character, a pimp wanting to find out exactly what her background was like. And she herself might have decided to introduce him to the Pritchards to give the impression she was going steady with him. Very respectable, that would have looked. And mentioning him to her mother – she might even have had some weird female idea of actually marrying him and turning him respectable. Would you think she might, my lad?'

'I'm slightly dubious, guv,' said Ross.

'So am I,' said the Chief Inspector. 'I think Maureen Flanagan had sense enough to play her cards carefully. You'd better toddle off to Vine Street.'

'Vine Street station?'

'Yes. Get round there and find out what they know about the pimps of the West End, and if they've got anything on one we only know as Godfrey. If they have, we want his address. Make sure you get it.'

'Right, guv.'

'Off you go, then,' said Dobbs.

'I'm on my way,' said Ross, and departed. His head and shoulders returned. 'Might I ask if you consider Pritchard's now an also-ran?'

153

'No, he's still in the running,' said Dobbs.

'Reasonable,' said Ross, and went.

Ross returned later, notebook marked with scribbles.

'Sit down,' said the Chief Inspector. Ross seated himself. 'Well?' said Dobbs.

'Pimps mostly stay under the surface—'

'I know that.'

'But they bob up occasionally.'

'I know that too, don't I? Get on with it.'

'There's a file at Vine Street—'

'I'll chuck my inkwell at you in a minute,' growled Dobbs.

'There's several names,' said Ross, 'but no Godfrey Who.'

'I hope you can do better than that,' said Dobbs.

'On the happy side, guv, it's recorded that a woman called Maureen Flanagan was stopped in Drury Lane one evening and given a warning on suspicion of being a street-walker and accordingly a public nuisance.'

'Yes, that's a lot better,' said Dobbs. 'When was this?'

'The evening of 15th October,' said Ross, 'which—'

'Hold on,' said Dobbs, 'what's going on at Vine Street? Maureen Flanagan's name must have been printed on the front page of every newspaper when she was murdered. Why didn't Vine Street pick it up and let us know they'd got a mention of her in some constable's notebook?'

'My point exactly when I put the question,' said Ross. 'It seems the name didn't register. It might have done with the constable in question, but he

154

happened to be on his last week of duty when he stopped and warned Flanagan, and he's now halfway to Canada with his family. He's emigrated.'

'You look as if you think that's helpful information,' said Dobbs. 'It's not, it's the worst case of inconvenient emigration I've ever heard of. But let's see, she was warned on the 15th of October?'

'That's the date,' said Ross, consulting his notebook.

'Well now, my son, 15th of October was the day when I think the unfortunate lady got the wind up. So what did she do? I'd say she had a meeting with her pimp and pointed out she wasn't going to risk being arrested. That would have meant an appearance in court and her name in the papers. Her pimp, of course, treated her to a bucketful of reassurance, along with his most charming smiles. That may have eased her worries for a little while. But I'd say she had another go at him, perhaps several, and during the last one he went over the top, like pimps do when they're crossed.'

'Whoever he is, he's not known to Vine Street,' said Ross.

'Perhaps, my lad, we've got his name wrong.'

'Not according to Pritchard and his old lady,' said Ross.

'Did you list known names?' asked Dobbs.

'Such as were given, guv, and such being standard practice according to—'

'Yes, I know. Read 'em out.'

'Right. Gus Robbins, Pinky Schmidt, Frankie Zapparelli, Jimmy Morris and Sidney Whelan. They're known. Then there's two suspected of pimping. Baz Gottfried and Walter Reynolds. Looks like Godfrey Who has never broken surface.'

155

'Does it look like that?' asked Dobbs.

'You asking or saying, guv?'

'I'm asking,' said Dobbs. 'And I'm asking who's got a name like Baz?'

'It's what Vine Street's got as the first name for Gottfried,' said Ross. 'German immigrant, I suppose.'

'Gottfried,' said Dobbs.

Sergeant Ross hit himself with his notebook.

'Well, I'm a ruddy cuckoo,' he said. 'Godfrey, of course.'

'Well, it's what Flanagan called him,' said Dobbs. 'Right, telephone Vine Street this time. Ask them if they've got the address of this suspected pimp, Gottfried. If they haven't, ask them for the addresses of a couple of known West End ladies of the bedchamber. One of them might know Gottfried and where he keeps himself under the surface. Get through now. Give 'em my compliments.'

'That'll help, of course.'

'Hurry it up,' said Dobbs.

Sergeant Ross made the call and came back with the information that Gottfried's address wasn't known, but the addresses of two West End ladies of the bedchamber had been given.

'Shall we go to work, guv?'

'Yes, put your hat and coat on,' said the Chief Inspector.

Chapter Ten

Constable Fred Billings, coming off his first beat of the day, spoke to Sergeant Gough about a lady resident's complaint concerning a suspect loiterer who began to follow her. Wisely, he omitted any mention of her female intuition.

'Come off it, Billings,' said Sergeant Gough.

'Thinkin' about it,' said Fred, 'I considered it me duty to report it.'

'You're reportin' that some lady friend of yours was follered last night in Back Church Lane?'

'The same, sarge.'

'Any lady in Back Church Lane at that time o' night can expect to be follered,' said Sergeant Gough. 'And much as it grieves me, some of 'em like to be follered. For purposes of a licentious nature, with money changing hands. Unfortunately, it don't always happen like that, as you know, or should know. Some of 'em get laid out, their 'andbags nicked and their wearables removed. That's on account of what we call the recipients bein' in need of overgarments and undergarments, and not too proud to put 'em on for Sunday church. I wouldn't be surprised if 'alf the hard-up females in Bow Bells on Sundays ain't wearin' what don't rightly belong to 'em.'

'I know all that, sarge,' said Fred, 'but I think what this partic'lar lady was on about didn't concern 'er wearables. I think she meant 'er virtue.'

'Eh?'

'Virtue, sarge.'

'You feelin' ill?' enquired Sergeant Gough.

'Right as rain, sarge.'

'D'you mean that after three years on yer present beat, you've found a female in Whitechapel that's still in ownership of 'er virtue?'

'I wouldn't rightly say I've found her, sarge, I've known 'er for years.'

'Who is she?'

'Bridget Cummings, sarge.'

'Bridget Cummings?' Sergeant Gough eyed Fred pityingly. 'The middleweight champion of Petticoat Lane, Caledonian Market, Whitechapel and Mile End? Constable Billings, any suspect geezer that takes to follering Bridget Cummings home is liable to be found in a mortally wounded condition.'

'Beg to differ, sarge.'

'You beg what, Billings?'

'Well, I grant Bridget Cummings is a bit quick to get aggravated, but under all that it's me genuine opinion she's got a warm heart and good intentions.'

'You're off yer rocker,' said Sergeant Gough. 'Bridget Cummings is 'ighly fortunate not to be in jug for participatin' in that riot.'

'She was only there by accident, sarge.'

'Billings, if you've gone weak in the head, get yerself a job openin' cab doors for the gentry. By the way, how'd you come to be speakin' to the middleweight champ first thing this morning?'

'I'm lodging with her and 'er family, sarge, 'aving moved in yesterday evening. It's already in the records.'

'Billings, see a doctor,' said Sergeant Gough.

'Sarge—'

'It's an order.'

Lulu Swann shared a flat with a lady friend in Albany Mansions off Shaftesbury Avenue. Albany Mansions looked as if it had seen its better days long ago. The stone stairs were pitted, the tiled walls dull with neglect. On the first floor, a woman stood in the open doorway of her flat. There were curlers in her fair frizzy hair, and she wore a pale green feathery wrap that looked as if it was struggling to survive constant wear. It also looked as if it was on its own.

'Hello, darlings, heard you coming up,' she said to the two men as they reached the top of the first flight of stairs, 'but no daytime clients, sweeties – oh, 'elp.' Her tone changed. She'd recognized two arms of the law. She vanished, closing the door fast.

Chief Inspector Dobbs and Sergeant Ross traversed the landing and climbed the second flight of stairs, their boots treading stone. They were looking for flat number seven. They found it and Sergeant Ross knocked. The door opened after a short interval. Another woman appeared, another gaudy feathery wrap, another head of hair, but loose in the absence of pins or curlers. A pretty face, a face that looked as if it had just had a lick and a promise, took on an expression of caution.

'Good morning,' said the Chief Inspector breezily.

'Er?' said the woman, in her mid-twenties.

'Would you be Miss Swann?'

'Who's askin'?'

'I am. We are.'

'What for? I ain't done nothing.'

'Why d'you say that?' asked the Chief Inspector.

''Cos yer coppers, ain't yer?'

'Very observant of you, Miss Swann. I'm Chief Inspector Dobbs of Scotland Yard, and this is Detective-Sergeant Ross. Might we come in and talk to you?'

''Ere, this ain't fair, Scotland Yard comin' it 'eavy on a gel,' said Lulu Swann.

'You're in no trouble as far as the Yard is concerned,' said Dobbs. 'We're simply making enquiries about a certain gentleman you might know.'

'Me?' said Lulu Swann. 'I don't know no gentlemen, except—well, a gel can never tell who's a gentleman and who ain't. You sure you ain't after layin' something on me?'

'Sure,' said Sergeant Ross.

''Ere, you're nice-lookin' for a copper, did yer know that?' said Lulu.

'Yes, Sergeant Ross knows it,' said Dobbs. 'Can we come in?'

'Well, all right, only I ain't prepared for visitors, not this time of the day I ain't, and Irene, me flat-mate, is still in bed.' Lulu stood aside and the men entered. Sergeant Ross closed the door for her and she took them into a living-room, cluttered and untidy. There was a faint aroma of scent and musk. 'Well, this is me sumptuous abode,' she said. 'Still, we don't get the mice up 'ere like they do down-stairs. What certain gent was you wantin' to ask about?'

160

'First,' said Dobbs, 'would you know a woman called Maureen Flanagan?'

'Is that Irish?' asked Lulu, drawing her wrap closer over a fairly capacious bosom.

'Yes, Irish,' said Ross.

'Never 'eard of her,' said Lulu.

'Sure?' said Ross.

'Positive,' said Lulu, 'never met any Flanagans in me life. Is she a gel that gets arrested occasional?'

'One of the arrestable kind, you mean?' said Ross.

'If yer like,' said Lulu.

'We've no record that she's ever been arrested,' said Dobbs.

'Well, I still don't know 'er,' said Lulu.

'D'you read the papers?' asked Ross.

'Papers? No, only picture magazines.'

'D'you know of or have you heard of a man called Baz Gottfried?' asked Dobbs.

'Baz what?' said Lulu. 'Who's 'e with a monicker like that?'

'A gentleman engaged in procuring,' said Dobbs.

'Oh, blimey,' said Lulu, 'you're 'ot stuff, you are, mister. A gentleman, you said? That's a good one, that is. But I've never seen 'im, spoke to 'im or 'eard of 'im.'

'Who looks after you, Miss Swann?' asked Ross.

'Give over, you know the game, don't yer?' said Lulu. 'I ain't comin' across with 'is name. He's me insurance.'

'You've never heard anyone mention the name Baz Gottfried?' asked Dobbs.

'No, honest I ain't,' said Lulu.

'How about Godfrey?' suggested Dobbs.

161

'No, nor 'im, either,' said Lulu.

'Your friend Irene,' said Ross, 'd'you think she might help us, Miss Swann?'

'She's in bed,' said Lulu. Her wrap, loose, gaped a little. Abundance made a fleeting attempt at emergence. 'Oh, beg yer pardon, gents,' she said, and forestalled revelation by adjusting her wrap and holding on to it. 'Irene had – well, a busy night. But she wouldn't be able to 'elp, she's new and a bit green. Me insurance man only brought 'er up from the country a week ago.'

'Your insurance man's heading for a nasty fall,' said Dobbs.

'Yes, ain't some people wicked, mister?' said Lulu.

'People like Baz Gottfried?' said Ross.

'Blimey, that one sounds like a circus knife-thrower that's 'it 'is target when he shouldn't 'ave,' said Lulu. 'Sorry I can't 'elp you gents, I never met nicer coppers. 'Ere, listen, handsome,' she said to Ross, 'you got any money? Only you could buy me out for a hundred quid, and I'd come and 'ouse-keep for yer, and do yer washin' as well.'

'I'm short of money in the bank,' said Sergeant Ross.

'Well, if yer luck changes and a windfall lands on yer doorstep,' said Lulu, pert and saucy, 'just come and knock.'

'And if you should hear of a man called Baz Gottfried,' said Ross, 'get in touch with us at the Yard.'

'Crikey, I don't want to be seen at the Yard,' said Lulu.

'There'll be a couple of quid for any useful information,' said Dobbs.

'Two quid?' said Lulu, looking pained.

'Four,' said Dobbs. 'Good day, Miss Swann. Stay off the streets.'

'Yes, be a good girl,' said Ross.

'Nice to 'ave met yer, I'm sure,' said Lulu, hugely relieved she'd hadn't been copped for soliciting. She saw them out, opening the door for them before suddenly sparking into life. ''Ere, half a tick, wait a bit. Baz you said? Baz? You sure you don't mean Basil?'

'You're saying there's a Basil Gottfried?' said Dobbs.

'Well, you said four quid and I remember I did 'ear a gel mention 'im once.'

'Dear, dear,' said Dobbs, shaking his head. Lulu gave a very good impression of not understanding. 'You've been naughty,' said Dobbs.

'Lying, guv, is that the word?' said Ross.

'Me?' said Lulu.

'Didn't you say you'd never heard of any Gottfried?' said Ross.

'It's me memory,' said Lulu, 'it goes blank sometimes.'

'Dear, dear,' said Dobbs again.

'Look, mister,' said Lulu, 'anyone could go blank about a name like that.'

'The reverse, I'd say,' said Ross.

'I told yer, though, that I've managed to remember,' said Lulu. 'By the way, could yer make it a fiver?'

'That depends,' said Dobbs.

'Well, could yer 'old on a minute while I see if Irene's still asleep? Only it ain't clever to talk about names if someone's listening.' Lulu moved down the corridor, carefully opened a door and looked

163

in. Satisfied, she quietly closed the door and returned. 'Dreamin' of country chickens, I expect,' she said. 'Anyway, Basil Gottfried's got gels, but I 'eard he's a bit nasty. He scarred one gel for life when she crossed 'im. Mind, that's only what I 'eard.'

'Where's he live?' asked Ross.

'I don't know that, honest,' said Lulu, 'he sort of keeps 'is head down, he sort of disappears and re-appears, but 'e still keeps 'is eye on 'is gels, all of 'em.'

'You sure you don't know where we could find him?' said Dobbs.

'Honest,' said Lulu.

'I think you're withholding information,' said Dobbs.

'No, I ain't,' said Lulu.

'Tck, tck,' said Ross.

'Mind, I could find out for yer,' said Lulu, 'I could find out this afternoon, if you 'ad a fiver up yer sleeve.'

'How?' asked Dobbs.

'Mister, I know one of 'is gels that likes me a lot. D'you mind if I don't tell yer any more?'

'I won't mind too much if you can come up with the man's address,' said Dobbs.

'Could yer come back 'ere tomorrer mornin'?' asked Lulu.

'We could do that,' said Ross.

'With me five quid?'

'If you're worth it,' said Dobbs.

'Could yer make it six quid?' asked Lulu.

'Two quid was a fair start, four quid was hand-some, a fiver's a promise, but six quid is coming it a bit,' said Dobbs.

'Still, it ain't a fortune,' said Lulu, 'and you didn't mind me askin', did yer, mister?'

'Well, we all like to have one more go at the lucky dip,' said Dobbs. 'Good day, Miss Swann, we'll be back tomorrow morning.'

'I won't let yer down,' said Lulu, 'specially if yer going' to put Basil out of business. He's a real nasty insurance man, 'e is.'

'That's only what you've heard, of course,' said Ross.

'Yes, that's right,' said Lulu.

Chief Inspector Dobbs and Sergeant Ross said nothing as they descended the stairs to the tiled hall. Leaving the building and entering the flow of the West End's busy life, Ross said, 'Saucy little madam, that one.'

'Fighting for survival, my lad,' said Dobbs, 'which is why she and her kind get into a habit of telling fibs.'

A weak sun had given up the attempt to brighten the misty air. Barrow boys were active, horse-drawn traffic rolling up from Piccadilly Circus, and the colourful adornments of ladies' large hats challenging the sober hues of winter. The Chief Inspector's brown bowler sat squarely on his head, while Sergeant Ross's black bowler was worn at a slightly rakish angle, which would not have pleased the Chief Superintendent.

'The offer of a few quid changed that,' said Ross. 'Do we make a call on the second lady, Mary Smith? I've got her address down as Wardour Street.'

'Right, with luck, Mary Smith might save the Yard five quid,' said Dobbs.

That piece of wishful thinking fell apart. Mary Smith, if such was her name, had departed from the

Wardour Street address two weeks ago, and the present occupant, a coloured lady in pink swansdown and very little else, knew nothing of her or of anyone called Baz Gottfried or Basil Godfrey.

'That puts Lulu Swann back on course for tomorrow,' said Ross, as he and the Chief Inspector retraced their steps to Shaftesbury Avenue.

'And there's still Mrs Pritchard and her fidgets,' said Dobbs.

'Any further thoughts on her old man, guv?'

'Basil's favourite at the moment,' said Dobbs.

'Odds-on, would you say?' asked Ross.

'Evens, sunshine, evens,' said Dobbs.

'They 'aven't come back, the police,' said Mrs Pritchard, when her husband walked in for his midday bite to eat.

'Well, if they do,' said Mr Pritchard, 'don't open yer north-and-south too much. Even opening it a bit ain't clever, not when it's in front of coppers from the Yard. Uniformed rozzers that walk the beat 'ave got the looks of the law, but not a lot up top. Yard coppers are artful sods.'

'You didn't 'ave much up top yerself when you told 'em you didn't go out that night,' said Mrs Pritchard.

'You 'ad even less when you said I did.'

'It just slipped out, it was me state of mind,' said Mrs Pritchard. 'I 'ope them coppers ain't been askin' questions down at the pub.'

'Ruddy 'ell, did you 'ave to mention that?' said Mr Pritchard.

'It's on me mind, ain't it?' said Mrs Pritchard. 'They might of found out you was there.'

'If they 'ad,' said Mr Pritchard, 'they'd 'ave been

back 'ere to ask a lot more of me. Listen, I dunno why we 'ave to 'ave troublesome lodgers.'

'For their rent, of course,' said Mrs Pritchard. 'And they ain't troublesome. It's you that is. Goin' after Maureen Flanagan at your age, that was trouble all right, you an old married man and all.'

'Leave it alone, will yer?' said Mr Pritchard.

Bridget was not given the opportunity to have another set-to with Constable Fred Billings that evening, for along with other constables he'd been despatched to investigate a disturbance at a lodging house in Crispin Street. Everyone in the place seemed to be fighting everyone else, women clawing, scratching and shrieking, men wading in on each other in attempts to break bones. It took the little band of uniformed policemen quite some time to quell the brawl and to save the lodging house owner from having every stick of furniture broken up.

Daisy had cooked a rabbit stew not only for herself and Billy but for their lodger as well. However, she kept Fred's helping hot, and he enjoyed it later, paying the agreed sum of sixpence for it. Bridget by then was at work, so Fred ate his supper in welcome peace.

The fog returned, not thickly, but in drifting rolling masses of pale brown mist. It searched for the alleys of Whitechapel, and for whatever doors that were open. It was the kind of fog that curled, crept and sneaked. It followed people into the ever-open pubs, causing drinkers to offer up violent protests.

'Shut that bleedin' door!'

It was a night which some people thought would tempt Old Nick to emerge from nowhere and prowl about in search of those who belonged to him. They were everywhere, Old Nick's own, seen one moment and gone the next, the drink-sodden, the degraded doxies and the men of ill repute. Imaginative people might have said the gentleman who walked with a measured tread did so in the way of the devil himself, as if evil had no fear for him.

He turned into New Road from Whitechapel Road, and from a doorway came the sound of a voice he knew.

'Lookin' for someone nice, are yer, dearie?'

He was ready for her this time.

'How much?' he asked.

She had her back to the door. It was slightly ajar and a thin streak of light showed. She was dressed in a red velvet bodice and a black skirt, her fair hair piled and dully gleaming. The pale brown fog curled around the gentleman, but she could see enough to place him as a toff.

'Four bob to you, love,' she said. 'I'm fresh, and only accept gents.'

'Upstairs?' he said, his voice a deep murmur.

'In me own room, ducky,' said Poppy Simpson. 'Here, do I know yer?'

'I gave you sixpence a few nights ago,' he murmured.

'Why, so yer did, and it was 'andsome of yer. I'll be really nice to you for that and four bob.'

'Lead the way.'

She turned and pushed the door open, revealing a passage partially illuminated by a small boat-shaped flame from a gas jet. He stepped in. She looked at him, a clean-shaven man. He smiled. He

168

was a gent all right. He placed his walking-stick against the wall and closed the door.

'Come on up, lovey,' she said.

He heard the sounds of people, little sounds. She turned again towards the stairs. Silently, he placed his bag on the floor, took one long stride, whipped his left arm around her from behind and clapped a gloved hand hard over her mouth, pulling her head back. She gurgled and choked. From his pocket of his coat he drew a knife with a thin, razor-sharp blade. With one fierce slashing incision he cut her throat wide open. Her blood spurted as he let her drop, retreating fast from her. He bent, wiped the knife clean on her skirt, and put it back in his coat pocket. He picked up his bag, put his stick under his arm, opened the door just wide enough to let himself out, then closed it silently behind him. He took hold of his stick and walked away, into the floating clouds of fog, his footsteps those of a man who felt no need to hurry.

Bridget, hastening home, entered Commercial Road, making for Back Church Lane, which led to Ellen Street. As usual, she had ridden to Aldgate on the underground tube train, the City Line, the fare three ha'pence. From Aldgate, she walked. The fog could have been a lot worse than it was, and the street lamps in Commercial Road were visible, even if they did seem to be floating in the misty pall. Into the patchy light of one walked a man, tall, over-coated, and carrying a bag and walking-stick.

'Oh, 'ello, doctor, how'dyerdo?' said Bridget.

'I beg your pardon?' He stopped and loomed.

'Oh, I don't suppose you recognize me,' said

Bridget, 'it was 'orrible foggy that evenin', when the workers was set on by the police and someone knocked me out.'

'Oh, yes, I remember, young lady.' The gentleman smiled. 'How's your head now?'

'Well, I'm still carryin' it about,' said Bridget.

'Should you be carrying it about at this late hour?'

'Oh, I'm just goin' 'ome from me evening's work in the West End,' said Bridget.

'The West End? I see.' He peered at her, taking note of her full figure. 'I see,' he said again. 'Well, this neighbourhood isn't to your taste, I dare say, so hurry along. Or would you like me to see you to your door?'

'Well, yer a kind gent offering,' said Bridget, 'but I'll be all right.'

'Are you sure? It's no bother.'

'Thanks, but I'll manage,' said Bridget.

'Goodnight, then.'

'Goodnight, doctor.'

They parted, Bridget resuming her walk to Back Church Lane, and he going his own way thinking well, well, her work is in the West End? Well, well.

As Bridget approached Back Church Lane, a policeman turned out of it. She glimpsed his helmet and uniform.

At this moment, a woman was making her frantic cries heard in New Road.

'Murder! Murder's been done!'

The cries did not reach Commercial Road, where neither Bridget nor Constable Fred Billings heard them as he came face to face with her amid the floating mist.

170

'Fred Billings, what're you doin' 'ere? asked Bridget.

'I though I'd come and meet you,' said Fred.

'What for?'

'To see you safely 'ome,' said Fred, 'and to make sure that you didn't get follered again.'

'Look, when I need a copper to walk me 'ome, I'll ask for one,' said Bridget.

'No need to ask, Bridget,' said Fred, 'I'm 'appy to volunteer. Besides which, I feet it's me duty as a policeman and me privilege as yer lodger.'

'As a policeman you ain't my kind of bloke,' said Bridget, 'and as me lodger you can take yerself off as soon as yer like.'

Fred wouldn't be put off, however, and insisted on seeing her home. Bridget told him not to think he was doing her any favours, and she also told him she'd seen that doctor again, the one who'd attended to her that evening of the riot. Fred said a doctor who had patients in Whitechapel was a bit of a rarity.

By this time the Whitechapel police station had seen the arrival of a man and woman, both of whom were white-faced as they reported the finding of a murdered prostitute, one Poppy Simpson, in what they said was their lodging house in New Road.

Chapter Eleven

Roused out of his bed by a uniformed police sergeant who had arrived in a cab, Chief Inspector Dobbs accompanied him to the scene of the crime in New Road. He kept his feelings to himself during the drive. A second murder similar to the first was bad enough. To have happened in Whitechapel and to a known prostitute made it far worse, since nothing would now hold Fleet Street back from suggesting Jack the Ripper had returned, even though neither victim had been mutilated.

The Whitechapel police had the house closed off to people. The Chief Superintendent of the Metropolitan Police, responsible for summoning Dobbs, was on the spot and waiting for him, along with a police surgeon. The Chief Superintendent was frankly alarmed. Dobbs was frankly disgusted. The hounds were going to be at his back now with a vengeance.

Inspecting the body and the pool of drying blood, he said, 'How long dead?'

'Not long,' said the surgeon. 'Say a little over an hour, say about eleven-thirty. Just the one wound, a clean slicing of the throat.'

'Poor bloody woman,' said Dobbs. He frowned

and mused. 'It doesn't look as if this one was carried from somewhere else.'

'You're thinking of the woman found in Tooley Street, the Flanagan woman?' said the Chief Superintendent.

'This one was done for right here,' said Dobbs.

'That's obvious,' said the surgeon.

'Who lives in this house?'

'It's a brothel,' said the Chief Superintendent, 'and the man and woman who own the place and live here, on the ground floor, were the ones who found the body. There are three women upstairs, and one had a customer with her at the time. He's still there, but swears he heard nothing. In fact, everyone in the house swears the same.'

'I think I'll still have a word with the owners,' said Dobbs, and did so. They were a coarse couple, both as hard as nails, which was one way of surviving in the sleazy jungle of the East End, where dog ate dog. But they were a shaken couple at the moment, insisting they heard nothing that would have made them suspect murder was taking place in the passage. The only sounds had been those from upstairs, where two women had been drinking gin, and a third had been entertaining a client.

'And gawd 'elp us if that ain't the truth,' said the man.

'Where might the murdered woman have picked up a client herself?' asked the Chief Inspector.

'From the doorway. That was 'er pitch, the doorway. She wasn't keen on walkin' no street.'

'Unfortunately, that precaution didn't help her in the end,' said Dobbs.

'He's come back, the bleeder,' said the woman.

'Who's come back?' asked Dobbs.

173

'The Ripper,' said the woman, white-faced.

'If you say that again, I'll lose my temper,' said Dobbs.

'Bloody 'ell,' said the man, 'if you're out of sorts, 'ow d'yer think we feel?'

'That Poppy, done for in our own 'ouse,' said the woman.

It was some time before Chief Inspector Dobbs allowed himself to return home. Daphne got up, and at four o'clock in the morning she made him a hot toddy, and a cup of tea for herself. He painted a picture for her of the murder.

'Horrible,' she said. 'Charlie, you're really up against it now, aren't you?'

'You could say so, Daffie.'

'"A policeman's lot is not a happy one".' said Daphne. 'Well, not according to Gilbert and Sullivan.'

'It's not as bad as the lot of Poppy Simpson or Maureen Flanagan, taken off to their Maker without even the chance to say a prayer, probably.'

'Charlie, back to bed for you. You can get some sleep before breakfast. You'll need it.'

The late editions of morning papers carried news of the murder in Whitechapel. Chief Inspector Dobbs, on arrival at the Yard, was shown how the papers had sensationalized the fact that the victim was a known prostitute attached to a small brothel and had been murdered within the area that had once been Jack the Ripper's hunting ground. Dobbs said he'd had a bad night, and that the day didn't look too good, either.

The Chief Superintendent had a word with him, letting him know the Commissioner himself had already been in touch and wanted a quick arrest before the whole thing blew up out of proportion. Further, he wanted some kind of action that would take the minds of Fleet Street and the minds of the public off any association with the crimes of the Ripper, otherwise every national newspaper would feed the public with rehashed stories of the Ripper that included conjectures on his identity.

'The gentlemen of the press will swarm into the Yard any moment,' said the Chief Superintendent. 'I'll deal with them, Charlie. You get busy. I've taken Inspector Davis off the arson case, and he and Sergeant Swettenham are to make up your investigating team. Have you decided, by the way, to work on the assumption that one man committed both murders?'

'I'm still giving that thought,' said the Chief Inspector, 'but what I'd like as a favour is for you to inform the press that the Yard has reason to believe a bloodthirsty lunatic went to work last night to copy the first murder.'

'Good idea, Charlie. I'll feed the hounds.'

In his office, Chief Inspector Dobbs and Sergeant Ross were joined by Inspector Davis and Sergeant Swettenham. Dobbs brought the latter men up-to-date with the file on Maureen Flanagan, then told them to do the rounds in Whitechapel, with the assistance, if necessary, of the local uniformed branch.

'Askin' after who might've seen or heard Poppy Simpson pick up the murderer?' said Inspector Davis.

'That's it, George, start at the beginning,' said Dobbs, 'it's the only way of starting for all of us, at the beginning. And Whitechapel teems with eyes and ears, even at that time of night.'

'You're not goin' to Whitechapel yourself?' said Davis.

'Not just now,' said Dobbs, 'I've got an appointment concerning Flanagan's murder.'

'Point is,' said Davis, 'is it a double murder by the same man or a case of sep'rate identities?'

'As far as the press and public are concerned, we're investigating two unconnected murders,' said Dobbs. 'If any reporters follow you about, get Sergeant Swettenham to tread on their feet. Has he got his best boots on?'

'I'm appropriately shod, guv,' said Sergeant Swettenham.

'Right, off you go, George,' said Dobbs.

Inspector George Davis left, taking Sergeant Swettenham with him. Sergeant Ross took a look at the Chief Inspector, whose rugged countenance was not at its best.

'We've got a bit of a swine here, guv,' said Ross.

'Don't I know it,' said Dobbs.

'You're still giving priority to the Flanagan case?'

'If we can solve that, I'll lay a pound to a penny we'll solve both,' said Dobbs.

'I can't see it myself,' said Ross. 'Well, I ask you, guv, if either Pritchard or the pimp did for Flanagan, what would be the motive of one or the other for giving the same treatment to Poppy Simpson?'

'Don't ask me questions like that,' said Dobbs. 'Just take it that I've got a feeling about this second murder.'

'Is that instinct, guv, or intuition?'

'As I don't happen to be a woman, my lad, drop

176

words like those into your wastepaper basket,' said Dobbs.

'So do we get after Lulu Swann now?'

'No, give her time to get the sleep out of her eyes,' said Dobbs. 'Listen, my lad, we're going to be chased from pillar to post, and crucified if we don't lay quick hands on the bugger who did for Poppy Simpson. And it'll be the Government that nails us to the cross.'

'Why?' asked Ross.

'Well, someone'll have to pay for what the papers will rake up about the Ripper and his identity. Read that.' Dobbs passed a photographic copy of a sheet of lined notepaper to Ross, who read its contents.

'Copy of Statement by George Hutchinson concerning the description of the man he saw talking to Mary Jeanette Kelly on the evening of her murder.

'Age about 34 or 35, height 5ft 6 ins. Complexion pale, dark eyes and eyelashes, slight moustache curled up at each end, and hair dark. Very surly looking. Dress: long dark coat, trimmed astrakhan, and a dark jacket under. Collar and cuffs, light waistcoat, dark trousers, dark felt hat turned down in the middle, button boots and gaiters with white buttons. Wore a very thick gold chain, white linen collar, black tie with horseshoe pin, respectable appearance.'

The statement was signed, *Geo. Hutchinson.*

Sergeant Ross looked up.

'Guv, where'd you get this from, and what's it mean?'

'Never mind where I got it from,' said Dobbs. 'What it means is that our lords and masters in high places have got serious objections to the newspapers interesting themselves in the Ripper inquiry, which they will do if we can't lay his ghost in respect of these present murders.'

'What I'd like to know,' said Ross, 'is why our lords and masters have got these objections, and if this description helped the police at the time to find and interview this flash-looking geezer.'

'The description doesn't mean anything to you?' said Dobbs.

'It reminds me of certain rumours,' said Ross.

'Well, let me tell you, Sergeant Ross, that that description, both in regard to looks and clothes, fits the late Duke of Clarence to perfection, particularly as per the hat, the moustache and the white buttons of the gaiters.'

'Christ,' said Ross. 'Did the Yard get to interview him?'

'Is that a serious question?' asked Dobbs. 'Interview Queen Victoria's grandson, heir to the throne after his father, the Prince of Wales? Fortunately for this country, and for himself, come to that, he passed away in 1892.'

'Fortunately for himself? Christ,' said Ross again, 'was he the Ripper, then?'

'Was it proved?' said Dobbs. 'No, it wasn't. After the murder of Mary Kelly, the last victim, the Duke of Clarence was sent on a visit to India, where he distinguished himself in the slaughter of tigers, boar and deer – he speared the boar to death. It turned his boots gory, but he didn't mind that. The Ripper investigation faded away. The high and mighty don't want the newspapers to interest themselves in it again. If we don't stop them by solving these two murders quickly, my son, we'll be for the Tower of London and the block.'

'I've got a headache, guv,' said Ross.

'You're not the only one,' said Dobbs. 'Well, grin and bear yours, and let's keep our appointment with Lulu Swann.'

Elsewhere, Constable Fred Billings was at the Commercial Street police station, a hive of activity, and Bridget and Daisy Cummings were trying not to believe the news that had flown through every keyhole of every house in the East End.

'Bridget, it just don't bear thinkin' about,' said Daisy for the tenth time.

'It don't bear thinkin' about by me personally,' said Bridget, 'not seein' it 'appened about the time I was on me way 'ome.'

'Lord Almighty,' said Daisy, 'ain't you glad Fred went to meet you and safeguarded you?'

'He's got some uses,' said Bridget. 'Daisy, if only I could get a decent-paid job, I'd see to it that we all moved out of Whitechapel.'

'I'd like to live next door to a park,' said Daisy, 'I'm a bundle of nerves livin' 'ere. Bridget, it just ain't fit for decent people, livin' on top of the worst slums.'

'We all know it, Daisy,' said Bridget. 'When you're settled in yer laundry job, and Billy's 'ad promotion to behind the counter of the grocers, we'll see if we can get a place in Walworth, say.'

'Walworth?' said Daisy. 'That's the other side of the river. Bridget, it's foreign.'

'That's where we'll go, to a foreign place, like Walworth or Lambeth,' said Bridget.

'I don't know 'ow we'll get on with foreigners,' said Daisy.

'We'll learn,' said Bridget. 'Round 'ere, Daisy,

there ain't any blokes you or me would even look at a first time, never mind a second.'

'There's Fred,' said Daisy.

Bridget muttered something. Since she never muttered, being given to speaking her mind whatever her mood, Daisy asked her if she was out of sorts. Bridget said no, she wasn't out of sorts except when Constable Fred Billings was mentioned.

'But I think 'e fancies yer, Bridget,' said Daisy.

'That's it, now make me spit,' said Bridget.

Lulu Swann opened the door to her flat. She was dressed all the way up to a hat and coat.

'Hello, going out, were you, Miss Swann?' said Sergeant Ross.

'Not till you arrived,' said Lulu, looking respectable rather than tarty. She came out, closing the door behind her. 'It ain't safe to talk to you in there, not with me flatmate around. Nor don't I want to walk down Shaftesbury Avenue with yer, not with two coppers I don't. I'll get noticed. No offence, mind.'

'None taken,' said the Chief Inspector.

'Downstairs, in the hall, we can talk there,' said Lulu. 'There's not many comings and goings in the mornings. Well, night work makes us gels sleep late. Let's go down, then.'

They descended to the draughty hall. The morning was clear of fog or mist, but the cold air was chilly with sharp winter. December was on its way.

Lulu tucked herself into the corner on one side of the closed door to the building.

'Take your time,' said the Chief Inspector.

'Kind of yer,' said Lulu, 'I never met kind police

before, I didn't know there was any.' She smiled at Sergeant Ross. 'I wouldn't mind walkin' out with yer in Hyde Park one Sunday,' she said.

'Unfortunately, Sergeant Ross walks out on Sundays with a nurse,' said Dobbs.

'A nurse?' said Lulu. 'Crikey, he must be 'ard-up, poor bloke.'

'Not all that much,' said Sergeant Ross. 'Have you got the information we want?'

'Would yer mind if I 'ad me six quid first?' asked Lulu.

'We'll pay on receipt of the information, young lady,' said the Chief Inspector, 'and we settled for a fiver.'

'Did we? You sure?' said Lulu.

'I'm sure,' said Dobbs. 'I'll just say that if the information leads us nowhere, we'll be back to charge you with fraud. We'll be sorry to, of course, but won't be able to help it.'

'Crikey, would I cheat yer, mister, would I?' said Lulu. 'Listen.' Her voice dropped to a whisper. 'Yer'll find Baz Gottfried that some gels call Godfrey at number four, Medway Road, Bow.'

'Medway Road?' said Dobbs. It was a little way south of Victoria Park.

'That's it, and I ain't flamming yer, mister, honest,' said Lulu. 'You won't 'ave to come back and knock me off. Mind, it won't break me 'eart if you knock Basil off. Where's me dibs, mister?'

The Chief Inspector took five pound notes from his wallet and handed them to her.

'Don't spend any of these just yet,' he said.

'No, all right,' said Lulu. She lifted her coat and skirt, and tucked the banknotes into the pocket

181

sewn to her petticoat. ''Ere, 'alf a tick, you won't mention my name, will yer? I begs you won't, or I'll 'ave me looks spoiled for good, and me legs broke as well.'

'Trust us, Miss Swann,' said Sergeant Ross.

'Oh, you're a real decent bloke, you are,' said Lulu, 'and if you'd like it for free sometime, I'd be very obligin', only not in me flat nor at night. Daytime somewhere. Say Highgate Cemetery, and when they ain't burying someone.'

'Make a note, Sergeant Ross,' said Dobbs. 'Thanks for your help, Miss Swann. By the way, d'you ever think of going back to your family?'

'Not much I don't,' said Lulu, 'me mum 'ud kill me. Well, she 'alf-killed me when she found me with me first bloke. So I left 'ome before she murdered me. 'Ere, what about that poor gel that got done in round Whitechapel last night?'

'I thought you didn't read newspapers,' said Dobbs.

'You don't 'ave to read newspapers to 'ear about a Whitechapel murder,' said Lulu.

'That crime is under investigation,' said Ross.

'Well, I 'ope you cop the bugger,' said Miss Swann. 'That kind make me forget I'm a lady.'

They took a growler, a four-wheeled cab, to Medway Street, Bow, the Chief Inspector musing, Sergeant Ross fidgety.

'Is something bothering you, sergeant?'

'I'm having a hard time trying to work out how to connect the murder of Flanagan with the murder of Poppy Simpson,' said Ross.

'Well, do the sensible thing, let it work itself out,' said Dobbs.

'I've never known any investigation that worked itself out,' said Ross.

'It's what they call waiting for things to fall into place,' said Dobbs.

'Bit of a lottery, I'd say, guv. By the way, I don't walk out with Nurse Cartright on Sundays.'

'Why not, my lad?'

'On Sundays, if she's not on duty, she likes to give her feet a rest.'

'I see,' asked Dobbs. 'By the way, is it a serious relationship?'

'Not yet,' said Ross. The cab was approaching Medway Road. 'Regarding Basil of Bow, how'd you feel about prospects?'

'I've a feeling, sunshine, that this time Lulu Swann wasn't fibbing. So we'll go straight for it.'

The four-wheeler drew up outside number four Medway Road, a not unpleasant thoroughfare. The two men alighted, and Sergeant Ross paid the cabbie.

'That's exact,' said the cabbie, looking at the silver shilling.

'Good,' said Ross.

'I ain't exactly used to it bein' exact.'

'I know what you mean.' said Ross.

'Well, so yer should, mister, bein' a Yard copper, if I ain't mistook.'

'Try this,' said Ross, and handed up a threepenny bit.

'Now yer talkin',' said the cabbie. 'So long, guv, and may yer lay all the villains and nobble all the artful dodgers.'

Off he went. Chief Inspector Dobbs and Sergeant Ross climbed the few steps to the front door of the house, and Dobbs knocked. A little time elapsed before they heard heels clicking on stairs. Seconds later, an attractive, well-dressed woman of about thirty opened the door. She regarded them coolly.

'Yes?' she said distantly.

'Where's Basil? asked Dobbs.

A haughty eyebrow went up.

'I beg your pardon?'

'Where's Basil?'

'I think you've come to the wrong address. This is my house and I live alone. I don't know any Basil, and I don't know you, either. Go away.'

The Chief Inspector shouldered his way past her and contemplated the hanging lace curtains that fronted the stairs.

'This way, I think, my lad,' he said to Sergeant Ross, and walked to the stairs through the divide in the curtains. He began to ascend. Ross entered the house. The woman ran to the stairs and yelled up at Dobbs.

'Oh, yer bleeder, come down, will yer!'

That brought a smile from the Chief Inspector.

'This is a friendly visit,' he said, halting halfway up the stairs and turning.

'Tell me another. You're interfering coppers, it's written all over the pair of you.' The woman's rageful expression and change of tone and accent didn't quite go with her stylish coiffure and fashionable dress. 'And where's yer search warrant?'

'What do we need a search warrant for, madam?' asked Ross. 'There's no stolen goods here, are there? We're only looking for Basil.'

'And all we need from him is some information on a friend of his,' said Dobbs, which was merely an opener.

184

'I said I didn't know him, didn't I?' countered the woman.

Dobbs regarded her well-attired handsomeness.

'I'm Chief Inspector Dobbs from Scotland Yard, and this is Sergeant Ross,' he said.

'Pleasured, I don't think.'

'I suppose you know the penalty for obstructing police enquiries, do you?' said Dobbs, looking as if he was cheerfully considering a cell for her.

'What police enquiries?'

'Concerning a friend of Basil's,' said Dobbs.

The woman, looking less hostile, said, 'Just one of his friends?'

'Just one,' said Ross, who knew his guv'nor meant Maureen Flanagan.

'Well, hard luck, he's not here.'

'Take a look, Sergeant Ross,' said Dobbs.

'Go on, then, take a look,' said the woman, 'but you won't find 'im.'

'He's out?' said Dobbs.

'Gone to visit an aunt in the country, if you must know.'

'Well, it's a fact that we have to know,' said Dobbs. 'What's the name and address of his aunt?'

'I don't know her name, or her address.' The woman had reverted to carefully modulated speech. 'She happens to be Basil's aunt, not mine.'

'Are you Mrs Basil?' asked Dobbs. 'Mrs Basil Gottfried? Or Godfrey?'

'No, I'm not. Baz isn't the marrying kind. I keep house for him.'

She's his mistress, thought the Chief Inspector, and he dresses her in style. That was the way of it with a well-off pimp. Nothing tarty in appearance adorned his private life.

'What's his business?' asked Ross.

'You don't know?' There was a suggestion of relief in her expression.

'What's your name?' asked Dobbs.

'Margaret Donaldson.'

'Well, Miss Donaldson, we don't know everything, which is why we frequently have to ask questions,' said the Chief Inspector amiably. 'Asking gets to be second nature with us.'

'Well, you can ask all day,' said Margaret Donaldson, alias Maggie Stubbs, 'but I still couldn't tell you anything about Basil's aunt, and I don't know what his business is, either. He's never told me. I just keep house for him.'

'When did he leave on this visit to his aunt?' asked Ross.

'Four days ago. He was called away suddenly.'

'By his aunt?' said Dobbs.

'That's what he said.'

'Four days ago?' said Dobbs.

'Yes.'

Dobbs glanced at Ross. Basil had chosen to go absent the morning after the murder of Maureen Flanagan.

'That's very inconvenient, Miss Donaldson,' said Dobbs. 'We'd like very much to speak to this friend of his. He told you, of course, when he'd be back?'

'He said he didn't know how long he'd be away.'

'Pity,' said Dobbs. 'Well, we'll have to try another source, we can't wait indefinitely. We'll find this friend of his through someone else we know. Unless, well, would you know a man called Gus Robbins?'

That, Sergeant Ross knew, was the name of one

186

of the known pimps listed by Vine Street police station.

'Me? Gus Robbins? Who's 'e when 'e's out?' The woman, flustered, reverted to type.

'Never mind, we'll find him,' said Dobbs, coming down from the stairs. 'Thanks for your help, sorry to have startled you, Miss Donaldson.'

'Sorry to have bothered you as well,' said Ross.

'Sorry I couldn't help,' said the woman.

'Sorry all round, eh?' said Dobbs. 'Good morning.'

He and Ross left.

'You let her off a bit lightly, didn't you, guv?' said Ross.

'Wake up, my lad. No point in putting the fear of God into her. Handsome woman, I thought. But there's no aunt, of course. Basil panicked and did a bunk and now he's lying low. And he did a bunk either because he murdered Flanagan or because, knowing she'd been done in, he guessed we'd find out she was a part-time pro and that this could lead us to him. Now, according to Lulu Swann, he can be vicious. That reputation would make a suspect of him. Either that or the fact that he's guilty caused him to panic. His woman denied knowing what his business was, but she knows it all, of course, and she probably knows other pimps, including Gus Robbins. What brought his name up, by the way?'

'I think you pulled it out of your hat to deceive the lady into thinking Robbins is the one we're after, and that Basil's in the clear,' said Ross.

'Glad to know you're up with me, my lad. Very refreshing. The lady, I'd say, will now let Basil know it's safe to come home to her bosom. He's under the surface somewhere. As soon as we get back to the Yard, arrange for the house to be watched from this evening onwards. The moment Basil's return is reported, we'll pay another call, this time with a search warrant, which will help us look for a very sharp knife and Flanagan's handbag.'

'And if there's no such knife or handbag, guv, and he comes up with an alibi?'

'Don't make me fret, sunshine, tell me another Scotch joke.'

'Under the circumstances,' said Ross, as they stood on the corner of Medway Road, looking for a cab, 'I don't feel jokes are in order. Still, did you hear about the suicidal Scotsman who broke into the house next door to gas himself?'

'Well, I've heard about him now,' said Dobbs, 'but don't mention him again.'

They took a cab to Trafalgar Square and found a pub that provided them with a sandwich each, a glass of beer for Ross and a whisky for the Chief Inspector, who said his need for it was greater than his need for any more jokes, Scotch or otherwise.

'Well, you've got your own kind of Scotch, guv,' said Ross, 'and that's not a joke, that's a world-wide medicine highly esteemed.'

'Stop showing off,' said Dobbs, and wondered how Inspector Davis and Sergeant Swettenham were progressing in Whitechapel. His bet was nowhere.

Chapter Twelve

The man who looked and spoke like a professional gentleman was again out and about at lunchtime. He approached a pub off the Strand, stopped, pushed the door open and looked in. The place offered to the eye a typical picture of polished mahogany, mirrors, glassware, an array of bottles containing whisky, gin, brandy or other spirits, and couched beer barrels. A painting of Sir Henry Irving hung on a wall, and the place was crowded with people who looked like Bohemian men and women of the theatre. The gentleman was tempted to put himself among them, but felt his ears would be dinned by the loud buzz of many voices. He let the door swing back and retraced his steps, electing for a restaurant in the Strand, which offered a different picture, one of colour and elegance. Not that he responded to colour and elegance at the moment, no, hardly at all. It was the fog-infested streets of Whitechapel at night that quickened him.

He enjoyed a quick one-course lunch, not allowing himself to be distracted in any way by the striking tableaux of beautifully dressed women seated beneath their hugely round hats. One could have said they were seated under feathered

189

canopies. His interest in them was lukewarm, however, for he had in mind an encounter with a woman quite different from any of these, a woman whom he had chanced upon more than once in the mist and fog of Whitechapel.

He mused very pleasantly on prospects, while still warm with satisfaction at the effectiveness of last night's swift strike. He finished his meal, paid his bill, and when he re-emerged into the Strand he was a gentleman who looked warmly handsome with well-being. The Strand was choked with horse-drawn traffic and alive with the shouts and noisy impatience of cabbies and the drivers of carts. A huge beer dray, pulled by a shaggy, strong-legged four, was impeded by a standing kerbside barrow laden with polished apples and pears. The vendor, flat-capped and aproned, had been selling to passing Saturday shop workers who fancied taking some fruit back to their places of employment for afternoon munching. He was now trying for a quick getaway push, with the driver of the dray bellowing at him. He had spotted approaching representatives of the law, two police constables. On they came, and the gentleman from the restaurant almost walked into them.

'Ah, so sorry,' he said, 'I'm not looking where I'm going.' The constables nodded in acknowledgement, then walked smartly up to the vendor to have several words with him. The gentleman stood where he was, listening.

'It's you again, Fruity, and right in front of my eyes,' said one constable.

''Ello, 'ows yerself, officer? And yer can't nab me, I ain't standing', I'm movin', as yer can see. Fruit barrers that ain't stationary but is movin' with the traffic is legal. 'Ere, and something oughter be done about this traffic and the size of it. It's near drownin' me barrer. A barrer's got rights on 'Er Majesty's 'ighways, yer know.'

'Not when it's causing an obstruction,' said the second constable, 'so keep yours moving.'

'Course I will, bless yer lawful 'eart. Me and me missus'll see yer at the policemen's ball with yer lady wives for a knees-up, eh?'

'Hoppit, Fruity.'

'I am, ain't I? But could yer do something about that there beer dray that's tryin' to climb up me back?'

'Hoppit.'

The cocky vendor and his barrow moved on. The gentleman smiled and began a saunter, thinking about a recently published book that was an attempt to theorize on the mysteries of minds that plotted murder.

Misty darkness cut short the winter afternoon, and by four all the street lamps were alight south and north of the river. Mr Pritchard accordingly was home by five. Damned if a minute later a knock on his front door didn't herald the arrival of Scotland Yard's nosiest pair of flatfooters.

'Ere, what's the game?' he growled.

'Game, Mr Pritchard?' said Chief Inspector Dobbs. 'What game?'

'Your bleedin' game,' said Mr Pritchard with bruising frankness.

'You're trying to tell me a murder investigation is on a par with hopscotch?' said Dobbs mildly.

'No, course I bleedin' ain't,' muttered Mr Pritchard. 'I'm just sayin' I ain't in favour of you

191

comin' after me like this. Why ain't yer gettin' after the bloke that done a Ripper job on a Whitechapel female last night?'

'We happen to be still after the person who finished off your lodger, Maureen Flanagan,' said Sergeant Ross.

'Blimey, more questions?' growled Mr Pritchard.

'There are a few,' said Dobbs.

'Oh, all right, come in, then, but me missus ain't goin' to like it.'

Mrs Pritchard didn't like it one bit, especially as the interview took place in the cold parlour in the light of a single gas mantle. The parlour was her husband's choice, and she hoped the coldness of the room would discourage these policeman from overstaying their welcome.

Her red face blanched when the Chief Inspector opened the proceedings by informing her husband that it was now known he had definitely been out on the night of the murder. In the Borough Arms, where he was served beer.

'It's unfortunate for you, Mrs Pritchard, that you stated otherwise. Very unfortunate. Dear, dear, eh? What a mess.'

'It's a bleedin' lie, I was 'ere all evenin',' said Mr Pritchard.

'It'll work against you, sir, and your wife, if you don't come up with the truth,' said Sergeant Ross.

'Oh, yer stupid man,' said Mrs Pritchard, 'you'll 'ave to tell 'em now, or get yerself in real trouble.'

'Well, sod it,' said Mr Pritchard. 'Well, all bloody right,' he said, 'but I didn't kill Maureen, and that's the truth to start with.'

'Well, let's have the rest, shall we? said Dobbs affably.

Mr Pritchard delivered himself of a large number of words. All right, yes, he had taken a fancy to Maureen, and he went up to her room that evening to see if she wanted any little odd job done, and to try his luck. He'd told his wife he was going to take up part of Miss Flanagan's lino that was worn and replace it for her. Well, she didn't want any odd jobs done, she was dressed for going out, and she didn't think much of him trying his luck with her, not even for ten bob.

'You at your age, you ought to be ashamed, a respectable woman like Flanagan,' broke in Mrs Pritchard. 'I'm ashamed meself.'

'Leave it, will yer?' said Mr Pritchard, and continued.

The fact was, he took hold of Maureen, trying his luck with her a bit closer, like, and saying she had time to be nice to him before she went out, didn't she? She kneed him in the belly and hit him with her handbag. She let him know she was a hard-working and respectable laundress, and with that she went straight downstairs and complained to his wife.

'That's correct, Mrs Pritchard?' said Sergeant Ross.

'Oh, lor', yes, she complained all right,' said Mrs Pritchard. 'Me 'usband come down 'isself and tried to make out he 'adn't meant no 'arm, but Flanagan said she wasn't goin' to 'ave 'er reputation ruined by 'im. So we – well, we said she could 'ave 'er room rent-free for the next two weeks, which was worth seven bob to 'er, and I said I 'oped the bit of trouble wouldn't go no farther. She said she'd accept that bit of recompense, like, and went back up to 'er room.'

'What time did she go out?' asked Dobbs.

'Well, she was all ready to go, dressed in 'er nice winter coat and 'at, but we didn't 'ear 'er leave. Well, we—' Mrs Pritchard hesitated.

'Well what, Mrs Pritchard?' asked Ross.

'I was goin' it 'ammer and tongs with Ted, givin' 'is ears a beltin' to learn 'im manners, and 'e was tryin' to shut me up by hollering at me. Oh, gawd, I never thought then that we'd seen the last of Maureen Flanagan, I never thought she was lyin' dead all night in Tooley Street.'

'Mrs Pritchard, I want you to think very carefully before you answer my next question,' said Dobbs.

'Yes, all right,' said Mrs Pritchard. 'You can understand why we didn't give yer the right answers before, we thought you might think me 'usband had 'is own back on Flanagan by waitin' for 'er that night, and – and cuttin' 'er throat.'

'Which I didn't, and that's me oath on it,' said Mr Pritchard.

'Mrs Pritchard,' said Dobbs, 'exactly what time did your husband get back from the pub?'

'Oh, before ten,' said Mrs Pritchard.

'Are you sure?'

'Yes, it's gawd's truth.'

'And what did he look like?'

'Eh?'

'In what condition were his clothes?'

'Same as always, of course – oh, yer rotten copper, yer tryin' to make me say they were all over blood.' Mrs Pritchard swelled up. 'Well, they wasn't, and you can look at all 'is clothes and mine as well, in our wardrobe, if yer want. Me 'usband might 'ave upset Flanagan, but 'e didn't kill her. You're worrying me something chronic, you are.'

194

'I suppose this is unpleasant for all of us,' said Dobbs.

'Don't make me cry me eyes out,' said Mr Pritchard, 'it ain't unpleasant for you like it is for me and me missus. It's a job to you, and you ain't goin' to lose no sleep if you put the wind up every poor bleeder you talk to. You've give me missus a bloody 'ard time, you 'ave.'

'I don't think I did, Mr Pritchard,' said Dobbs, 'I think you did, from the moment you decided to try your luck with Maureen Flanagan.'

'Leave off, will yer?' muttered Mr Pritchard.

'One last question,' said Dobbs. 'Was Miss Flanagan wearing her scarf?'

'Yes, so she was, I remember now,' said Mrs Pritchard.

'I think that's all, don't you, Sergeant Ross?' said Dobbs.

'We can always come back, guv, if we've missed anything,' said Ross.

'Oh, gawd, you ain't goin' to come back again, are yer?' begged Mrs Pritchard.

'Not as things are at the moment,' said Dobbs. 'I don't want to sound too much like a policeman, but the fact is straightforward stuff pays better than fairy stories. Fairy stories lead us up the garden and make me late home for my supper. Well, we'll let you get on with yours. We'll see ourselves out. Goodnight.'

On their way to London Bridge, with mist dampening the air over the river and the night in its first stages of poor visibility, Sergeant Ross said, 'If Maureen Flanagan hadn't wanted to keep up a front of respectability, Pritchard might have had some return for his ten bob.'

195

'You think so?' said Dobbs. 'I've a feeling she wasn't a ten-bob touch, particularly as she was contracted to a West End pimp.'

'I noticed you didn't suggest searching Pritchard's house for a knife and a handbag, guv. You're putting him in the clear now?'

'Not a hundred per cent,' said Dobbs. 'There's still something that doesn't satisfy me.'

'And what's that?'

'I wish I knew,' said Dobbs. 'All I do know is that I'm beginning to suspect Maureen Flanagan was murdered this side of the river. It won't stand up, my lad, a carrying job over a bridge to Tooley Street. Didn't I say before that she'd have been dropped in the river?'

'How about if her pimp brought her home, had a hell of a row with her on the way, and simply did for her somewhere? How about if he then mopped up the blood and then dumped her in Tooley Street?'

'Why would he do that, mop up the blood and take her to Tooley Street?' asked Dobbs, as they began to cross London Bridge. Embankment lights and dockside lights were beginning to dim in the rising mist. 'Let's say he did the job. It wouldn't have mattered where Flanagan was found south of the bridge. In the West End somewhere, yes, that would have pointed a finger at him.'

'I think we've got two cut-throats,' said Ross. 'Either Pritchard or Basil Gottfried for the Tooley Street murder, and a different bloke for the Whitechapel one. And I'd say the Whitechapel bugger did a copy-cat job.'

'And I'd say you're close to being correct, my lad. Well done. I'm appreciative of an assistant who's as close as you are to being all present and correct. Well, let's get back to the Yard and see if anything has come out of Whitechapel.'

Constable Fred Billings, along with many other uniformed men, had had a taxing day, helping CID officers in the plodding work of conducting enquiries. The people of Whitechapel were far more forthcoming than they were were normally. Normally, as soon as they found coppers at their doors, they were inclined to shut those doors with a bang before a single question could be asked. Further, their kids threw orange peel at first sight of a helmet. Some kids, who always ate whatever orange peel came their way, threw kipper skeletons or mouldy cabbages picked out of the gutters.

The general attitude of these desperately hard-up people was different today, even if many of them had recently been involved in a battle with what they saw as the uniformed army controlled by factory bosses. An unacceptable type of murder had been perpetrated last night, and they wanted the villain caught and hanged. Their answers to questions were the fanciful kind of the over-helpful.

'Yes, I 'eard some screams, just like those of a pore woman bein' done in.'

'What time was this?'

'I dunno, I was in me bed, wasn't I? Them screams woke me up. They'd 'ave woken anyone up, includin' Old Nick 'isself.'

'You sure, missus? They weren't heard by people in the house itself.'

'Bleedin' deaf lot, then. And when I got out of me bed and looked out of me winder, there 'e was,

197

running, a great big bloke with a carvin' knife.'

'You saw him from yer window, with a carvin' knife, missus? In the darkness and through the fog?'

''Orrible, 'e looked, so did 'is knife.'

Then there were those who swore the murderer had run past their doors waving a blood-stained razor, their descriptions of him varying from a crooked hunchback to a tall and bearded monster.

Fred and his colleague received no real help at all, only a large amount of wishful thinking. Similarly negative results were the lot of all the other uniformed men. For that matter, Inspector Davis and Sergeant Swettenham fared no better during the morning and most of the afternoon. Residents who claimed to have seen a skulking figure in last night's fog around the time in question, were all naturally inclined to believe they had glimpsed the coming or going of the Ripper. Inspector Davis let them know in no uncertain terms that the murder was not the work of the Ripper. The Ripper was dead. There were caustic responses to that.

'So's yer Aunt Fanny.'

'Come out of 'is grave last night, did 'e, then?'

'Well, you coppers might think 'e's passed on to 'is friend, Old Nick, but as yer never caught 'im and didn't know who 'e was, yer talkin' like an ignoramus, ain't yer?'

'The Ripper's dead? That's me grandmother over there, and she's splittin' 'er sides.'

Inspector Davis and Sergeant Swettenham knew they were up against the problem posed by the darkness and the fog of last night, and the fact that the deed had been done inside the house, with the

198

front door almost certainly closed. And it had been done silently, if the people in the brothel were to be believed. So far, the CID men had found no-one who'd witnessed the encounter between victim and murderer, and no-one who'd seen a man emerging from the house at the relevant time. Nor had any such possible witness come forward. Sergeant Swettenham suggested it might be worth considering the owners of the brothel house as suspects. That's worth sweet Fanny Adams, said Inspector Davis, since Charlie Dobbs cleared them at the time.

'And where's the ruddy motive, eh?' he said sourly.

'Search me,' said Sergeant Swettenham.

'It's goin' to give the Chief Inspector grey hairs, all this belief that the Ripper's come back,' said Davis.

'Nor won't he like it if the Chief Superintendent takes over,' said Swettenham. 'Bit of an unlucky come-down that'll be after last month, when he 'ad the newspapers paying 'im compliments for the way he showed the Old Bailey just how William Good had poisoned his wife.'

'We all suffer hard luck,' said Davis, 'but I don't want to suffer too much on this case meself. Come on, keep goin'.'

It was towards the end of the afternoon when they were in Underwood Street, north of Whitechapel Road, that a slatternly woman came running after them.

''Ere, you coppers!'

About to knock on one more door, the CID men turned. Up came the unkempt woman in the misty dusk.

'Got something else to say, have you?' asked Inspector Davis. They'd already talked to the woman and listened to nothing helpful from her.

'It's Archie Binns what lives in me back yard,' she said. ''E's just told me 'e done it, and 'e could 'ave, 'e's got funny ways and 'e showed me the razor 'e used. Come on, come and git 'im before 'e hops it or does one of me lodgers in.'

Inspector Davis didn't argue. He and Sergeant Swettenham followed the hurrying woman back to her dingy house.

Chapter Thirteen

When Chief Inspector Dobbs and Sergeant Ross got back to the Yard, Inspector Davis and Sergeant Swettenham were waiting for them.

Inspector Davis, who had already reported to the Chief Superintendent, now reported to his immediate superior that a suspect had been arrested.

'Is that a fact?' said Dobbs.

'A bloke by the name of Archie Binns,' said Davis.

'Where is he?'

'In a cell. He's confessed. And look at this.' Davis unwrapped a cut-throat razor. The blade showed a rusty stain.

'That's the weapon?' said Sergeant Ross.

'He says so.'

'What's his confession worth?' asked Dobbs.

'You'd better decide that, guv,' said Sergeant Swettenham.

'Let's have a look at him,' said Dobbs, and they made their way to the cells. The suspect was locked up in number three. A uniformed constable unlocked the door and the four CID men went in. The suspect, seated, glanced up. He was a cadaverous-looking man who might have been any age from thirty to forty. His chin and jaws were covered with dark stubble, his eyes hollow. He wore a ragged unbuttoned coat over a darned grey jersey and patched black trousers, and his boots were dirty and cracked. His uncovered head was black with a profusion of greasy hair. At the sight of his visitors, an inane smile parted his mouth to reveal an array of bad teeth, alternating with gaps.

''Ello, gents, ain't I a wicked bloke?' he said.

'Are you?' said Dobbs. 'How wicked?'

'Well, I'm the one, ain't I? I done it, didn't I?'

'And what did you do?' asked Dobbs.

'Good as cut 'er napper off, didn't I?'

'Whose napper?'

'Poppy's. In 'er doorway. Just like that.' He effected a slashing movement of his right hand. 'With me razor.' He smiled again, a foxy smile this time.

'What's your name?' asked Dobbs.

'I ain't givin' me name, not till I've 'ad a cup of tea and a meat pie.'

'He's Archie Binns,' said Inspector Davis, 'and he lives at fourteen Underwood Street, in an old watchman's hut in the back yard. We picked him up there, on information given by a Mrs Flint, who rents the house and has lodgers.'

'He lives, sleeps, eats and walks about in an old watchman's hut in a backyard?' said Dobbs.

'More or less, accordin' to Mrs Flint,' said Davis.

'She ain't a bad old cow,' said Binns. 'What about me tea and a pie?'

'We'll see what we can do,' said Dobbs.

'I'm 'ungry,' said Binns.

'When was it you used your razor on Poppy Simpson?' asked Dobbs.

'Last night, didn't I?' Binns sounded pleased with himself. 'In 'er doorway.'

'And what time was this?' asked Dobbs.

'Late, wasn't it? I don't read times. I can read writin', I can't read times.'

'What made you do it?' asked Dobbs.

'Well, I 'ad me razor with me, didn't I? 'Ere, you should've seen the blood.'

'You want to make a full confession, do you?' asked Dobbs.

'You write it down and I'll sign it,' said Binns. Again he smiled, ingratiatingly this time. 'But not till I've 'ad me pie, an 'ot one. And will I git some breakfast?'

'You'd like to make your confession, sign it and stay here, would you?' said Dobbs.

'Well, I would, wouldn't I?'

'The board and lodging is free,' said Dobbs, 'and we'll see now about some food.'

'I ain't goin' to complain,' said Binns.

The CID men left. Back in his office, the Chief Inspector said, 'Well?'

'The bloke's a half-wit, guv,' said Ross.

'Could've done it, though,' said Inspector Davis. 'Had to pull him in.'

'He'd like to stay,' said Dobbs, 'so we'll let him.'

'And charge him?' said Sergeant Swettenham.

'Let's think about what we've got,' said Dobbs. 'We've got a gift horse, a suspect who's offered a confession, a local Whitechapel man.'

'Hold on, guv,' said Ross, 'we all know the confession's not going to stand up. The bloke's a crackpot.'

'But the Fleet Street hounds don't know it,' said Dobbs, looking cheerful. 'I'd say that as Archie

Binns would like to be our guest indefinitely, we could use him to take the pen-and-ink hounds off our backs. My back particularly, I might say. So we'll keep him under arrest and let the press know we're making enquiries into the details of his confession. That'll quieten Fleet Street. Binns won't worry how long we keep him in a cell as long as we feed him tea and hot pies.'

'Good idea, guv,' said Sergeant Swettenham.

'Which reminds me, sergeant,' said Dobbs, 'go and organize the required food for our guest.'

'What, go and find a pie shop, you mean, sir?' said Swettenham.

'That's the ticket,' said Dobbs. 'Hurry it up.'

Sergeant Swettenham left.

'What's our next move?' asked Inspector Davis, and Dobbs put him in the picture concerning the day's developments in respect of the suspects Pritchard and Basil Gottfried. Pritchard, he said, could be in the clear now.

'Yes, could be,' he added. 'But I've still got peculiar suspicions about him.'

'We could all turn peculiar over any case of double murder,' said Davis.

'Tomorrow,' said Dobbs, 'you and Sergeant Swettenham carry out the watch at Bow.'

'Tomorrow's Sunday,' said Davis.

'Yes, hard luck,' said Dobbs.

'I knew some of that would come my way,' said Davis. 'What'll you be doin'?'

'Taking my family to church,' said Dobbs.

''Ope you enjoy the sermon,' said Davis.

Constable Fred Billings was late going off duty. By the time he reached the house in Ellen Street, the winter evening was dark, damp, and patchy with fog. In the street, kids were gathered around a coke fire contained in an old dustbin patterned with holes. The contraption had been pinched that day from a coke yard.

Daisy and Billy were pleased to see Fred. Fred, however, wasn't too pleased to hear from Billy that Bridget had gone to her washing-up job as usual.

'I'll have to talk serious to that sister of yours,' said Fred.

'But she can't afford to give 'er job up,' said Daisy.

'A job that keeps her out late at night is the wrong sort of job,' said Fred, thinking about the kind of villainy that lurked around Whitechapel at the witching hour. 'Yes, I'll have to talk serious to her.'

'Can I listen in, Fred?' asked Billy. 'It could be worth as much as tuppence, listenin' to anyone talkin' serious to Bridget. 'Ere, how did the police get on today about last night's murder?'

'Being as I am, a constable of the law, Billy, I'm not in a position to come up with confidential details,' said Fred, 'but I did 'ear a suspect's been taken in.'

'Crikey, the Yard's laid their mitts on the bloke?' said Billy.

''Ave they, Fred?' asked Daisy.

'So I 'eard from me station sergeant,' said Fred.

'Oh, who is he?' asked Daisy.

'Well, Daisy,' said Fred, 'even if I knew, I wouldn't be at liberty to give yer his name and address.'

'Still, ain't it a relief 'e's behind bars?' said Daisy. 'Billy and me didn't like to think of 'im prowling about lookin' for other unfortunate women that's come down in the world.' Daisy, for all that she knew of Whitechapel's street walkers, always referred to them in charitable terms, and although Ellen Street rubbed elbows with the streets of ill repute, she remained uncontaminated by what went on in brothels. 'Billy says 'e's goin' to meet Bridget at Aldgate tube tonight.'

'I'll do that, Billy,' said Fred, 'it's a man's job. And it'll give me the chance to do my bit of serious talkin' to her.'

'That's ever so kind of yer, Fred,' said Daisy.

'Well, didn't I tell yer, Daisy, that we could rely on Fred to do some safeguardin'?' said Billy.

'So yer did,' said Daisy. 'Fred, I've kept yer supper hot on the hob. It's mutton stew with suet dumplings. Take yer 'elmet off and sit down and I'll serve it up.'

'I'll appreciate that, Daisy,' said Fred. He placed his helmet aside and sat down at the oilcloth-covered table, on which stood a cheap cruet. Daisy took a knife and fork from a dresser drawer, and a tablespoon. She put the cutlery in front of Fred.

'The spoon's for the gravy, Fred,' she said.

'I also appreciate that, Daisy,' said Fred. 'I'm partial to gravy when there's dumplings as well. You're treatin' me very 'ospitable.'

'Yes, and only sixpence a time,' said Billy.

Daisy took a large plate out of the oven and placed it in front of Fred. Then she lifted the iron saucepan off the hob of the range fire and with a ladle filled the plate. Amid the meat and the pot-cooked vegetables there were two creamy-looking dumplings sitting roundly in the thick gravy.

'Well, I like the look of that,' said Fred. Hungry, he set to with his knife and fork, and found the dumplings tasty and succulent.

'Bridget's thinkin' about us movin',' said Billy.

'Bridget's thinkin' sensibly, then,' said Fred. 'Where to, might I ask?'

'On the other side of the river,' said Billy, 'only Daisy ain't sure she'll like it among foreigners.'

'Foreigners?' said Fred, stalwart-looking in his uniform.

'Anyone that lives on the other side of the river is a foreigner to Daisy,' grinned Billy.

'Oh, not like French or German, though,' said Daisy, 'and, anyway, I'll get used to them. We all will. Bridget thinks conditions is better in Southwark, and that me and 'er will 'ave a chance of meetin' men that's more respectable than those round 'ere.'

'I see, she's suddenly thinkin' about gettin' herself a bloke, is she?' said Fred.

'Well, I don't think she wants to be an old maid with just a parrot for company,' said Daisy.

'I dunno why you can't be 'er bloke, Fred,' said Billy. 'I mean, you ain't walkin' out with a skirt, are yer?'

'Well, I suppose I'm what you call available,' said Fred, 'and you're welcome to let Bridget know that.'

'Can't you let 'er know it yerself?' asked Billy.

'Unfortunately, that kind of talk comin' from me personally is liable to aggravate Bridget and earn me a quick funeral,' said Fred, 'and I ain't ready for that yet. I'd like to live on for a bit.'

'Fred, you don't 'ave to take all Bridget's remarks serious,' said Daisy.

'I don't mind her remarks,' said Fred, his appetite doing full justice to Daisy's cooking, 'it's 'er saucepans that make me nervous.'

'Well, I'll admit it,' said Billy, 'when she take 'old of one I always start running meself.'

'Still, 'aven't yer noticed, Billy, she 'asn't chucked Fred out, nor any of 'is things,' said Daisy.

'There y'ar, Fred,' said Billy, 'Bridget's bark is a lot worse than 'er saucepans.'

Fred laughed and finished his stew, whereupon Daisy served him a helping of rice pudding from the dish she took from the oven.

'All for sixpence, Daisy?' he said.

'Well, when I cook for me and Billy,' said Daisy, 'it don't cost much more to include you. And you can sit round the fire with me and Billy afterwards.'

'Home from home, Daisy, bless yer warm 'eart,' said Fred.

Bridget, wrapped in a thick apron, was enveloped in clouds of steam as she worked her way through a mountain of crockery in the kitchen scullery of the restaurant.

Oh, blow this, she thought, it's breaking me back and ruining me lily-white hands. I'd like a decent daytime job. It's not natural at my age slaving away at a sink till eleven at night. And what's more, walking home from Aldgate about half-eleven every night, and in the fog most nights, ain't what I call cosy. It's beginning to make me feel like one of them women that walk the streets. I'll get horrible men propositioning me. Or following me and dogging me footsteps, like I'm sure happened a few nights ago. Bridget Cummings, it's time to move out of Whitechapel with Daisy and Billy, and get yourself work in a nice shop somewhere in Lambeth or Southwark. Daisy ought to have a

208

chance of meeting a decent feller with a decent job. There's not many fellers like that in Whitechapel. Not that it's their fault, there's no decent jobs going, poor blokes. I'll have to do some looking for a place across the river, especially seeing that's where Daisy's going to work. I'll start looking quick. As for Fred Billings, that crafty copper's getting his feet under the table at home, I suppose.

Much to her disgust, the patchy fog had thickened by the time she reached Aldgate on the tube train. It had crept into the station, and the booking hall was misty with it. She hurried through and stepped into the dark night. The street lamps were veiled, but their dim glow was some help. The number of lamps had been increased following outcries about badly lit streets during the time of the Ripper.

He was waiting for her, the man who looked like a professional gentleman. He was tucked against the wall on the other side of the entrance to Back Church Lane as she turned into it from Commercial Road. He was quite invisible. He heard her footsteps and recognized them. He smiled. Back Church Lane was a place of silence at this hour, and only in the pubs of Commercial Road were there local people not yet abed. She crossed the street and he began to follow, moving at a quick silent pace through the fog. He carried no bag, nor did he have his walking-stick with him. In his right hand was his razor-sharp, thin-bladed knife.

Bridget heard nothing of him, but all her nerves were tautly strung, her every instinct alive to the threat posed by the veiled night, the silence and a sense of the lurking unknown. Up to a week ago, the lateness of her homegoing journeys hadn't been any real worry to her. She wasn't of a nervous disposition. Only during this last week had she let imagination and sensitive instincts take hold of her, and last night's murder had increased her unusual apprehension.

She froze as a figure loomed up in front of her.

'Is that you, Bridget?' asked Constable Fred Billings, and Bridget's stalking shadow silently checked.

'Oh, me gawd,' gasped Bridget, 'what d'yer mean by scarin' me to death?'

'Give over,' said Fred, 'I'm 'ere to walk you home. I'd 'ave met you at Aldgate, only I ran into a night duty sergeant on his beat with a constable, and that delayed me. This has got to stop, Bridget Cummings. It's dangerous for any woman to be on the streets at this time of night. Sooner or later you'll get jumped on and dragged into an alley. I never knew a more aggravatin' woman than you in the way you don't take good advice and give up this night-time job in that West End restaurant.'

'Me? Me aggravatin'? Talk about the pot callin' the kettle black, what bleedin' cheek,' said Bridget. Behind her, at a distance of no more than ten yards, the gentleman, hidden by the fog and the doorway of a house, put his knife back into his coat pocket and smiled resignedly. It hardly mattered now, in any case. She wasn't a prostitute. He had thought she was, that she went street-walking in the West End each evening.

'We don't want any language,' said Fred, 'just a bit of commonsense.'

'Kindly don't talk to me like me keeper,' said Bridget. 'Mind, I ain't saying it wasn't thoughtful to come and meet me. I'm gettin' to imagine things lately in all this fog, and it ain't doin' me nerves one bit of good.'

'Well, it's not very clever, is it, wandering about after what 'appened in New Road last night,' said Fred sternly. The fog and darkness that surrounded them allowed each only a vague picture of the other, but Bridget's taut nerves had relaxed at what she felt was the solidity of his presence.

'Wandering about?' she said. 'Don't come it, Fred Billings, the next time I wander about will be the first. Don't you get 'igh and mighty with me just because you've got yer 'elmet on.'

'Never mind that,' said Fred, 'just come along with me, my girl, and I'll see yer safe home.'

'Do what?' said Bridget. The hidden gentleman smiled again.

'Just come along with me,' said Fred.

'I'm 'earing things,' said Bridget, but she began walking with him.

'Now,' said Fred, 'about you movin' with Daisy and Billy across the river—'

'None of yer business,' said Bridget, 'and who told yer, anyway?'

'Daisy and Billy,' said Fred. 'First sensible idea you've 'ad for ages. I'll ask around and see if I can point yer to a decent place in Lambeth or Southwark. It'll suit Daisy, seeing she'll be workin' across the river at Guy's laundry.'

''Ere, who put you in charge of us?' demanded Bridget.

'Just consider me yer 'elpful lodger,' said Fred.

'I ain't considerin' anything of the kind,' said Bridget, and argued with him through the fog all the way to her front door.

211

The gentleman, meanwhile, had departed.

It was when he reached Tower Hill that the risk he himself was constantly taking in being out late at night reared its menacing head. Out of the fog came a large man with a sepulchral voice.

''Old yer 'orses, cully.'

'What d'you want?' The gentleman stiffened.

'Yer watch and chain, and yer bleedin' wallet, and I want 'em quick, or I'll beat yer brains out.'

A cudgel thrust at the gentleman's chest.

'A moment,' he said.

'Come on, divvy up.'

'Here,' said the gentleman, and delivered a violent kick to the footpad's left knee. A hoarse bellow signified pain, but an arm swung, and the cudgel lifted high. In the darkness, a knife dimly flashed, and the blade rushed across the raised wrist. Blood spurted.

'Oh, yer bleeder!' The cudgel dropped, and the footpad clasped his slashed wrist. If he couldn't see his own blood running, he could feel it, and he went lurching and limping away in the fog, howling for help. The gentleman took out his handkerchief, cleaned the knife, and when he began to cross the footbridge he dropped the handkerchief into the unseen river below.

Chief Inspector Dobbs found sleep difficult to come by that night. The relation of the first murder to the second might make sense to those who had a copy-cat Ripper in mind, but as far as a suspect for both crimes was concerned, who could relate the murder of Poppy Simpson to either Pritchard or Basil Gottfried, whom Maureen Flanagan had called Godfrey? What motive would either of those

212

men have had for polishing off the Whitechapel prostitute? He knew what the Chief Superintendent might say. That a copy-cat Ripper needed no motive beyond that of a weird kind of bloodlust.

So the point was, thought Dobbs, lying awake, if he caught the murderer of Maureen Flanagan, had he also caught the murderer of Poppy Simpson? He didn't think so, not if Flanagan's slayer was either Pritchard or Godfrey.

It was gone two before he finally fell asleep beside Daphne.

Just prior to retiring, the Prime Minister spent a few moments reflecting on how to avoid questions being asked in the House about the possible re-emergence of the Ripper or his successor. That would bring to the fore the conditions of want and privation still existing in the East End, conditions that some awkward members might suggest were responsible not only for turning women into prostitutes but invited the attentions of twisted minds bent on murder. There would be uproar and another huge press campaign condemning the authorities. Most upsetting. Her Majesty, failing in health though she was, would send for him.

Under no circumstances did he want her waving newspapers at him, newspapers that had dredged up the rumours and insinuations that had been whispered in high circles twelve years ago, rumours and insinuations concerning the possible implication of her grandson, the late Duke of Clarence, in the Ripper murders. That kind of thing would put the frail old lady on her deathbed.

It was some comfort to know Scotland Yard had taken a prime suspect into custody.

Such comfort helped welcome sleep to claim him.

Sergeant Ross had no problems at all once his head touched the pillow in his police flat. He'd had a cosy evening with Nurse Cartright and her parents, playing whist in front of a warm coal fire. Whist relaxed a bloke and took his mind off the unpleasant nature of murder cases, particularly with Nurse Cartright as his partner.

Chapter Fourteen

Constable Fred Billings, uniformed, was stopped by
Bridget as he came down the stairs at nine o'clock
on Sunday morning.

'You on duty today?' she asked.

'Not yet, officially,' he said, 'but I've got to report
to the station, along with other men, to see if we're
wanted for special duties. In case people start a riot
about the murder and the arrest of a local suspect.'

'You didn't tell me last night that a suspect's been
arrested,' said Bridget accusingly. Her wondrous
mop of black hair was combed, brushed and piled
high, and held in place with pins.

'I was busy tryin' to stop you burnin' me ears and
gettin' you home in one piece,' said Fred.

'Well, I wasn't ungrateful about you meetin' me
to see me home, it was a nerve-rackin' night,' said
Bridget, 'but you were comin' it a bit all the way to
me door.'

'So were you,' said Fred, 'and I felt fortunate to
'ave got here without bein' wounded.'

'You'll finish up wounded in six places at once
if you keep answering me back in me own dwelling,' said Bridget. 'Anyway, Daisy and Billy told me
you said a bloke 'ad been arrested. Did 'e do it,

then, did 'e murder Poppy Simpson?'

'Unfortunately—'

'I keep 'earing that word too much lately,' said Bridget.

'Unfortunately,' said Fred, 'I didn't arrest the suspect meself, nor was I given official details of how it came about, but I did 'ear a public-minded resident informed on 'im and was told by the Yard subsequent to the arrest to keep 'er north-and-south shut on the grounds that she was in line for bein' a star witness.'

'Fred Billings, when you've got that uniform on, you're a pain in both me ears,' said Bridget. 'Can't you talk like a human being?'

'I was explaining to you—'

'Showin' off yer copper's lingo, you mean,' said Bridget, scowling at him.

'Don't do that,' said Fred.

'Don't do what?'

'Put creases in yer face,' said Fred, 'it spoils yer looks.'

'Oh, beg yer pardon, I'm sure,' said Bridget. 'Anyway, it's a relief the Yard's got the bloke. It's about time they did something useful instead of 'elping the bosses to tread on the workers. Look, we're scrapin' something together to make a fairly decent Sunday dinner, with apple dumplings for afters, so if you ain't wanted for special duties, I dare say we could find enough for you.'

'Well, that's an 'eart-warming invitation, Bridget,' said Fred.

'Don't let it give you ideas,' said Bridget.

'No, of course not,' said Fred, 'I know where I stand with you, Bridget.'

'Yes, and just remember I'm still only lettin' you

lodge 'ere on sufferance, and me sufferance'll die a quick death if you get fancy ideas,' said Bridget.

'Never mind that,' said Fred, 'just do yerself the favour of gettin' a job that doesn't keep you out late at night.'

'Stop 'aving these other ideas about thinkin' you're entitled to safeguard me,' said Bridget.

'Well, I'm admirin' of yer valiant character, Bridget, and don't want yer to come to grievous harm,' said Fred.

'Very kind of you, Fred Billings, I'm sure,' said Bridget. 'Go on, you'd best get down to the station now.'

'I'm off,' said Fred. 'See you later, and thanks for the offer of dinner. I'll put the usual sixpence in the kitty.'

'Did I ask for any sixpence, did I?' said Bridget.

'I thought—'

'Hoppit,' said Bridget.

Fred left. At the station he was told the Yard required no help from the uniformed branch today, so he went for a long walk, crossing London Bridge to the south side of the river, and on to some police stations in Southwark, to find out if any constables on regular beats knew of a small house to rent in a fairly decent street.

Chief Inspectors Dobbs, in his best suit, took his family to morning church. There, a pretty eleven-year-old girl, Edith Baxter from next door, dislodged herself from her own family and slipped into the pew beside twelve-year-old William, an engaging boy who was fighting the sudden onset of freckles fairly dormant up to now. Ten-year-old

Jane, next to her dad, rolled her eyes.

'William's starting early, Dad,' she whispered.

'Never too soon to get acquainted with troubles,' murmured Charlie. 'Helps you to learn to cope with 'em before you're old and grey.'

The service began, with Charlie thinking again about the complications of trying to decide if he was up against one murderer or two.

Daphne, knowing what his faraway expression meant, whispered in his ear, 'Perhaps a prayer might help, Charlie.'

'Well, I'm in the right place for a prayer and a half,' he whispered back.

On arrival home, he found Inspector Davis on his doorstep.

'Hello, George, what's brought you from Bow?'

'If I could have a word?' said Inspector Davis. 'Morning, Mrs Dobbs.'

'Good morning, George,' said Daphne.

'Sorry about bargin' in on a Sunday,' said Davis. 'And how are you two?' he said, addressing himself to Jane and William.

'Oh, quite well, thank you,' said Jane.

'Except she's got a pink nose,' said William.

'Looks all right to me,' said Davis.

'Come in and have something hot, George,' said Daphne. The morning was damp, grey and cold.

'I won't say no,"said Davis, and Daphne made a hot toddy for both men before resuming preparation of the Sunday dinner, which would be eaten at two o'clock, as was customary with most London families.

Davis, in the parlour with the Chief Inspector, watched as Charlie Dobbs gave the fire a poke, and then advised him that the man known as Basil Gottfried or Godfrey had shown up. He had entered his house at Bow midway through the morning. Well, at least a man answering his description had. Dressed in a posh overcoat and hat, and looking very self-assured, he let himself in with a key. A woman appeared as he did so. Then the door closed. Sergeant Swettenham was still keeping watch, and if the suspect left the house, Swettenham would follow, although he was hoping to be relieved before the afternoon was over.

'I'm much obliged, George,' said Dobbs, enjoying his hot toddy, 'but as it's Sunday, go back, and if Sergeant Swettenham is still there, let him know he can go off duty. So can you. I'll call on Basil tomorrow morning.'

'You'll risk him givin' us the slip,' said Davis, his own hot toddy creating a glow in his stomach.

'I don't think so,' said Dobbs, 'I don't think he'd have put in an appearance if he suspected we were after him and not one of his feller pimps.'

'It'll be your funeral if you're wrong,' said Davis.

'I'll chance it,' said Dobbs. 'You and Sergeant Swettenham pop off home. I know you've both missed morning church, but you can still go to Evensong.'

'The joker in you 'asn't given up, has it?' said Davis.

'Don't you go to church, then?' asked Dobbs.

'Now and again,' said Davis. 'For weddings and funerals.'

'Church is a good place for praying,' said Dobbs.

'Someone just informed you of that?' said Davis.

'Yes, Daphne,' said Dobbs.

'Anything on Binns come through?'

'Such as?'

'Well, I've been wondering if the Chief Superintendent has 'ad him certified, and might have sent you a message about same.'

'The idea, George, is to class him as a case for serious investigation until we lay our hands on the genuine person unknown,' said Dobbs. 'I hope Binns is getting hot pies for his Sunday dinner. I left instructions.'

'D'you think the pimp Gottfried is our man?' asked Davis, finishing his toddy.

'If he's not,' said Dobbs, 'we'll have problems. At least, I will.'

'You've got them already,' said Davis, 'on account of the double murder.'

'Don't I know it. See you tomorrow, George.'

Constable Fred Billings arrived back at Ellen Street in time to sit down with Bridget, Daisy and Billy to a dinner of sausages, mashed potatoes and tinned peas.

'I'd like to mention again I'm very appreciative of this kind of 'ospitality,' he said.

'So am I,' said Billy, 'I 'appen to be fond of sausages and mash.'

Domestic events had made Daisy a bit reckless with the limited amount of housekeeping. What with Fred's weekly rent of five bob and her forthcoming job at the laundry, she'd felt she ought to splash out. There were three plump sausages each, a snowy mountain of mashed potato on every plate, and a generous helping of shining tinned peas. And there were apple dumplings to follow.

''Eatin' like we're prosperous, well, it's welcome,' said Bridget, 'but I can't 'elp thinkin' there's families in the worst slums probably only gettin' something like bread and drippin'. For Sunday dinner too. I could spit every day for a week.'

'Bridget, you don't 'ave to talk like that,' said Daisy, 'specially on a Sunday and when we've got company.'

'Constable Fred Billings ain't company,' said Bridget, 'he just 'appens to be 'ere. On sufferance, I might add.'

'Well,' said Billy, 'passin' by yer comment on Fred—'

'What you talkin' about, passin' by?' asked Bridget.

'Overlookin' it,' said Billy. 'And I was goin' to say wantin' to spit ain't what you call unmentionable, Daisy. It ain't nothing like what old Mother Figgins across the street comes out with at times. It's 'er age, yer know, Fred. Sixty years she's lived as girl and woman, and in that time she's picked up words that even old Sailor Joe from down the street ain't ever 'eard of. Bridget's got a long way to go to catch 'er up.'

'If I could say something,' ventured Fred, 'it's that your sister Bridget shouldn't be encouraged to be like Old Mother Figgins, Billy. With a bit of right encouragement, Bridget could turn her hand to talkin' more like a lady.'

'Turn me 'and to talkin' like what?' said Bridget.

'It's me serious contention there's always been a lady tryin' to get out from under yer stays and blouses, Bridget,' said Fred.

Billy choked on a mouthful of sausage and mash. Daisy giggled over a mouthful of peas. Bridget's forkful of mash halted halfway up from her plate.

'Fred Billings, am I 'earing things?' she asked. 'Did you remark on me personal wearables?'

'Only out of me firm beliefs,' said Fred, well into his tasty meal.

'How would you like me dinner in yer lap?' suggested Bridget.

'No, you eat it,' said Fred, 'I've got me own. By the way, I 'appened to be talkin' to a constable in Blackfriars Road across the river this mornin', and he put me in the way of a vacant house in Pocock Street, which is off Blackfriars Road. I said that's a bit of luck, I know a fam'ly that's thinkin' about movin'. So I made me way to Pocock Street, and there it was, empty all over, and lookin' like it was three up, three down, which could suit you. Of course, it's not like the Garden of Eden, but I noticed the kids all 'ad boots on their feet and didn't look starvin'. It's a step up from Whitechapel.'

'Oh, we could go and look at it, Bridget,' said Daisy.

'Not 'alf,' said Billy. 'While I wouldn't mind something like the Garden of Eden, I fancy a step up from Whitechapel and work in a Blackfriars' grocers. I'm in the way of likin' groceries, and gettin' a job behind a counter in a white apron.'

'Well, you get the job first and then we'll think about movin',' said Bridget. 'Fred Billings, did you 'appen to be across the river accidental or on purpose?'

'As I wasn't needed for any special duties, Bridget, I did take a walk,' said Fred.

'On account of us talkin' about movin' across the river?' said Bridget.

'I thought about that when I was talkin' to the constable,' said Fred.

'Oh, it was a nice thought, Fred,' said Daisy.

'Fred's a decent copper,' said Billy.

'I've got suspicions 'e's tryin' to make 'imself a bit too useful,' said Bridget.

'Well, that's a lot better than makin' 'imself a bit too awkward,' said Billy.

'Oh, yes,' said Daisy, 'I'm sure Fred's goin' to be ever so useful, Bridget. Well, there's things a useful man can do for us women, ain't there?'

'I could ask what sort of things, but I won't,' said Bridget.

'Let's 'ave the apple dumplings now,' said Daisy. 'There's custard as well.'

'Crikey, you're gettin' to be a reg'lar marvel, you are, Daisy,' said Billy.

'Oh, what with 'aving an 'elpful paying lodger and me gettin' a job,' said Daisy, 'I thought I'd go a bit mad with Sunday dinner.' I just hope, she thought, that when I get to the laundry tomorrow, the Superintendent don't sack me before I start on account of me saying I knew that poor Maureen Flanagan when I didn't. It won't be in me favour that I had me fingers crossed. Oh, ain't life hard on a poor girl?

Sundays made very little difference to the lives of the people who dwelt in the slums of Whitechapel. The Sabbath did not bestow food, clothes and silver on them, or repair leaking roofs and fill fires with fuel. It did not even supply bare-footed kids with boots. It arrived and it went on its way as indifferent to want and privation as any other day.

Sunday evenings were much the same as weekday evenings, the dingy pubs catering for the drunks and the slatterns who had all kinds of crafty ways for obtaining the few coppers that would enable them to buy beer or gin. And the women who walked the streets were as active as ever. Sailors and merchant seamen found their way from the docks into the embrace of doxies.

The gentleman, however, did not take his usual measured walk around the area on which Jack the Ripper had left his gruesome mark. The evening was clear, the air sharp with the onset of crisp winter, and the smoke from chimneys rose to discharge itself without hindrance. Whitechapel on a clear night held no excitement for him. He spent the evening reading a published version of papers issued by Sir William Gull on the causes, the symptoms, and preventive measures relating to syphilis. Sir William Gull had been physician to the Duke of Clarence, once the heir to the throne of the United Kingdom. His papers also dealt with the effects the disease had on the actions and behaviour of the afflicted persons.

The gentleman smiled at intervals over his reading. He did not have the disease himself. Accordingly, he did not suffer moments of savagery, as certain syphilitics did. He merely had a need for strange excitement and the pleasure of doing Scotland Yard and Chief Inspector Dobbs in the eye.

Chapter Fifteen

Daisy arrived at the laundry well on time on Monday morning. She was quaking nervously all over. She entered through the large sorting room where men were delivering sackfuls of Monday's items, including bed linen and nurses' uniforms. She dodged around them.

''Ello, 'ello, not seen you before,' said a young man, heaving a sack from his shoulders onto a long table.

'Oh, I'm new 'ere,' said Daisy.

The young man shifted his flat cap back, scratched his curly brown hair, took a friendly look at her, liked what he saw and said, 'What's yer name, then?'

'Daisy Cummings.'

'Well, good on yer, Daisy. I'm Percy Townsend. I'll meet yer outside the Elephant and Castle Theatre at 'alf-seven tonight and take yer in to see the show.'

'Crikey, you don't waste time, do yer?' said Daisy, delighted.

'Can't afford to, it's a short life and a merry one, yer know,' said Percy. 'Well, merry is as merry comes, like the music hall.' Someone bawled his name and a warning to get on with his job. 'There y'ar, you can see what I'm up against.'

'Yes, and I've got to get upstairs,' said Daisy.

'See yer tonight, then, Daisy?'

'You'll be lucky,' said Daisy, and went on to the sorting room, where the actual washing took place in hydroves, machines that looked like large tubs. The place was the province of men. They did all the washing. Up went Daisy to the next floor, where the calender room was situated, where the laundry was dried and pressed, and where Maureen Flanagan had worked. Laundresses already there greeted Daisy in friendly fashion, and when the forelady arrived she took Daisy in hand, explained that she would be taught exactly what to do, supplied her with a white cap and apron, and then placed her in the charge of a motherly woman for instruction.

Daisy's day began on quite an encouraging note, the atmosphere of the kind established by chatty women glad to be in work and accordingly cheerful and gossipy. She was shown how to fold sheets and put them through a calender machine, the equivalent of a large mangle. The sheets had to be put in tightly flat and then pulled through the other side. Daisy applied herself happily and diligently, the calender taking two sheets at a time.

She quaked again, however, when the forelady came up and told her the Superintendent wanted to see her.

The formidable lady turned as Daisy knocked on the open door of her office.

'Come in.'

In Daisy went, nerves travelling up and down so acutely that they seemed to put a strain on her stays, and that made her bosom go up and down as well.

'Good mornin', mum.'

'Ah, there you are, Cummings,' said the Superintendent. 'You're under instruction?'

'Yes, mum.'

'Good. You'll soon get your hand in, and I hope you're finding the laundresses have got over the worst of the unpleasantness. Do you feel a little better yourself?'

'Oh, yes, mum, and ever so glad to be at work,' said Daisy, wondering why the chopper hadn't quickly come down on her neck.

'Um – were you able to help the Scotland Yard gentleman?' asked the Superintendent.

'Beg yer pardon, mum?'

'Well, as you were a close friend of poor Miss Flanagan, I suppose you were able to tell the Chief Inspector all you could about her?'

Oh, happy day, thought Daisy, he didn't tell the Super I didn't know Maureen Flanagan. She crossed her fingers.

'Oh, he come and spoke to me, mum, and we 'ad a long talk about poor Maureen. 'E was a kind man, and I do 'ope he catches the one who – who –'

'Yes, I understand,' said the Superintendent, 'and I'm sure you were able to help him a little about any particular man friend.'

'Oh, I wasn't able to 'elp him a lot, mum.'

'Never mind, a little is sometimes enough for the police. That's all, then, you can return to your work.'

'Thank you, mum,' said Daisy, and returned to her work relieved of her quakes and with her fingers uncrossed.

The Chief Superintendent had a word with Chief Inspector Dobbs first thing. His opinion of the detention of Archie Binns was succinct.

'You've laid an egg,' he said.

'Well, it needn't turn out to be bad, providing it keeps Fleet Street quiet and gives us time to catch the real villain,' said Dobbs.

'The morning papers look as if Fleet Street's accepted the egg,' said the Chief Superintendent. 'They've concentrated on the fact that we're holding a suspect, and they'll probably turn him by implication into a tough old chicken, or at least an egg that's hard-boiled, just to keep things going. As to the real villain, Charlie, you're still not sure if you're looking for one or two, are you?'

'Yes, I'm looking for the one who did for Flanagan,' said Dobbs. 'Well, I've got a feeling that if we catch him, we'll also catch a lead to the second murder, even if he's not responsible for that himself. I'm interviewing Basil Gottfried this morning, and taking a search warrant with me. Inspector Davis and Sergeant Swettenham are keeping the house under observation.'

'Well, get on with it, Charlie. We've got the Assistant Commissioner breathing down our necks.'

'I can feel it,' said Dobbs. 'By the way, I think I'll let Binns in on details of Flanagan's murder.'

'You'll do what?' said the Chief Superintendent.

'It could be a help,' said Dobbs. 'Once I've given him details, I'll ask him if he did it. He'll say yes, poor old Archie. Well, we've met his kind before. His confession to both murders will make Fleet Street's interest in the return of the Ripper as cold as leftover suet pudding. At the time of the Ripper, Archie Binns was a down-and-out in Portsmouth.'

'How d'you know that?' asked the Chief Superintendent.

'Saw the old codger first thing this morning,' said Dobbs.

'Charlie, a double confession? Touch of genius. But it'll all blow up if you don't solve both cases in reasonable time.'

'Don't I know it,' said the Chief Inspector.

Five minutes later he and Sergeant Ross were talking to Binns, who professed himself happy about the regular supply of hot meat pies. The Chief Inspector said that if he was happy, then so were the police. Further, the police would like his help concerning the death of a woman called Maureen Flanagan, who had lived in Tanner Street, near the south side of London Bridge. She'd had her throat cut last Monday night, and was found in Tooley Street. Archie Binns listened with a peculiarly idiotic smile. Dobbs said the police would appreciate it if he'd assist them with their enquiries.

'Course I will,' said Binns, and tapped his nose.

'Did you do it?' asked Sergeant Ross.

'Course I did,' said Binns, 'with me razor, didn't I? And I know Tooley Street, don't I? 'Ere, can I 'ave mash again with me midday meat pie?'

'Double portion, if you'd like,' said Dobbs, 'and this afternoon we'll take full statements from you and get you to sign them. How's that?'

'Suits me,' said Binns cheerfully. 'I can write me name, yer know. O' course, I'm what yer call unsound of mind.'

'That'll count in your favour, Archie,' said Dobbs.

'Mind, I ain't daft,' said Binns.

'No, but you're a great help,' said Dobbs.

Before he and Sergeant Ross left for Bow, the leading news agency of Fleet Street had been advised that the suspect being held in connection with the Whitechapel murder had also confessed to the murder of Maureen Flanagan, and that the Yard were checking his verbal statements. The Yard would release his name when they were in a position to charge him.

'Got your nut-crackers with you, guv?' asked Ross, when they were on their way to Bow in a growler. The morning was as clear as the night had been.

'For cracking a hard one, my lad?'

'Basil Gottfried could be tough,' said Ross.

'I don't know why you can't cheer me up now and again,' said Dobbs. 'Try another Scotch story.'

'I think I've run out, guv,' said Ross, 'except that as Christmas is coming it's reminding me of the Scotsman who fired a revolver outside his house on Christmas Eve, then ran indoors and told his kids that Santa Claus had committed suicide.'

'Look here, my lad,' said Dobbs, 'you're making a regrettable habit of being unfair to the Scotch.'

'Scots, guv. Scotch means whisky.'

'Anyway, and whatever, sunshine, don't take any of those unfair stories North of the Border with you.'

'Right you are, guv.'

The growler took them through the Strand and Fleet Street, through the city to Aldgate, and then by Whitechapel Road and Mile End Road to Bow, the Monday traffic thick all the way, the street cleaners shouldering the burden of a workload indigenous to horse-drawn vehicles. The cabbie, under instruction, halted on the corner of Medway Road. Inspector Davis, on the lookout, came up as Dobbs alighted, followed by Ross, who paid the cabbie.

'No movement,' said Davis.

'He's having a Monday morning lie-in, perhaps,' said Dobbs. 'Well, you and Sergeant Swettenham keep yourselves handy, while Sergeant Ross and I knock on the door.'

'Is that in order?' asked Davis.

It was what Dobbs preferred, but not what was correct. It was not for inspectors to stand and stare while sergeants took the honours.

'I see your point, George,' said the Chief Inspector, and glanced at Sergeant Ross. Ross, understanding, nodded.

'Right, if he does a bunk, guv, I'll get after him, with Sergeant Swettenham,' he said. Sergeant Swettenham was some way down the road, but out of sight.

Accompanied by Inspector Davis, Dobbs knocked on the door of Gottfried's house. Again it was opened by the woman, the good-looking woman who called herself Margaret Donaldson. Her mouth dropped open and a hissing breath escaped.

'Good morning,' said the Chief Inspector. 'Oh, and this is Inspector Davis. We'd like to see Mr Gottfried.'

'I told you, he's away!' The woman shouted the words. There was the sound of a chair crashing over at the rear of the house.

'Kitchen,' said Dobbs, 'in you go, George.'

Inspector Davis threw himself into the hall and rushed.

''Ere, what's the bloody idea?' shouted Margaret Donaldson.

'Sorry about the hurry, lady, but we do have a search warrant,' said Dobbs, and went striding through the house to the open door of the kitchen. There, the table was laid for a late breakfast, and the aroma was that of grilled kippers. Two plates showed half-eaten specimens. The kitchen was large, the range extensive, its fire glowing, the furniture excellent, although one table chair lay on its side. Against a wall stood a man with a fulsome moustache, a head of thick wavy brown hair, and an expression of irritation on his broad face. Dressed in a grey suit, with a cutaway jacket, he looked close to forty. Inspector Davis had a hand on his chest, keeping him pinned to the wall. He voiced his irritation.

'Leave it be,' he said, 'I'm not going out.'

'You looked as if you were,' said Davis. The scullery beyond the kitchen showed an open door to a small garden much in need of a gardener's hand. In the brick wall at the rear of the garden was a green door. 'Sorry if I made a mistake,' said Davis, and took his hand away. The man adjusted his tie and pulled his jacket into place.

Chief Inspector Dobbs stooped and righted the fallen chair, then gave his suspect a friendly smile.

'Mr Gottfried? I'm Chief Inspector Dobbs of Scotland Yard. My colleague is Inspector Davis. Sit down, Mr Gottfried. You and your – um – house-keeper can finish your breakfast, if you like.'

'Thanks very much,' said Margaret Donaldson bitingly.

Nevertheless, Basil Gottfried sat down, took a cosy off a handsome china teapot, and poured himself a cup of tea. He added milk and a little sugar. Margaret Donaldson, taking her cue from him, seated herself on the opposite side of the table, and she too poured herself tea.

'Well, now you're here, Chief Inspector, carry on,' said Gottfried.

'How's your aunt?' asked Dobbs.

'Spare me that stuff,' said Gottfried.

'Are you German-born?' asked Dobbs.

'Do I sound like it? If you could ask my grandfather that, he'd say yes, but as he's dead, you can't.'

'Let me ask you, then, how well did you know a woman called Maureen Flanagan, recently found dead with her throat cut?'

'Who?' said Gottfried, sipping his tea.

'Don't play games, sir,' said Dobbs. 'We've witnesses who'll confirm you knew her. A Mr and Mrs Pritchard. She lodged with them, and you met them one evening. Was that about the time when you were – um – establishing a business relationship with the deceased?'

'Business relationship?' Gottfried looked blank.

'Yes, was she one of the ladies you manage in the West End?'

'Now wait a minute, what are you after?' asked Gottfried.

'Well, briefly, the person who cut her throat,' said Dobbs. 'Tell me about her and then we might have a better idea of who we're looking for, say perhaps a client of hers or someone she considered a friend.'

'You're looking for me,' said Gottfried.

'Did you do it, then, Mr Gottfried?' asked Dobbs. 'Is that why you disappeared in the direction of your aunt somewhere in the country?'

233

'No, I didn't do it, but I guessed you'd come after me,' said Gottfried. 'I'm easy meat, easy enough to be put in the dock and found guilty. Very convenient for you, one more case solved, but deadly for me.'

'Why are you easy meat?' asked Inspector Davis.

'All right, so I did know Maureen Flanagan. She needed help or she'd have ended up in the gutter.'

'Took her under your 'elpful wing, did you, sir?' asked Inspector Davis.

'If there was no-one to help these girls, they'd all end up in the gutter,' said Gottfried.

'With your help, where do most of them end up?' asked Dobbs, and Margaret Donaldson gave him an offended look.

'Mr Gottfried treats all his girls well,' she said.

'Yes, I daresay,' said Dobbs, 'but where do most of them end up?'

'I can tell you some have made very advantageous marriages,' said Gottfried, 'but what's that got to do with a murder enquiry?'

'Just a point of interest,' said Dobbs. 'Would you like to tell us about Maureen Flanagan or not?'

'I don't trust you, not after the way you foxed my housekeeper,' said Gottfried. 'You led her to believe you were looking for a professional acquaintance of mine.'

'You can accompany us to the Yard, if you'd prefer, sir, and make a statement there,' said Inspector Davis.

'Yes, I'd like that, wouldn't I?' said Gottfried. 'Once there, I'd be laughing, I don't think. All right, about Maureen Flanagan, then.'

He met her, he said, through one of the ladies he

was managing. Maureen was willing to be looked after and given use of a room in a house of his in Wardour Street on the occasions when she came up to the West End. She felt she needed security. Chief Inspector Dobbs admired the way that word slipped easily from Gottfried, who went on to say Maureen was a clean woman, looked very attractive in her outfits, but didn't want to entertain except during evenings, and then only two or three evenings a week. He respected her wishes, knowing she wanted to go back to Ireland eventually. She was a little unlucky one evening, she had her name taken on the grounds she was suspected of street-walking, and that scared her.

'That made her want to give up being an entertainer, did it?' said Dobbs.

'No,' said Gottfried brusquely, and Margaret Donaldson said something naughty under her breath.

'I suggest you told her she couldn't give up without your permission, Mr Gottfried,' said Dobbs.

'We merely discussed it,' said Gottfried, 'and I told her I'd give her further help.'

'Such as finding clients yourself for her?'

'I am able to introduce gentlemen of the West End to ladies who like to entertain them,' said Gottfried.

'I suggest she had a go at tryin' to break with you,' said Inspector Davis.

'What's coming next, another suggestion?' said Gottfried. 'That she walked away from the business, and that I cut her throat later on? I thought it would come to that, that you'd try to land a murder charge on me. Well, it won't wash.'

'Where were you on the night she was murdered, Mr Gottfried?' asked Dobbs.

'In Scott's bar in the West End with Miss Donaldson, my housekeeper,' said Gottfried.

'You'll confirm that, of course, Miss Donaldson?' said Dobbs.

'Yes, I bloody well will,' said the lady. 'It's true.'

'Well, in view of what you might call a cast-iron alibi, Mr Gottfried,' said Dobbs, 'could I ask you again why you disappeared?'

'My answer's the same,' said Gottfried. 'I knew I'd be the first one you'd look for once you found out about Maureen being an entertainer and connected to me.'

'That's the word for it these days, entertainer?' said Inspector Davis.

'For the select kind of ladies,' said Gottfried.

'But you still had your alibi,' said Dobbs.

'What's a housekeeper's word worth to an Old Bailey judge?' retorted Gottfried.

'It's the jury that decides, not the judge,' said Dobbs. 'I think, Mr Gottfried, that we'll have to search your house. We've got a warrant.'

'Turn the place inside-out, if you want,' said Gottfried.

'Basil, you'll make them put it to rights again, won't you?' said Margaret Donaldson.

'We'll see what their manners are like,' said Gottfried.

Inspector Davis fetched Ross and Swettenham, and the three of them went through the house from top to bottom, looking for a sharp knife and a lady's handbag. They found several knives in the kitchen, of course, two of which were sharp enough to cut a throat, but such could be turned up in many households. They also found two handbags, both of which were in the main bedroom, one on the dressing-table, the other in a tallboy drawer. Margaret Donaldson coldly explained where she had bought them, and just as coldly described them in every detail.

Sod it, thought the Chief Inspector, we haven't got a thing on him, not even a small piece of decent circumstantial evidence. And who could prove that Maureen Flanagan had obviously reached a stage where she wanted to back away from organized prostitution? That kind of attitude was known to turn pimps spiteful, but again who could prove in this case that Gottfried had turned murderously spiteful? We could charge him with living off immoral earnings, but that's like making do with dry bread when we're after a full-course meal.

'Mr Gottfried, before you and Miss Donaldson took yourselves off to Scott's, you saw Maureen Flanagan, did you?'

'No, I didn't. I saw the girls in the house I own in Wardour Street, and then left them to their own ways of seeing the night through. Maureen wasn't among them.'

'But we know she went out that night,' said Sergeant Ross.

'Not to the West End,' said Gottfried. 'That is, not to Wardour Street. It was a bloody foggy night, anyway.'

'Was she due to turn up?' asked Inspector Davis.

'That night?' said Gottfried. 'Yes, she was, but she didn't. I put her absence down to the fog.'

'On the other hand,' said Inspector Davis, 'you knew where she lived, you'd been there. You could 'ave met her somewhere nearby.'

'And cut her throat?' said Gottfried. 'Don't be childish.'

'In any case, he was in Scott's with me,' declared Margaret Donaldson acidly, 'and I'll put that in me best writin' if you want.'

I'm chasing rainbows, thought the Chief Inspector. And what's more, there's not a chance in hell that this prosperous pimp did the Whitechapel murder.

'What time did you leave Scott's?' he asked.

'A little after ten,' said Gottfried.

'That's it, a little after ten,' said the woman.

'I see.' Dobbs glanced at Davis. 'Is everything tidy?' he asked Inspector Davis.

'Fairly,' said Davis.

'Would you like to check, Miss Donaldson?' asked Dobbs of the simmering lady.

'Yes, I would,' she said, and got up and left the kitchen. She inspected the house upstairs and downstairs before returning. 'There's some loose ends,' she said.

'Could we criticize their manners?' asked Gottfried.

'We could,' she said.

'But we'll let it go,' said Gottfried.

'In that case, we'll say good morning.' Dobbs looked as if his brisk and outgoing approach to life and its problems had taken a little beating. 'I hope you understand why we had to interview you, Mr Gottfried. Sorry to have spoiled your breakfast. Kippers, I see. I've a fondness for the occasional kipper myself. That's all, then, thanks for putting up with us. By the way, don't disappear again.'

'Does that mean you'll be back?' asked Gottfried. 'If so, let me know in advance, and I'll see that a grilled kipper will be ready for you.'

'That's a kind thought,' said Dobbs. 'Good morning, then.'

He left, and the others followed him out. Margaret Donaldson closed the front door on their going.

'You satisfied, guv?' asked Sergeant Ross on the way to the main road.

'Not much,' said the Chief Inspector.

'He's the kind that could've done it without blinkin' an eyelash,' said Sergeant Swettenham.

'While he was in Scott's?' said Sergeant Ross.

'I'll grant that needs workin' on,' said Swettenham.

'The two of them, Gottfried and his so-called housekeeper, 'ardly turned an 'air,' said Inspector Davis, 'except the woman got a bit irritable. He's a cool customer, Gottfried. I wouldn't trust him any farther than one of 'is tarts could throw him.'

'That's what I said,' observed Sergeant Swettenham.

'I think I've got a headache,' said Dobbs.

'I think we all have, guv,' said Ross.

'George,' said the Chief Inspector, 'do me a favour. There must be someone in Whitechapel who noticed a man who didn't belong, but who didn't think anything of it at the time. I'm convinced Poppy Simpson wasn't done in by a resident, even if some of them might drown their own mothers for the price of a pint. Ask around at the pubs, and ask the known doxies if any of them were approached that night by an unusual kind of customer.'

'Unusual?' said Davis.

'They've all got a nose for the unusual,' said

Dobbs. 'Take Sergeant Swettenham with you.'

'Well, it's a fact it won't do to spend all our time lookin' for Flanagan's murderer,' said Davis. 'That'll just let the trail go cold in Whitechapel. In any case, I'd still bet on Gottfried as the cove we want for the Tooley Street job. I wouldn't give a monkey's tail for 'is alibi.'

'A jury might,' said Dobbs, 'but I think I'll call in at Scott's.'

'I'd go for Gottfried meetin' Maureen Flanagan definite that night,' said Sergeant Swettenham.

'Yes, that's still on the cards,' said Dobbs. He and Sergeant Ross parted company with Inspector Davis and Sergeant Swettenham when their growler reached Aldgate. The Chief Inspector and Ross continued on to the West End. 'What's keeping you quiet, my lad?' asked Dobbs.

'I was with Nurse Cartright last night,' said Ross.

'Again? Have you got intentions?'

'Just my feet under the table at the moment, guv,' said Ross. 'What I was thinking about was that Nurse Cartright suggested that as the fog was a real pea-souper on the night of the Tooley Street murder, perhaps Flanagan didn't go out at all. I said she must have, seeing she had to be out when she copped the knife. My lady friend said that knocked her supposition on the head a bit, but, frankly, I'm wondering now if she wasn't right.'

'Jesus Christ,' said Dobbs as the growler jostled for position on crowded Ludgate Hill.

'Hit the bull's-eye by accident, have we?' said Ross.

'It's been right under our noses from the beginning,' said Dobbs. 'Flanagan didn't go out, not in that pea-souper. She was murdered in her lodgings and dumped in Tooley Street. That was why there was no handbag. Remember, the Pritchards said they didn't hear her leave. They were having a ding-dong, and thought that was the reason why they didn't. But she stayed in her room, of course she did, and we ought to have guessed that days ago. The man who did for her wasn't going to leave her in her lodgings, was he? That would have pointed us immediately at either a friend or acquaintance.'

'Pritchard or Gottfried,' said Ross.

'Buy Nurse Cartright a large bunch of flowers, and a box of chocolates as well,' said Dobbs. 'Our next stop, by the way, will be Scott's. Let's see if they can help us to put some kind of a dent in Basil's alibi.'

The growler, reaching Trafalgar Square eventually, moved into the maelstrom of traffic and went on to Piccadilly Circus. From there it continued on to Scott's bar and eating-place, where it dropped the CID men.

There, two members of the staff struck a blow favourable to Gottfried. He was a regular patron, and yes, he had been there on the evening in question. He had a lady with him, but because of the fog they left earlier than usual, just before ten.

'I've got the dead hand of bad luck resting heavy on my shoulders,' said Dobbs, growling a bit as he and Sergeant Ross departed. 'A little before ten's not much different from a little after ten. Gottfried said after ten to put himself well on the safe side.

'There's still Pritchard,' said Ross.

'He's favourite now,' said Dobbs, 'but let's find some food first, sunshine. I'm not at my best on an empty stomach. Also, my headache's worse and I need a whisky.'

'Well, after a Scotch, would you fancy a hot meat pie at Joe's in Covent Garden, guv?' asked Ross.

'That'll do,' said Dobbs. 'Which reminds me that Archie Binns's confession to both murders will be taken down in writing this afternoon. Which means the Commissioner and Fleet Street will expect him to appear at a magistrates' court for committal once we've finished checking details.'

'I thought that was only bluff,' said Ross.

'So it is, my lad. Checking details only means giving ourselves more time to lay our hands on the real villain or villains. By the way, we'll put ourselves on Pritchard's doorstep at six this evening. He'll be home by then.'

'His old lady will either faint or reach for her port,' said Ross.

'If she faints, he's our man,' said Dobbs, 'but will that solve the Whitechapel murder as well?'

'Search me, guv,' said Ross.

As they made their way to a pub, a light mist began to creep into London.

When they returned to the Yard, a uniformed constable from Whitechapel was waiting to see Chief Inspector Dobbs. His station sergeant had sent him. He was Constable Fred Billings, and he had something to tell the Chief Inspector.

'The fact is, sir, it occurred to me only this morning what ought to 'ave occurred to me at the time. That is, on the night Poppy Simpson was murdered.'

'Let's have it, then,' said Dobbs.

Fred explained that he was lodging in Ellen Street with two sisters and their brother, name of Cummings. On the night of Poppy Simpson's murder he'd left the house about eleven-fifteen to meet the elder sister, Bridget Cummings, who worked in the evenings at a West End restaurant. It was very foggy, but he came face to face with her in Commercial Street. She told him she'd just met a doctor, a gent who'd attended to her when she was knocked out during the Whitechapel riots, and who said he had patients in the district that he had to see. Fred described him, tall and good-looking and probably in his early forties, well-dressed in a bowler hat and overcoat, and carrying a walking-stick and a Gladstone bag.

'Typical of a doctor,' said Sergeant Ross.

'Yes,' said Fred, 'but I don't recollect Whitechapel ever 'aving a well-dressed doctor doin' the rounds of patients, nor attendin' to any late at night. Whitechapel people that get sick usually end up dyin' in their beds or in the Infirmary, mostly without ever 'aving seen a doctor. And I know now that when Bridget Cummings bumped into this one, it wasn't long after Poppy Simpson was found with her throat cut.'

'He's in his early forties, you say?' queried the Chief Inspector.

'That's the age I'd give him, sir,' said Fred.

Early forties. That meant he would have been about thirty, say, twelve years ago. Chief Inspector Dobbs thought what that could point to. A return of press and public interest in a resurrected Ripper. Bugger that.

'Sergeant Ross,' he said, 'take Constable Billings to your desk and get him to write down every detail he can remember about this doctor. Do that for us, will you, constable?'

'Very good, sir,' said Fred.

'And when you get back to Whitechapel, give your station Superintendent my compliments and ask him if he could put some extra men on the beat tonight.'

'To keep a lookout for the doctor bloke, sir?' said Fred.

'That's it,' said Dobbs. 'By the way, compliments to you too for having a head on your shoulders.'

Later that afternoon, Archie Binns made a statement that was taken down in writing and signed by him over a cup of tea sugared to his liking. Subsequently, the Chief Superintendent himself gave the press the kind of information that led them to believe a down-and-out would be formally charged with both murders, providing his confession had no holes in it.

The information was relayed to the Prime Minister, who expressed gratitude and relief.

Chapter Sixteen

Daisy, her first day's work over, left in company with other laundresses. She was more than pleased with her day, especially as the forelady had received a good report about her efforts. Passing through the sorting-room, she heard a voice she recognized, that of the young man, Percy Townsend.

''Old on a tick, Daisy gel, and I'll see yer 'ome.'

'I can see meself 'ome,' said Daisy.

''Ello, Percy's got 'is eye on yer already, 'as he, Daisy?' asked a laundress.

'He don't waste time, does 'e?' laughed Daisy, and out she went with her new friends into the rising fog of the late afternoon. Percy's voice followed her.

'See yer, Daisy gel.'

'Well, 'ard luck if I see you first,' said Daisy. Crikey, she thought, me prospects could be a lot better here than in Whitechapel. She said good-night to the other laundresses and set off for London Bridge. When she reached it, it was full of people coming home from the City, and the bridge and the home-goers all looked dim and ghostly in the dark shrouds of winter. But she had a little bit of spring in her step.

When she arrived home, both Bridget and Billy were there.

'Bridget, ain't you goin' to work?' she asked.

'First, 'ow did you get on?' asked Bridget.

'Oh, there wasn't no trouble at all,' said Daisy.

'Not from the Superintendent?' said Bridget.

'No, she was ever so welcomin', them police officers mustn't have told on me, that was kind wasn't it?' said Daisy. 'And everyone else was ever so kind and 'elpful. They nearly all live that side of the river, but they wasn't a bit like foreigners. The forelady said that if I was satisfact'ry at the end of a month, I'd be kept on and me wages made up to ten shillings. Won't that be a boon, Billy?'

'I ain't goin' to complain,' said Billy. 'All of us earning something, and Fred's rent on top. And Bridget ain't doin' any more night work, which shows she ain't as much short of sense as we thought. Or Fred must've talked serious to 'er.'

'Fred Billings talks through his 'elmet mostly,' said Bridget.

'Bridget, you doin' day work, then?' asked Daisy.

Bridget said she'd been out during the morning. She'd been able to talk to the kitchen manager of the restaurant, telling him that her sister was failing for want of necessities and that her brother was getting consumptive. They couldn't be left of an evening. The kitchen manager said troubles that never came singly ought to be looked after in hospital, and that it was fortunate that she herself looked in prime condition. Bridget assured him looks were deceptive, that her night work was wearing her out. Not that she wanted to give it up, not while there was still breath in her body, but she'd be forever grateful if there was day work she could do in the kitchens. She nearly fell down when the manager said all right, start this afternoon and work from one till five, washing-up, clearing-up and helping to get the restaurant ready for the evening patrons.

'Bridget, oh, today's our luckiest one,' said Daisy blissfully.

Bridget said it was about eleven when she left the restaurant during the morning, so she took a tram along the Embankment and down Blackfriars Road, and when she got off she decided to go among south-London foreigners and walk to Pocock Street, to look at the empty house that Fred Bluebottle had mentioned.

'Bridget, that's not nice, callin' Fred that,' said Daisy.

'He's lucky I ain't smothered 'im in his sleep,' said Bridget.

''Ere, 'old on,' said Billy, 'as the man in this fam'ly, Bridget, I ain't standin' for you gettin' into bed with Fred, and then tryin' to smother 'im once he's fell asleep.'

'Oh, yer saucy monkey,' said Bridget, and darted. She plucked the frying-pan from its hook above the hob, and turned. Billy, however, wasn't there any more. He'd vanished. She sped from the kitchen. 'You Billy,' she yelled up the stairs, 'you come down 'ere and take yer medicine, or I'll come up there and give it to you, you 'ear me?'

'If yer don't mind, Bridget,' called Billy from the landing, 'I'm just about to lock meself in Daisy's room to keep meself alive. Mind you, I still ain't 'aving you gettin' up to larks wiv our lodger. It ain't decent, not in this fam'ly it ain't. Call me when supper's ready.'

247

'Oh, yer young cuss,' yelled Bridget. 'Me gettin'
up to larks with a copper? I'd chop me own 'ead off
first.'

'Bridget, stop shoutin',' called Daisy.

'That Billy needs takin' in hand,' said Bridget,
coming back into the kitchen and replacing the
frying-pan.

'You didn't finish tellin' me about the 'ouse
across the river,' said Daisy.

Bridget said she'd looked at it. It had railings and
a gate, it was quite a nice terraced house with a bay
window, and the kids around didn't try to nick her
handbag, they just wanted to know why she was
looking at the house. At least, she thought that was
what they were asking about, only their south-
London cockney sounded foreign.

'It didn't, did it?' said Daisy. 'It didn't in the
laundry.'

'I'm pullin' yer leg, you silly,' said Bridget.
'Anyway, I asked who the landlord was and where I
could see 'im. They told me, so I've been thinkin'
I might go and talk to 'im one mornin'. Yes, I might.
That's if we think Billy might get a bit of a job in the
area.'

'Oh, ain't today been a promisin' one?' said
Daisy. 'Bridget, is there something cookin'?'

'Yes, a rabbit stew,' said Bridget, 'but it only went
on the 'ob 'alf an hour ago, after I got back from
me afternoon's work, so supper'll be a bit late.'

'Oh, that's all right,' said Daisy. Billy reappeared,
although in cautious fashion. Bridget frowned at
him.

''Ello, 'ow's yerself, Bridget?' he said. ''Ere, ain't
Fred 'ome yet?'

'No,' said Bridget, 'and this ain't 'is home, it's

248

where he 'appened to arrive one evening when me back was turned, and don't think I don't know who 'elped him.'

'Well, sometimes, yer know, Bridget, it's safer for some of us when yer back's turned,' said Billy. 'Oh, blimey.' Out he darted. Bridget was after him again.

In their house in Tanner Street, Mr and Mrs Pritchard were aghast. Mr Pritchard was facing the prospect of arrest and detention.

'I put it to you again, Mr Pritchard,' said Chief Inspector Dobbs, 'that after the scene with Miss Flanagan, after she had gone back to her room following her complaint to your wife, you went up again much later. You went up after you'd returned from the pub, with drink inside you. You took a knife up with you and cut Miss Flanagan's throat. I also put it to you again, Mrs Pritchard, that you knew this. Did you help your husband mop up the blood and to wash away all evidence?'

'Oh, me dear gawd,' gasped Mrs Pritchard, and tottered to the dresser and to her bottle of port. 'I'm goin' mad, I'm out of me mind already.'

'Following the murder, Mr Pritchard, you carried the body out of the house at some time during the night and left it in Tooley Street,' said the Chief Inspector. 'I think that's what happened. Am I right?'

'You're up the bleedin' pole,' said Pritchard, pale and shaking, while his wife sank quivering into a chair with her port bottle clutched in both hands. 'I ain't the kind to murder a woman just because she doesn't fancy me. Nor because I 'ad a pint of beer inside me. And 'ere, would me or anyone else 'ave done for Flanagan in 'er room when our other lodger was in at the time, rentin' the rooms next to Maureen's?'

'Other lodger?' said Dobbs, and Sergeant Ross blinked.

'We've all got lodgers round these parts, ain't we?' said Mr Pritchard. 'We 'ad two till Maureen run into a bloke with a nasty turn of mind that night. I'm tellin' yer, I don't 'ave nasty turns of mind about women, and nor ain't I bloody daft enough to slice one up when there's someone else close by. And on top of that, me missus said you searched Flanagan's room. As coppers, you'd 'ave noticed something, wouldn't yer? You'd 'ave noticed if the floor lino 'ad just been washed and cleaned, wouldn't yer?'

'Bloody hell,' said Chief Inspector Dobbs in exasperation, 'why didn't you let us know there was another lodger?'

'What for?' asked Mrs Pritchard woundedly. 'You didn't do no askin' about other lodgers, and I kept quiet about Mr Oxberry in case you started worrying 'im like you was worrying me. Mr Oxberry's a respectable and quiet gent that's a bit down on 'is luck. 'E was very grieved about Maureen Flanagan, like we all was, and besides, I didn't know you was goin' to come and accuse me 'usband of cuttin' 'er throat in 'er own room. She was out, wasn't she, and it was done when she was out, wasn't it?'

'We believe she didn't go out,' said Ross, 'not in that pea-souper.'

'But Ted did,' said Mrs Pritchard.

'Only down to the pub,' said Ross. 'If I remember right, you did tell us you didn't hear Miss Flanagan go out.'

250

'Well, I told yer me and Ted was 'aving a real up-and-downer, didn't I?' said Mrs Pritchard. 'Listen, you got to believe me, he didn't go up to Flanagan's room after 'e come back from the pub that night. If she was done for in 'er room, it wasn't Ted that was guilty.'

'Mrs Pritchard,' said Dobbs, 'tell me about your other lodger, Mr Oxberry.'

'Yes, 'e's Mr Jarvis Oxberry,' said Mrs Pritchard, holding on to her port for dear life after a needful intake. 'We let the two rooms to 'im about a month ago. 'E's a gentleman.'

'A gentleman?' said Dobbs.

'Very distinguished, like,' said Mr Pritchard, perspiring.

'Lodging here?' said Ross. Tanner Street was hardly salubrious.

'Why shouldn't 'e be?' said Mrs Pritchard, cuddling her bottle of port as close to her bosom as a lifebelt. 'Me and me 'usband is respectable, ain't we? We ain't robbed anyone's safe, 'ave we? Mr Oxberry, bein' down on 'is luck, is grateful we give 'im cheap lodgings.'

'He's an old gent, is he?' said Ross. 'Retired?'

'He ain't old, nor retired,' said Mr Pritchard.

''E works for a gents' outfitters in the Strand up to three in the afternoons, Saturdays as well,' said Mrs Pritchard. ''E looks like 'e's just turned forty.'

Dobbs glanced at Ross.

'A gent just turned forty who works at the outfitters in the Strand?' said Ross. 'I know the shop. Could you describe him, Mrs Pritchard?'

'What for?' asked the quivering lady.

'We'd like to know,' said Dobbs.

'Well, 'e's tall, 'andsome, and like me 'usband said, distinguished.'

Ross drew breath. Dobbs looked well and truly alive. Mrs Pritchard gulped another drop of port, and her lamplighter husband wiped a little perspiration from his brow with his hand.

'What kind of clothes does he wear?' asked Dobbs.

''Ere, what you gittin' at now?' asked Mr Pritchard.

'Just what kind of clothes he wears,' said the Chief Inspector.

'I ain't 'appy about this,' said Mrs Pritchard, 'but I can tell yer 'e wears a gentleman's suits, with a nice-lookin' overcoat and a smart bowler 'at.'

'I see,' said Dobbs. 'Is he in his rooms now?'

'No, 'e's out,' said Mr Pritchard, perspiring less. The penny was beginning to drop. These coppers had suspicions about Oxberry. Christ.

''E goes out most evenings,' said Mrs Pritchard. 'I think 'e said once 'e does a bit of part-time work in the evenings as well as 'is part-time day work to 'elp with 'is income. Well, 'e don't usually get back till me and me 'usband is in bed. Mind, 'e don't come in noisy, 'e's very quiet and thoughtful, like. What you askin' all these questions for? Ain't you asked enough?'

'Not yet, Mrs Pritchard.' The Chief Inspector did some rapid thinking. 'I'd like to have another look at Miss Flanagan's room,' he said.

'Well, all right,' said Mrs Pritchard, 'but there ain't no evidence up there that'll show me 'usband done her in.'

'And we ain't touched it,' said Mr Pritchard, 'it's

252

like it was since she last used it. I give yer me oath on that.'

'Noted, Mr Pritchard,' said Dobbs, and went up to the room with his sergeant. He struck a match and applied the flame to the gas mantle. Light spread and glowed. He inspected the floor linoleum. 'Would you say that looks as if it's recently been washed, sergeant?'

Sergeant Ross went down on his hands and knees, and crawled about.

'No, I wouldn't say so, guv,' he said, coming to his feet. 'What I would say is that we've picked up a lead that beats all others.'

'Picked it up?' said Dobbs, scanning the linoleum. 'More correctly, it jumped into our laps. Let a prayer said in church be a lesson to you, my lad.'

'Eh?' said Ross, looking around with eyes turned into gimlets.

'I said one myself on Sunday. Pritchard was right. When we went all over this room the morning after the murder, we noticed nothing to make us think it had been committed here.'

'On the other hand, guv, we weren't looking for those kind of signs,' said Ross.

'No, we weren't,' said Dobbs, 'but we did turn everything over. This gentleman lodger now, Jarvis Oxberry. Has he been in here? Did he try his luck with Maureen Flanagan, and did she turn him down too? Hold on, wait a minute, go down and ask the Pritchards if he was out that evening. If he wasn't, he'll be a prime case for investigation, since I'm sticking like glue now to the probability that Flanagan stayed in. I've got some serious thinking to do, and a feeling that when you get back we'll need to inspect Oxberry's rooms.'

'Right, guv,' said Ross, and down he went.

Dobbs wandered around the room. He opened the wardrobe. The late Maureen Flanagan's clothes were still there, on their hangers. And two hangers were still empty. He moved the clothes about, and noted that a blouse and a skirt were hung together.

'Charlie Dobbs,' he said, 'I think something's staring you in the face. The corpse now, that was staring you in the face to begin with, and so was the fact that there was no blood, just a faintly stained scarf, and a bit of a smudge on her blouse. That didn't make sense then, and it doesn't make sense now.'

The wheels of thought turned slowly. If the blouse and skirt Flanagan had been wearing when her body was found had occupied the same hanger, that would leave one hanger spare. Was it a spare, was it one hanger she hadn't needed to use? Or had it been in use? If so, what had been on it? A dress? Another combination of blouse and tarty skirt?

Balls of fire, was that it, was there a blouse and skirt missing, and were they missing because they related to the murder? A gashed throat. Spurting blood. And a blouse that was only marked by a faint pink smudge, and a skirt not marked at all. Nor the coat. Bloody impossible.

If Flanagan had died under the knife in this room, there would have been a hell of a mess to be cleaned up. What with? Her towel, hanging over the washstand roller, could have been used to mop up blood, but it was clean. A small worn rug beside her bed, there to protect her bare feet from the cold lino when she rose each morning, could also have been used. But it obviously hadn't been. Jesus, had her skirt, blouse, petticoat and drawers been ripped off to do the job?

I'm going for that, and I'm going for the bugger dressing her in a spare blouse, skirt and petticoat after he'd cleaned her body up. And I'm also going for her coat being off when he sliced her.

No, wait a moment, there'd be some signs, even if only small ones, if it had all taken place right here. We'd have noticed something when we searched the room. Further, it would have reeked of murder.

He sat down on the edge of the bed and applied himself to the mental strain of dredging up further suppositions and theories. Feet sounded on the stairs, and when Ross came in, he had Mr Pritchard with him.

Looking haunted, the man said, ''Ave yer cottoned on to anything, guv? I 'ad to come up with yer sergeant and ask, I'm that worried. So's me old lady.'

'I've got my own problems,' said Dobbs.

'Oxberry was in that evening, guv,' said Ross. 'Mrs Pritchard's quite certain she heard him moving about.'

'Yes, and she mentioned to me 'e was in for a change,' said Mr Pritchard. 'That was after our ding-dong, and she said she 'oped Mr Oxberry 'adn't been listening. What's more, I 'eard 'im meself when I come back from the pub. The fog didn't usually bother 'im, 'e'd go out most evenings whatever, yer know. But 'e was in all right that evening.'

'Well now, be a helpful bloke,' said Dobbs, 'and

tell me what Miss Flanagan was wearing under her coat at the time you were up here trying your luck with her.'

'I can't,' said Mr Pritchard, ''er coat was done up.'

'Was she wearing the scarf?'

Mr Pritchard screwed his suffering forehead up in concentrated thought.

'Yus, she was,' he said, and Dobbs thought that perhaps at that stage she was still thinking about going out. Basil Gottfried had said she was expected in the West End.

'So you couldn't see the neck of her blouse?' he asked.

'Yus, I could,' said Mr Pritchard. ''Er scarf was 'anging loose, she 'adn't wound it round 'er neck yet. I remember seein' a touch of yeller, or a sort of lemon colour.'

'Sure?' said Dobbs.

'Yus, I remember that touch of colour,' said Mr Pritchard.

'Well, that's some help,' said Dobbs. The blouse on the body of Maureen Flanagan had been white.

'Me old lady's sufferin' chronic, guv.'

'Well, you can tell her I think you've finally put yourself in the clear,' said Dobbs. 'With your mention of a touch of colour.'

'I dunno 'ow that counted in me favour,' said Mr Pritchard.

'All the same, it did,' said Dobbs.

'Thank gawd for that,' said Pritchard. 'Listen, guv, might I ask yer if you got suspicions about Oxberry?'

'I can tell you my enquiries are proceeding in every direction,' said Dobbs.

'As the saying is,' said Ross.

'I got yer,' said Mr Pritchard, and went down to rejoin his old lady and to inform her he was as good as in the clear. Mrs Pritchard stopped palpitating on his behalf, poured herself a full glass of port, drank some of it, and then, because of new developments, began palpitating on behalf of her gentleman lodger, Mr Jarvis Oxberry.

Upstairs, Dobbs said, 'Well, Sergeant Ross, now what've we got?'

'You tell me,' said Ross.

'I will,' said Dobbs, and detailed the conclusions he'd drawn.

'Stone my Aunt Beatie's cockatoo,' said Ross, 'what an eye-opener. I'd say that makes Oxberry a highly promising suspect.'

'But where did it happen, eh?'

'Not in here,' said Ross, 'not in this room.'

'Somewhere else, of course,' said Dobbs, 'and what we might find there could lead us to Whitechapel as well. He went out most evenings, never mind the fog. That's it, he did for Maureen Flanagan somewhere close, and later that week for Poppy Simpson. I'll lay my Sunday shirt on it. You realize, don't you, he answers the description given by Constable Billings of the man who called himself a doctor?'

'I did happen to recognize Mrs Pritchard's description as being as good as one and the same,' said Ross.

'When you asked the Pritchards if Oxberry was in or out that evening, I suppose you also asked them if he owns a walking-stick and a Gladstone bag?'

'Well, no, I—'

'Dear oh dear,' said Dobbs, and shook his head at his sergeant.

'Come off it, guv,' said Ross.

'Do me a favour, go down and ask them now,' said Dobbs.

Ross went. He was back almost at once.

'Yes, a black ebony walking-stick and a brown Gladstone bag,' he said.

Dobbs put his bowler on.

'I think we'll take a look at his rooms,' he said, and led the way out. On the landing he called, 'Mr Pritchard?'

Out came Mr Pritchard from the kitchen.

'I'm 'ere, guv.' His mood now was almost respectful.

'We're going to take a look at Mr Oxberry's rooms.'

'Eh?'

'Any objections?'

'Bloody 'ell, you got that far in yer suspicions?' said Mr Pritchard hoarsely.

'You could say it would help our enquiries if we examined the rooms. We're going in now.'

'No objections, guv,' said Mr Pritchard, 'but it's goin' to give me missus another bad turn.'

'Sorry about that,' said Dobbs.

Sergeant Ross tried the door of the front room. It was locked. He fished into his jacket pocket and took out a bunch of keys. He tried three. The fourth one turned the lock, and he opened the door. The room wasn't in complete darkness. There were two gas mantles, one on each side of the wide chimney breast, and one was alight but turned low, offering a mere glimmer. Dobbs went in and turned it fully on. Light sprang. The room was warm. A cumbersome-looking gas fire stood in the hearth, its jets burning low. A sofa fronted the hearth, and a table stood under the curtained window. The furniture generally, old and unhandsome, was that of a living-room. A cupboard that could have been used as a larder was empty on inspection except for a packet of tea and a can containing a little milk. Additionally, on the cupboard floor, tucked back, were newspapers, several of them, and all neatly folded.

Dobbs brought them out and took a look at them. They were all recent issues of the *Daily Telegraph*, the earlier issues containing reports on the murder of Maureen Flanagan, the later ones dealing with the Whitechapel murder and suggesting the one was possibly linked to the other. Comments implied that the Scotland Yard man leading the enquiry, Chief Inspector Dobbs, was baffled.

'Who's arguing?' said Dobbs.

Sergeant Ross, foraging around and turning things over, said, 'Not me, guv, I haven't said anything.'

'These newspapers have,' said Dobbs. 'Now why is the Pritchards' gentleman lodger hoarding papers that begin with the news of Flanagan's murder? Is your pulse beginning to jump about?'

'Not yet,' said Ross, 'this place looks like anybody's lodging.'

'What about the floor?' asked Dobbs, peering.

'I've looked,' said Ross, 'and that's anybody's floor too.'

'Well, let's try the bedroom. There's always more secrets in a bedroom than anywhere else.'

The bedroom door was also locked. Sergeant

Ross and his ring of skeleton keys made short work of that obstacle. The CID men entered. Darkness enveloped them. Dobbs struck a match, and Ross pointed out a gas mantle above the fireplace. He turned the tap and Dobbs lit the mantle. The light uncovered bed, chair, wardrobe, tallboy, washstand and bedside table.

'This feels a bit more promising, wouldn't you say, my son?' said Dobbs.

'I tell you, guv, all my feelings are in my stomach now,' said Ross.

'What you need is a hot meat pie,' said Dobbs. 'What's that on the bed?'

'It's the walking-stick,' said Ross, and picked it up. Made of solid ebony, with a silver handle shaped like a leaping leopard, it was heavy. There were marks on the silver, and also on the stick itself. Dobbs examined it.

'Well, it's handy, of course, but you couldn't cut anyone's throat with it,' he said, his hat on, his over-coat unbuttoned. He opened the wardrobe, disclosing two suits, a mackintosh and a pair of shoes. In a drawer of the tallboy was underwear, male, together with socks. 'Anything under the bed, sunshine?' he asked, and Ross stooped.

'This,' he said, and brought out a Gladstone bag. He placed it on the bed and opened it. It contained small bottles of medicine, headache powders and a stethoscope.

'I call that something to blind the innocent,' said Dobbs, and examined the floor. Its old linoleum covering was cracked in places, but it seemed exceptionally clean. 'Take a good look, sergeant.'

Ross went down on his hands and knees again.

He looked, he moved about, and he dipped his nose close to sniff at the lino.

'It's been washed, guv, with soap and water,' he said, and sat back on his heels, his expression stark. 'Holy angels, this is where Flanagan copped it?'

'Where else? It was staring us in the face from the start, my lad, the fact that the only reason why she was dumped was because having been murdered here, the murderer had to remove her. If you'd had any gumption, you'd have come up with that conclusion as soon as Nurse Cartright suggested to you that perhaps Flanagan never went out at all.'

'Have a heart, guv, you didn't come up with it, either,' said Ross.

'I grant that, but I'm not as young as you are,' said Dobbs, 'I take time to work things out.' He remembered then that his young son had unconsciously given him a clue when he said no-one would want to go out in a pea-souper. 'Now, lift that linoleum at its edge and let's see if the cracks can tell us anything.'

Ross used his penknife to lever lino tacks free of the floorboards. He turned the lino back. On the floor, matching the lines of the deepest cracks, were faint stains.

'Bloodstains,' said Ross.

'Yes, I think we've as good as got the gent,' said Dobbs. 'Now, suppose it happened as follows, my lad. Suppose Oxberry also fancied Flanagan, but not in the same way as Pritchard. More as a handy victim. Suppose he brought her into his bedroom after she decided a distinguished-looking gent was more acceptable than a lamplighter, and could be relied on to be discreet and fairly generous. She

261

wasn't going to risk her front of respectability for a five-bob touch from a lamplighter, and Oxberry might have offered her as much as five quid. In fact, my lad, if he intended to do her in, he could have offered her ten quid, and she'd have been thinking she wouldn't have to pay her pimp Godfrey a percentage of however much it was. Under the circs, and with all that fog outside, throttling London, I'd say she found the invitation irresistible, as long as Oxberry convinced her it would all take place on the quiet in his bedroom.'

'Well, I've got to admire that chapter of suppositions, guv,' said Ross, 'but we're missing something. Why should he have wanted to do her in?'

'Wake up,' said Dobbs. 'Because he found out she was a pro and he fancied himself as a copy-cat Ripper, but without any gruesome touch.'

'Steady on, guv,' said Ross, 'that's the last thing you want, isn't it, another Ripper?'

'More to the point, have we got one?' said Dobbs.

'Well, guv, if he posed as a doctor in Whitechapel, I'd say it wasn't because of visiting the sick.'

'He's our man,' said Dobbs.

'But he was taking a chance, wasn't he, still lodging here after he'd done for Flanagan?' said Ross. 'Mrs Pritchard could have mentioned him when we first interviewed her, and we'd have had to interview him too.'

'You heard her say why she didn't mention him. And there's another reason why. Because she knew he had probably heard Flanagan going for her husband when he tried it on. In any case, Oxberry might have seen the risk as a challenge. He'd have known we'd be investigating an outside job, not a job in his bedroom. There's got to be a suitcase here somewhere. Find it.'

It was found standing up against the wall beneath the bed. Ross pulled it out, placed it on the bed and opened it. All it contained was a slim printed booklet, with neat stiff covers. Dobbs took hold of it and opened it. It was a published version of papers issued by a physician, Sir William Gull, the subject matter being syphilis. Dobbs leafed through it, perusing paragraphs here and there, and discovering Sir William did not spare the reader in describing the repellent effects of the disease on the actions and tempers of the sufferer.

'What's it all about?' asked Ross.

'The pox, and what it can do to a victim,' said Dobbs. 'Note the name of the author. Sir William Gull. Sir William, my lad, was physician to the late Duke of Clarence at the time of the Ripper murders, and when the Duke's behaviour was nowhere near what you'd call normal. I'd say Oxberry, in being in possession of this book, has got a feeling for the actions and behaviour of the Ripper. D'you know what that means, sunshine?'

'That he's got the pox?'

'Not necessarily,' said Dobbs, 'think some more.'

'Well, I could say it means his reason for murdering Flanagan and Poppy Simpson was because he knew they were both pros,' said Ross.

'Good on you, laddie, you've caught up,' said Dobbs. 'Have a look at this bedroom fire.'

Behind the bars of the fire was a heap of ashes.

'Burned clothing?' said Ross.

'There's no firewood in the fuel box, no coal in the scuttle,' said Dobbs.

'Well, who lights a bedroom fire unless someone's sick and needs a warm atmosphere, guv?'

'Very correct,' said Dobbs. 'I don't think you'll find any coal ashes among that lot. It's got to be clothing. Still, you might find what's left of buttons. You might. Wait a minute, it's been a week since Flanagan was murdered, and three days since Poppy Simpson was similarly victimized. And Oxberry's out, and the evening's foggy. On top of that, what haven't we found here?'

'The perishing knife,' said Ross.

'Then we can't afford to stand about having a chat, can we?' said Dobbs.

'Christ,' said Ross, 'are you thinking he's going after another woman tonight?'

'I'm thinking that if he's got the knife on his person, he's not going to use it for peeling onions,' said Dobbs. 'Where's he likely to be?'

'If he's copying the Ripper, where else but Whitechapel?' said Ross.

'I compliment you, my son. Let's get back to the Yard at the double. On our way out, we'll let the Pritchards know that this floor is out of bounds, and that we'll be sending a uniformed constable to stand guard up here. Come on, get moving, stop chewing your bowler.'

On the way to the Yard, Dobbs came up with another possibility, that the man mentioned in Maureen Flanagan's last letter to her mother wasn't Gottfried, alias Godfrey, but Oxberry. After all, she'd known Gottfried for some time, whereas Oxberry had only been lodging in the same house for a month. If he'd made himself especially pleasant to her, even discreetly entertained her

264

some evenings in his living-room, she'd have gone there happily on his invitation the evening she was murdered. Unfortunately for her, Oxberry had already found out she was a prostitute.

'I'll go along with that,' said Sergeant Ross.

'Thought you might,' said the Chief Inspector.

Chapter Seventeen

By nine o'clock, the fog hung high, gathering into itself the smoke from London's countless chimneys. At ground level it drifted and shifted, and was semi-opaque within the region of each street lamp. Traffic in the West End was crawling, and in the East End it was sparse. In the haunts of Whitechapel, it had all but disappeared. Figures moved in and out of the lighter patches of fog, and outside the pubs shawled women and flat-capped men argued or gossiped, while doxies fixed their painted faces in expressions inviting, hopeful or coy. Coy was a little difficult for most of them, but experience told them some men preferred coyness to witchery. Inside the pubs, other men and women drank what they could afford, and either brooded on their lot or let the drink loosen their tongues. If they had homes to go to, they were none of them eager to get there. Many homes were hovels, where not even tap water was laid on. The Government still hadn't passed legislation forcing the landlords in question to supply this basic amenity. But recent murders had brought Whitechapel and its un-civilized conditions into the news again, and

Parliament was having to consider some kind of legislation to compel landlords to improve that which was merely primitive.

The gentleman who called himself Jarvis Oxberry stood within the black lee of a house wall in Mitre Street, taking in the atmosphere created by the murder of Catherine Eddowes, the fourth victim of the Ripper twelve years ago. The crime had happened only yards from where he stood. He smiled to himself. The indulging of interest and inclinations was doubly exciting when it embraced such an atmosphere as this. He wondered how close Chief Inspector Dobbs was to him in his investigation. Mrs Pritchard had complained today that he was always on her doorstep. Jarvis Oxberry considered himself capable of keeping comfortably ahead of the Yard man. Tomorrow he would move, before plodding Dobbs finally hit the nail on its head and arrived at his living-room door.

He heard a man and a woman approach him. He heard them because they were quarrelling. That was the eternal way with such people in such a neighbourhood, where want, privation and slow death stalked so many of them. Quarrelling, shouting, swearing and coming to blows were as much in evidence as dumb apathy.

They passed him without seeing him, he invisible against the wall and the rolling fog making shapeless creatures of them. He moved away once they were at a distance, beginning his measured walk after satisfying his compulsive liking for being where the Ripper had been. He had walked in the Ripper's footsteps frequently of late, visiting each of the five places of gruesome murder more than once.

He was not far from Aldgate tube station. That was where he was sure a certain woman came from late at night, always hurrying, despite the fog. But unless he was mistaken, a plodding constable had decided to come and meet her each night. Not that he was bitter about having been thwarted. Frustrated, yes, because there had been something about her hurrying footsteps that tempted him to bring them to a sudden full stop and her life to its end. But it wasn't important, his failure, since he was sure from her conversation with the policeman that she wasn't a street-walker. She was no part of his pattern if she didn't sell herself. He could find one who did easily enough. They proliferated around the pubs and lodging houses in this neighbourhood. Those who plied their trade from the shelter of doorways or simply by walking the streets were not in evidence tonight, however. He knew why. The fate of Poppy Simpson had scared them, and they were electing to join their kind in or outside the pubs. There was comfort in numbers. He had no intention of approaching such groups and presenting himself to a dozen calculating eyes. He was sure one or two would risk walking the streets. They all knew that some men would rather approach a solitary street walker than select one from a flaunting bevy.

The foggy conditions, in his favour, were the kind in which he revelled. He had neither his stick nor his bag with him, just his knife. Without his stick, he was at risk himself in such a God-forsaken hole, but his left hand had to be free for the attack from behind. With the woman called Poppy, he had been able to place both stick and bag aside when the front door had been closed. He could not do that when following an intended victim in a street.

He had plenty of time to select one. And one would surely cross his path eventually. He sauntered in anticipation, keeping to the darkest ways, and hiding himself each time he became aware there were men about.

'Funny about Fred being called out,' said Billy.

'Yes, and not 'aving to put 'is uniform on,' said Daisy.

'I don't know why you two talk about 'im as if 'e was our best friend,' said Bridget, 'specially as 'e's probably been called out to 'elp victimize some starvin' workers that's makin' a protest about their stingy wages.'

'What, this time of night?' said Billy. 'Anyway, the strike's over, the workers 'ad to go back, poor bleeders.'

'The time of night don't matter,' said Bridget, 'the workers and their fam'lies are starvin' all the time. Their troubles don't stop at night, I'll 'ave you know. They've got empty stomachs twenty-four hours a day. If that copper, Fred Billings, is out there right this minute, kickin' and bashin' men and women near to death, 'e's goin' to get 'is head knocked off when 'e gets back 'ere. Then 'e's goin' to get chucked out, and all 'is goods and chattels chucked out after 'im.'

'Oh, lor', Bridget, I wish you wouldn't get so cross about Fred,' said Daisy.

'It'll spoil yer looks, Bridget, you bein' in a state of permanent vexation,' said Billy. 'It'll start showin', it'll make yer kind face look like a crosspatch. You got a very kind face when you ain't bein'' cross. Look at Daisy, she's always showin' a kind face. So am I. It's inherited, yer know, from our mum and dad, and we ought to take care of it and keep lookin' kind, specially you and Daisy. Decent blokes like women with kind faces and comfortin' bosoms. I expect Fred does too.'

'Just lately, Billy Cummings, you've 'ad more to say for yerself than you ever 'ad before,' said Bridget, 'and you're saucy with it.'

'Well, it's me advancin' age, and the fact I consider meself the man of the fam'ly now,' said Billy. 'I'd be obliged, Bridget, if you'd be a bit nicer to Fred, that's our one and only lodger and pays 'is way generous.'

'Where's the kettle?' demanded Bridget. 'Daisy, lift it off the hob and 'and it to me, so's I can drop it on Billy's 'ead.'

'But, Bridget,' said Daisy, 'Billy only asked yer to be a bit nicer to Fred.'

'Blow Fred,' said Bridget.

'You could start by puttin' his washin' in the copper with ours tomorrer,' said Daisy. Monday washing had been given a miss because of Daisy's new job and Bridget being out. Bridget was due to do it tomorrow morning. 'I'm sure Fred would be ever so grateful.'

'I can't believe me ears,' said Bridget. 'Me do that blue-bottle's washin' and hang it on the yard line as well? And then iron it in the evening?'

'I bet Fred 'ud be tickled to see 'is washin' hanging on the line next to yer stays and petticoats and things,' said Billy.

'Daisy, I'm goin' to break yer brother's leg in a minute,' said Bridget.

'Bridget, you can't,' protested Daisy, ''e won't be able to ride 'is groc'ry bike.'

'Do a lot to cure 'im of 'is sauce, though,' said Bridget. 'Mind, I'll admit it's a nice change bein' with you two of an evening instead of 'aving to be at work. I got fed up comin' 'ome late in the fog.'

'Fred was ever so pleased you managed the change to day work,' said Daisy.

'Look, if you don't stop keepin' on about that copper,' said Bridget, 'me kind face really will suffer.'

'It's still funny 'im bein' called out, though,' said Billy, 'and not 'aving to be in uniform. Something's goin' on somewhere, that's my opinion as the man in this fam'ly.'

Bridget rolled her eyes and changed the conversation by saying they'd all go and look at that house across the river on Sunday. Her announcement met with unalloyed approval, and Billy said she was sometimes good of nature as well as kind of face.

Inspector Davis and Sergeant Swettenham were among the plain-clothes men and local constables on duty, all of whom were keeping a low profile. Davis and Swettenham had experienced a useless day asking questions about strangers.

Now they were at their own particular station in a dingy street, keeping a lookout for a man answering the description obtained by Chief Inspector Dobbs from Constable Fred Billings and the Pritchards. The fog made the responsibility difficult not only for them, but for the rest of the police on duty.

'What's the bettin' the bugger don't show up?' murmured Swettenham.

'You suggestin' Chief Inspector Dobbs has got it all wrong?' said Davis.

'Not me, sir,' said Swettenham, 'it wouldn't be correct.'

It might be right, though, thought Inspector Davis.

At ten o'clock, Jarvis Oxberry was in Buck's Row, close to the spot where the Ripper's first victim, Mary Ann Nichols, had been found done to death. He had arrived there by a roundabout way that kept him clear of the turgid heart of Whitechapel. He had walked south through the Minories, turned left for Mint Street and Cable Street, then directly north up Cavell Street to Buck's Row. He was conscious as always of the dismal overtones of Whitechapel at night. No amount of fog could hide the East End's need of help. Somewhere a hungry urchin whined, an urchin perhaps too hungry to even to go bed. Somewhere a woman shouted. Another screamed abuse. A tired man called, 'Put a bleedin' sock in it, will yer?' Another man coughed outside his door to ease his diseased lungs. Not far away was a pub, and the sounds of drunken singing could be heard, although muffled by the fog.

Jarvis Oxberry moved to the corner of Buck's Row, and in the dim light of its street lamp he was observable for a moment or so. Then he was quite still again, listening to the drunks, to the men and women obviously out of the pub. Some of the women would be moving soon, those who had failed to pick up customers in the pub and would come looking for them. If fog kept some men away from Whitechapel, it did not keep away foreign merchant seamen or furtive characters eager for a woman.

He waited. From the shelter of a doorway on the corner of Darling Row opposite, a man and woman watched him. He was just visible to them through the semi-opaque fog at the edge of the patch of light. He moved again, becoming invisible, but they were sure he was still there. He was waiting, that was certain, for he'd arrived all of ten minutes ago.

A minute whisper arrived in the woman's ear.

'Going to try this bloke?'

'He'll be the fourth, blow you. Still.'

The woman, in a skirt, blouse and warm woollen shawl, a gaudy hat on her head, crossed the street, humming a song. Reaching the corner of Buck's Row she stopped in the light of its lamp, bent down, lifted her skirt and petticoat and pulled on the top of a gartered stocking.

'Cussed thing,' she said, then let her skirts drop. Straightening up, she looked over her shoulder. 'Oh, 'ello, ducks, lookin' for a nice time, are yer? I didn't see yer at first, or I wouldn't 'ave give yer a free look at me underpinnings. 'Ere,' she went on boldly, 'yer a 'andsome gent, and if me legs 'ave made yer fancy me, and you've got 'alf a crown to spare, I'm yer girl. Me lodgings ain't far. 'Ow about it, eh?'

'Not this evening, thank you,' said Jarvis Oxberry, sizing her up.

'Oh, come on, dearie, yer'll like me.'

'Here, take this shilling.'

'What for?'

'To buy you a good supper.'

'Well, I ain't goin' to say no. Ta, mister, and bless yer.' Her hand closed over the coin. 'Yer sure you don't want a little bit of what yer fancy?'

'No. You may go.'

'Well, a' right, ta again,' said the woman, and went on, up Brady Street towards the Jewish cemetery.

He was behind her within seconds, silent and sure, tracking her through the flirting fog, his right hand in the pocket of his coat. Someone close to Buck's Row bawled a sailor's song tunelessly. Jarvis Oxberry took no notice, he was too intent now. But the woman stopped, turned and made him out.

'Oh, 'ello again, ducks, 'ave yer changed yer mind?' she asked.

He leapt in sudden fury at having been discovered. It interfered with his method, which was to attack from behind, as he had with both Maureen Flanagan and Poppy Simpson, the former in his bedroom and the latter on her way to the stairs. That way, and if his knife slashed fast enough, he escaped the blood. Now his knife was out, his left hand ready to turn this new prey and to smother her mouth. However, she did a leap of her own that took her clean out of his path. He turned as swiftly as a cat and ran at her. A firm body came flying at him, crashed into his back and downed him. He thudded onto wet slimy cobbles, all breath knocked out of him, the knife slipping from his hand.

'Hold him,' said the woman, 'and watch his knife.'

'I've got him, and his knife,' said Sergeant Ross,

and snapped handcuffs on writhing wrists. Obscene imprecations hissed.

'Listen, you, whoever you are,' said Ross, 'I'm a police officer and you're under arrest. You'll be formally charged at Whitechapel police station.'

Jarvix Oxberry, seething, hissed, 'Who planned this?'

'Chief Inspector Dobbs of Scotland Yard.'

'May he rot in hell.'

'You'll be able to tell him that,' said Sergeant Ross. 'Well done, Miss Cartright.'

'I didn't like the way you sang "Barnacle Bill The Sailor",' said Nurse Cartright shakily. Her role as a dupe had originated in the lively mind of Dobbs, but although a little pale and visibly unnerved by what it had entailed, she was able to smile faintly as she added, 'It sounded bloody awful. You're better at whist.'

Constable Fred Billings, in mufti, returned to Ellen Street at eleven. Along with other constables he had been released from the evening's special assignment, that of looking out for a copy-cat Ripper. The suspect had been nabbed.

Bridget, Daisy and Billy were all still up.

'What's been 'appening, Fred?' asked Billy.

'Nothing to worry you,' said Fred.

'If you've set about the starvin' workers again, Fred Billings,' said Bridget, 'you ain't welcome in this 'ouse, and I'll 'ave to request yer immediate departure, with all yer bags and baggage.'

'Now?' said Fred. 'It's me bedtime. And I'm on the side of the starvin' workers, as you well know, Bridget Cummings.'

'No, I don't know,' said Bridget.

'You're lookin' real handsome tonight,' said Fred. Bridget's thick and lush hair, piled, was a shining crown of raven-black. She'd been giving it a lot of attention lately.

'I ain't receptive to compliments from a copper,' she said.

'Bridget, ain't you gettin' tired of bein' unkind to Fred?' protested Daisy. 'Can't we 'ave a change from 'earing you goin' on and on?'

'I don't want 'im bein' personal about me looks,' said Bridget.

'Still, when they're right in front of me peepers,' said Fred, 'I consider meself entitled to comment.'

Daisy giggled. Bridget gave her a straight look.

'Something up with you, Daisy?' she asked. 'And what're you grinnin' about, Billy?'

'Well, you been doin' yer hair up a treat recent, Bridget, and it suits yer,' said Billy. 'I dunno what you got called out for, Fred, but while we was talkin' about you, there was a mention that me, Daisy and Bridget 'ave all got kind faces that we inherited from our mum and dad. And Bridget's got a fine build as well, ain't she? Is it Bridget's kind face and fine build that makes yer think she's 'andsome?'

'I'm admirin' of all she's got, Billy,' said Fred.

'Where's the new copper stick?' yelled Bridget. 'I'll do for you, Billy Cummings, and you too, Fred Billings, while I'm at it.'

'Bridget, leave the new stick alone, there's a dear,' said Daisy, 'you'll only lose that one as well. And don't shout so much.'

'If anyone ever suffered more aggravation than me, it ought to be wrote down in a book for posterioty,' fumed Bridget.

'Posterity,' said Fred.

'Stop showin' off, will yer?' said Bridget. 'I 'ate show-offs.'

'Bridget,' said Billy, 'yer kind face is slippin' a bit again.'

'I'll strangle that boy in a minute,' said Bridget.

'Time we all went to bed,' said Fred.

'Is that an order?' asked Bridget.

'Not likely,' said Fred, 'trouble comes easy enough without me askin' for it. I'd be happy if you'd all consider me just a fam'ly friend. I'm pleased you're givin' sensible thought to that house in Pocock Street, Blackfriars. It's not Park Lane, but it's a sight better than Whitechapel. And Daisy's had a fav'rable start at Guy's laundry, so I 'ear. Things are lookin' up for all of yer, specially now Bridget's on day work.'

'I can't 'ardly believe this,' said Bridget, 'I must be 'earing things.'

'Sounds all right to me,' said Billy, 'and d'you know what, Daisy, something's just come to me.'

'What 'as?' asked Daisy.

'Well, 'aven't you noticed?' said Billy. 'Fred's got a kind face as well.'

'Oh, me gawd,' said Bridget, 'I'm goin' to bed before I fall sick.'

Chapter Eighteen

Nurse Cartright had received a commendation from Chief Inspector Dobbs before being escorted home. Her role as a decoy had been a dangerous one, but she had volunteered to take it on without hesitation. With Sergeant Ross always her shadow and guard, she had approached three possible suspects at intervals and in different streets, and quickly established they could not be identified as the man called Jarvis Oxberry, of whom a very good description had been obtained. Farce entered the realms of danger when one of these men said he couldn't afford a woman, but that he could offer her fourpence if she'd show him what she kept in her corset. She told him to keep his fourpence and went on her way, Sergeant Ross keeping her in sight all the while.

Regarding the fourth man, she knew she could rely on Sergeant Ross to understand this man was very much a possible in that she called him a handsome gent. Those were the key words, and she'd spoken them clearly enough for Ross to hear. Ross's drunken bawling of the sailor's song had been to let her know the man was on her tail after she had resumed her walk.

Dobbs, who had been in company with the Chief Superintendent during the discreet police infiltration of Whitechapel, not only expressed hearty admiration of Nurse Cartright, but subsequently suggested to Sergeant Ross that she was hardly a woman who should be encouraged to merely play whist.

The Chief Superintendent was present at the interview with the man called Jarvis Oxberry. It took place at Scotland Yard. Dobbs and his team regarded the suspect with a great deal of interest. Jarvis Oxberry, now recovered from his bruising encounter with Sergeant Ross, showed a calm demeanour. A good-looking man with a quite distinguished air, he appeared to be in his early forties, his handsome countenance marred only by a little scar on his left temple. Dobbs put the first question.

'You gave your name as Jarvis Oxberry at the Whitechapel police station,' he said. 'Is that correct, sir?'

'Of course.'

'You didn't give your address.'

'I don't concern myself with trivial questions.'

'We believe you to be residing in Tanner Street, the Borough, as a lodger of a Mr and Mrs Pritchard.'

'Who the devil are they?'

'We can get them here to identify you as their lodger, sir.'

'Do as you like. I've been accused of certain crimes. You can't prove I'm responsible.'

'You were arrested, Mr Oxberry, at a moment when you were attempting the murder of a woman.'

Jarvis Oxberry looked contemptuous.

'You can't prove that,' he said. 'I didn't lay a

finger on her. An attempt at murder is only an assumption of yours.'

'You were seen to follow her—'

'Seen? Through the fog?'

'It wasn't thick at ground level last night,' said Dobbs, 'and you were seen to run at her with a knife in your hand.'

'What knife?'

'This one.' Dobbs unwrapped the wicked-looking weapon.

'I've never seen it before, except in the hand of a man who claimed to be a police officer. I only know that after I was physically assaulted, he showed the knife to me.'

'You dropped it when you fell,' said Dobbs.

'That's what you say.'

'Mr Oxberry,' said the Chief Superintendent, 'are you denying you followed the lady and ran at her?'

'I followed her, yes, she had stolen a shilling from me. I didn't need a knife to prevail on her to give the coin back.'

'She – um – acquired the coin by picking your pocket, did she?' asked Dobbs.

'It was in my coat pocket. I occasionally keep a coin or two there.'

'I can't recollect that the lady is known for picking pockets,' said Dobbs.

'Well, you know now,' said Oxberry.

'Why were you in Whitechapel, sir?' asked Inspector Davis.

'What nosy people you are, but if you must know I've an interest in certain types of crime, and I've recently indulged that interest by making the rounds of the area notorious for being associated

280

with Jack the Ripper. May I go now?'

'I'm afraid not, sir,' said Dobbs, fiddling with his watch chain. 'There's the murder of Maureen Flanagan to be considered. Miss Flanagan also lodged with Mr and Mrs Pritchard. We suggest the crime took place in your bedroom.'

'That suggestion is pitiful. The woman was unknown to me.'

'Was she? Could she have been when she lodged on the same floor of the house as you?'

'Being aware of another lodger isn't the same as knowing her,' said Jarvis Oxberry dismissively.

'There are bloodstains on the flooring planks beneath the linoleum in your bedroom, Mr Oxberry,' said Dobbs, looking cheerful at being able to deliver that piece of information.

A little flicker disturbed Oxberry's lashes, but he said, quite calmly, 'There may be. I know nothing of them.'

'They're undergoing expert examination,' said Dobbs. 'Further, there are ashes in the fire and the pan. What did you burn there, sir?'

'I've lit no fires. Nor can you prove I did.'

'What d'you do for a living?' asked Dobbs.

'Very little. I mainly exist on my savings and what I earn as a part-time shop assistant.'

'In the men's outfitters in the Strand?' said Sergeant Ross.

'That's correct. I'm committed to a quiet and respectable life.'

The Chief Superintendent said, 'How respectable is it, sir, to indulge a morbid interest in the devilish crimes of Jack the Ripper?'

'I consider that a childish question,' said Oxberry.

Dobbs studied the man's features more intently, and surprised himself with a sudden feeling that they weren't completely unfamiliar. It wasn't a strong feeling, it was merely a vague stirring in his mind.

However, he said, 'Mr Oxberry, have we met before, would you say?'

'Never.' The answer was incisive.

'You surrendered your wallet at Whitechapel police station,' said Dobbs. 'It contained twenty-seven pounds, and nothing else, nothing to prove you are Jarvis Oxberry. I suggest you're hiding your real identity.'

'You can suggest what you like, but the fact is your accusations that I'm responsible for certain crimes are based on no proof, and my own suggestion is that you let me go.'

'You're being held very definitely in respect of your attack on a woman, Mr Oxberry,' said the Chief Superintendent. 'We'll resume interviewing you in the morning, and if you wish to have your solicitor present, you may do so. Overnight, you'll be detained in a cell.'

'You're making a serious mistake,' said Jarvis Oxberry, 'but I should at least like a cup of tea before I retire. No sugar, thank you.'

He was taken down and given a cup of tea, but not before the Chief Inspector had made another study of his features, a searching one.

'Charlie,' said the Chief Superintendent before leaving, 'he's going to be difficult to break.'

'We'll get him for the attempted murder of Nurse Cartright,' said Dobbs, 'and for the murder of Maureen Flanagan.'

'I think we'll succeed with the attempted

murder,' said the Chief Superintendent, 'but we can do with more than circumstantial evidence in respect of Maureen Flanagan. See you in the morning.'

Dobbs spoke to Sergeant Ross a minute later.

'About our guest, Archie Binns.'

'Yes, guv?'

'We won't release him yet, not until we've cracked Oxberry. Archie won't mind, as long as we keep feeding him. Oh, and search those ashes for buttons first thing in the morning.'

'We need buttons, guv, Oxberry's as tough as Gottfried.'

'Don't I know it. For instance, in respect of the buttons, who's going to be able to say a burned set belonged to one of Flanagan's blouses? Still, make the search. Goodnight. Compliments to Nurse Cartright.'

Mrs Daphne Dobbs was still up when her husband at last arrived home.

'Daffie, what's kept you out of bed?'

'Oh, just the fact of being a dutiful wife, Charlie. Would you like a hot toddy or d'you want to go straight up?'

'Let's have a hot toddy.'

'Has the man confessed?' asked Daphne. Charlie had telephoned to let her know he'd be exceptionally late on account of a suspect being charged. The Metropolitan Police had paid for the installation of a telephone last year.

'No, he's denying everything, and we're carrying the heavy burden of no real proof, sod it,' said Charlie.

'I'll overlook that,' said Daphne, and the two of

them transferred themselves to the kitchen, where she set about preparing the hot bedtime toddies. When they were ready, she and Charlie sat at the kitchen table to enjoy them. Charlie was thoughtful. 'Penny for them,' said Daphne.

'I had a funny feeling that I'd seen this bloke Oxberry somewhere before,' said Charlie. 'Not recently, sometime in the past.'

'In a police prison cell, perhaps?' suggested Daphne.

'You could be right on target,' said Charlie. 'You're a bright girl, Daphne.'

'Well, I was very bright once, when I married you instead of your rival, my charming floorwalker,' smiled Daphne.

'I've got fond memories of my lucky day,' said Charlie. 'I wonder now, has Oxberry got a police record?'

Chapter Nineteen

The cheap alarm clock woke Daisy at a quarter to seven. She was up at once, and roused Billy when she was washed and dressed.

'Come on, Billy, wake up, Christmas is comin'.'

'Well, it ain't gettin' me out of my bed,' said Billy drowsily.

'Yes, it is, and I'm doin' a beef sausage each for breakfast, with scrambled egg.'

Billy sat up, hair any old how, nightshirt rumpled.

'That's different,' he said. 'Crikey, all this rich livin' lately, ain't you a marvel, Daisy?'

'Just splashin' out a bit,' said Daisy. 'We'll let Bridget sleep on a while, and I'll put 'ers in the oven.'

Bridget woke up to an aroma. It drew her out of bed, and her bare feet hit the cold lino. She hissed with the shock of it, then thought of the many slum dwellings in which all lino had been ripped up to feed fires, and bare feet trod cold floorboards and suffered splinters. Putting a coat on over her old flannel nightie, she went downstairs and entered the kitchen, her hair loose and tumbling. She stopped to stare.

Daisy, Billy and Fred were all at table and eating a cooked breakfast. The large pot of tea stood on the table under its cosy.

'Excuse me,' she said, 'might I be informed what's goin' on?'

'Daisy's cooked a sausage each for us with scrambled egg,' said Billy, 'and me and Fred can 'ardly believe our luck. Yours is in the oven, keepin' 'ot.'

'Yes, you don't 'ave to get up as early as us,' said Daisy.

'Wait a minute, what's Constable Fred Billings doin', sittin' at our breakfast table?' asked Bridget.

'He's eatin' 'is sausage and egg,' said Billy.

'Our sausage and egg, if yer don't mind,' said Bridget.

'Morning, Bridget,' said Fred, uniformed.

'You've got a sauce, invitin' yerself to breakfast,' said Bridget.

'Well, no, I invited 'im,' said Daisy, 'seein' there was four sausages to the 'alf-pound that was in the larder. Yes, and Fred says he'll pay fourpence for any breakfasts we give 'im. He's give us 'is fourpence for this one.'

'I'm bein' undermined by me own sister,' said Bridget, 'and me own brother.'

'Come on, Bridget, sit down and 'ave yours now you're 'ere,' said Billy. 'We've near finished ours.'

Bridget sniffed.

'I don't 'appen to be dressed for sittin' down,' she said.

'It don't bother me,' said Fred. 'Mind, I'll admit this is the first time I've seen you not dressed for

286

sittin' down, but it still don't bother me. In fact, not dressed for sittin' down suits yer at this time of the morning.'

'Oh, it does, does it?' said Bridget.

'If I might be so bold as to say so,' said Fred, 'it goes with yer rosy flush of sleep.'

'Oh, 'elp,' breathed Daisy, alarm bells ringing at the look on Bridget's face.

'In my opinion,' said Fred, 'it ain't every woman that can show a rosy flush of sleep to go with—'

'Watch out, Fred,' said Billy.

As Fred bolted from the house thirty seconds later, a rolling-pin came after him. It flew through the air and knocked his helmet off. He could have gone back and arrested Bridget, but decided not to.

Fred was a wise copper, all things considered.

'Watcher, Daisy gel, I missed yer last night.'

So said Percy Townsend as Daisy approached the entrance to the laundry that morning. Percy was weighed down with a large sack of hospital washing, but still had a light in his eyes.

'What d'you mean, you missed me?' asked Daisy.

'Well, you wasn't where I 'oped you'd be, outside the Elephant and Castle Theatre,' said Percy, entering the sorting-room behind her.

'Oh, what 'ard luck,' said Daisy, 'and I can't stay talkin', except where d'you live?'

'Old Kent Road,' said Percy.

'Is that near Blackfriars Road?' asked Daisy, amid the hustle and bustle of bags and bundles and sacks.

'Stone's throw,' said Percy.

'Well, fancy that,' said Daisy, 'you might be just a

287

stone's throw from where I'll be livin' soon. So long for now.'

Get that man to the Old Bailey, and get enough proof to ensure a conviction.

That message came down to the CID from the Police Commissioner. The Minister for Home Affairs wanted the whole thing out of the way as soon as possible, and with it, all further reference to the case of Jack the Ripper and the dire poverty of the Queen's subjects of the East End.

'Well, guv,' said Sergeant Ross when he arrived at the Yard from his stint at the Pritchards' house, 'you might say I come bearing gifts, even if I couldn't find any buttons or button remnants in those ashes. First, what I *did* find was a smoky-looking handbag lodged up the chimney, and, second, a certain note in the pocket of one of Oxberry's jackets. There's the handbag. D'you like it?'

It was a brown, soft-leather handbag, dirty with soot and smoke. Ross had made no attempt to clean it. It contained the little items common to most ladies' handbags.

'Yes, I do like it, my lad,' said Dobbs. 'Yes, I can say that with confidence. My word, it does look filthy, doesn't it? Has it been identified as belonging to Maureen Flanagan?'

'Yes, by the Pritchards. Further, guv, as we left before we'd made a thorough search of Oxberry's bedroom last night, due to having to leave in a hurry, I did a bit more after locating the handbag. That's when I found this note.'

It was a folded slip of paper bearing the pencilled words, '*Collection of Published Writings of GULL. New Sydenham Soc.*'

'I see,' said Dobbs, 'yes, I do see. He made a note of something else he wanted to read, something published by the New Sydenham Society. Sir William Gull again. I think, my son, that our man was being what you might call self-seduced into the lamentable world of the Ripper, and probably mesmerized by who and what the Ripper was – hold on, where's that anonymous note we received?'

'On the file, guv.'

'Get it, there's a good bloke. Let's make sure we've got something to hit Oxberry hard with when we see him this time.'

The anonymous note, produced, was placed beside the note found in one of the suspect's suits. The Chief Superintendent and Inspector Davis entered Dobbs's office then, and each took his turn to examine the handwriting. The Chief Superintendent agreed that whatever little differences existed elsewhere, the formation of the capital letters in both notes was by the same hand. That needed to be confirmed by an expert, of course.

'Have we got enough to break him?' asked Inspector Davis.

'We've got bloodstains on his bedroom floor which I'm certain will have come from Maureen Flanagan,' said Dobbs. 'We've also got her handbag, found up his bedroom chimney, his knife, a note relating to a physician who was treating the Duke of Clarence at the time of the Ripper murders, and a publication on syphilis and its effects as written by that same physician, Sir William Gull.'

'Forget those last items,' said the Chief Superintendent brusquely.

'They're evidence of Oxberry's interest in the Ripper and his possible identity,' said Dobbs.

'They're inadmissable,' said the Chief Superintendent.

'On your orders?' asked Dobbs.

'The Public Prosecutor's,' said the Chief Superintendent.

'On what grounds, might I ask?' said Dobbs.

'You know damn well, Charlie.'

'On the other hand,' said Dobbs, 'there's no reason why we can't use them in our interrogation of Oxberry, is there?'

'I'll allow that,' said the Chief Superintendent, 'but no mention of them is to be made in the notes.'

'Tricky,' said Dobbs.

'I hope you'll be able to break Oxberry without reference to them,' said the Chief Superintendent.

'Well,' said Dobbs in optimistic vein, 'clouting him with the handbag might even knock him out.'

The Chief Superintendent, usually with Dobbs all the way, looked on this occasion as if the Chief Inspector's euphemistic comment was out of order.

'It might take more than the handbag to rattle him,' said Inspector Davis.

'Well, I grant you,' said Dobbs, 'he may be certifiable, but he's no half-wit.'

'And he hasn't asked for a solicitor,' said Inspector Davis.

'He likes the challenge of fighting us on his own,' said Dobbs.

'He liked the challenge of jumping Nurse Cartright from behind,' said Ross.

'Call that a challenge?' said Inspector Davis.

'It might have been to him,' said Dobbs.

'Let's have him up,' said the Chief Superintendent.

Jarvis Oxberry complained to begin with that he hadn't been allowed to shave. The Chief Superintendent said the supply of a razor to a prisoner was forbidden.

'To prevent me cutting my throat? That's laughable. Why should an innocent man think about doing away with himself?'

'Well, you are innocent, sir, until you're proved guilty,' said Dobbs, with Sergeant Ross taking notes. 'Are you sure, by the way, that you don't wish to have a solicitor?'

'Quite sure. I don't need one. All your questions are based on insupportable theories and accordingly ridiculous.'

'Not all, I hope,' said Dobbs briskly. 'Now, do you still say you had no contact with Miss Flanagan on the night of her murder?'

'I do say so, of course I do. I was out all evening.'

'So was Miss Flanagan, wasn't she?' said Dobbs. 'Was she out with you?'

'Out? You said last night—' The suspect checked. 'Never mind. I state categorically I had no contact with her.'

'Mr and Mrs Pritchard have assured us you were in, that they heard you.'

'If it's a question of my word against theirs,' said Oxberry, 'I doubt them being given the benefit of the doubt. People addicted to drink make unreliable witnesses. The man Pritchard is an unwholesome character altogether, make no mistake, and if it's true that this unfortunate woman, Miss – what was her name?'

'Maureen Flanagan,' said Inspector Davis.

'If it's true she was murdered in my bedroom while I was out you'd all be wiser to look closer at Pritchard than at me.'

Dobbs smiled.

'Ah, yes,' he said, 'we received an anonymous letter pointing us at Mr Pritchard. What a surprise it was to discover it was in your handwriting, sir.'

'You're an idiot,' said Oxberry.

'Oh, I've had my moments,' said Dobbs, 'and you've had a careless one. You left a note lying about.'

'You're mistaken.'

'No, we've got it, sir,' said Inspector Davis.

'You may say you have,' said Oxberry.

'We do say,' said Dobbs, 'and that and the anonymous letter have been under expert examination this morning.' Sergeant Ross hid a smile. 'You wrote them both, Mr Oxberry.'

'I deny it, naturally. What note are you talking about?'

Dobbs glanced at the Chief Inspector, who gave him a warning look.

'We'll come to that later, Mr Oxberry,' said Dobbs, and opened up the brown paper parcel to disclose the sooty handbag. 'This is Miss Flanagan's handbag. It was found in your bedroom chimney, lodged there. Can you explain how it got there?' It was the Chief Inspector's belief that the man had overlooked it when he left the house to carry the dead woman to Tooley Street.

'I can offer a guess that it was planted in an attempt to incriminate me, either by your men or by the man who dealt Miss Flanagan her death blow. Incidentally, haven't you forgotten something? As I understood it from newspapers, Miss Flanagan's body was found in a street, not my bedroom.'

'You're referring to the newspapers we found in your cupboard?' said Dobbs.

'Am I to be charged with keeping newspapers in a cupboard?'

'Didn't you further understand from their reports that Miss Flanagan wasn't murdered where she was found? She was carried there, and by you, I suggest, sometime during the night.'

Oxberry laughed.

'Dobbs,' he said, 'you're clutching at straws in the wild wind. You've no proof at all that I committed this murder, let alone any hope of proving I carried her to where she was found.'

'We'll see,' said Dobbs.

'By the way, sir, why 'ave you been posing as a doctor?' asked Inspector Davis.

Jarvis Oxberry shut his mouth tightly, and the small pink scar on his temple deepened in colour. He took time to speak.

'Is that a serious question, or is Scotland Yard staffed by idiots?'

'Oh, some idiots can ask serious questions, y'know,' said Dobbs, 'and we do happen to have a witness who heard you tell a young woman you were a doctor. She'd taken a knock during the riots in Whitechapel, and let you attend to her.'

'Nothing of the kind.'

'A police constable was present,' said Dobbs.

'He's the witness?' Oxberry looked caustic. 'A police constable? Well, he would be one of you, wouldn't he?'

'He and the young woman can identify you,' said Dobbs.

'Who could accurately identify anyone in that fog?' said Oxberry.

'He had his lamp on you and the young woman,' said Dobbs, 'and the young woman recognized you when she bumped into you in Whitechapel on the night Poppy Simpson was murdered. You spoke together, Mr Oxberry. You had with you a walking-stick and a Gladstone bag. Is this the bag, sir?'

It was Inspector Davis who produced it and placed it on the interview-room table. Oxberry regarded it calmly.

'It looks like mine,' he said.

'It was found under your bed, Mr Oxberry,' said the Chief Superintendent.

'Really? How interesting.'

'It contains bottles of cheap medicine, headache powders and a stethoscope,' said Dobbs. 'I suggest you adopted the look and title of a doctor to give yourself the commendable appearance of a pro-fessional gentleman above suspicion, and that in the case of the injured young woman you were unable to resist acting the part.'

'Above suspicion of what?'

'Well,' said Dobbs, 'let's say something like the murder of Poppy Simpson, a known prostitute.'

Oxberry laughed again.

'What comes next, Dobbs, my implication in the Gunpowder Plot?' he said. 'You're running around in demented circles.'

The Chief Superintendent reached and opened the Gladstone bag.

'Mr Oxberry, why have you been carrying these items in your bag?' he asked.

Oxberry took a look.

'These items are foreign to me, since I've never seen them before,' he said. 'I should like to know where such things and the knife and the so-called note come from.'

'I daresay we can sort that out,' said Dobbs. 'After all, you've heard of the Yard's fingerprint system of identification, haven't you?'

'You'll be lucky to find—' Mr Oxberry checked and shut his mouth tightly again.

'Lucky to find fingerprints on any of these items?' said Dobbs, who knew there were none. And the only fingerprints on the knife were blurred. 'You've handled everything with your gloves on?'

'Everything you've shown me are items I've never seen before.'

'A jury might not think so,' said Inspector Davis.

'You've no case to put before any jury,' said Oxberry. 'You can prove nothing. Dobbs has the wrong man, and he knows it.'

'Mr Oxberry,' said the Chief Superintendent, 'the lino of your bedroom floor has been washed clean with soap and water.'

'I'm delighted to hear it,' said Oxberry. 'Thank the landlady for me. Perhaps I should buy her a bottle of port, her favourite tipple.'

'Let's see,' said Dobbs thoughtfully, 'has the blood group of the floor stains been established, Sergeant Ross?'

'Same group as Miss Flanagan's,' said Ross.

'That doesn't look too good for you, Mr Oxberry,' said Dobbs.

'Nor for you,' said Oxberry, 'since it doesn't prove I was responsible for her murder. I stand on my statement that I was out all evening, pursu-ing my interest in the actions of Jack the Ripper. You may think that interest strange, but it's no more than the interest shown by any number of people over the years. I really think it's time you released me, for you're getting nowhere, and you know it. You must look for someone else, and I demand you let me go.'

'Not yet,' said Dobbs, 'no, I don't think so, not yet. There's your attempted murder of a woman as solid grounds for holding you.'

Oxberry's scar turned livid.

'Damn you for that put-up job,' he hissed.

'That scar of yours,' said Dobbs, 'how did it come about?'

'By reason of tripping and falling fifteen years ago,' said Oxberry. 'Any doctor will tell you it's an old scar.'

'It changes colour,' said Inspector Davis.

'Yes, so it does, I believe,' said Oxberry, 'but only when idiots strain my temper.'

'You wouldn't like to make a statement, I suppose?' said Dobbs.

'About a piffling scar?' said Oxberry.

'About your involvement in the murder of Maureen Flanagan and Poppy Simpson.'

'You're making a complete fool of yourself,' said Oxberry.

'Well, we'll give you time to think about a confession,' said Dobbs. 'D'you still not want the help of a solicitor?'

Oxberry smiled.

'You're the one who needs help, Dobbs, not I,' he said.

'We'll see,' said Dobbs. 'That's all for the time being.'

Oxberry was taken back to his cell. The Chief Superintendent regarded Dobbs soberly.

'Any competent defence counsel will make a good case for him,' he said, 'even for his attempted murder of Nurse Cartright.'

'We can't even be sure of proving he was in 'is lodgings when Maureen Flanagan had her throat cut,' said Davis, 'especially if his counsel makes mincemeat of the Pritchards.'

'Which his counsel will do if they say they only heard him,' said the Chief Superintendent.

'Well, somehow we've got to break him,' said Dobbs. 'He was close to blowing up once or twice. George, go to the outfitters in the Strand and find out if Oxberry really did work part-time there. Take Sergeant Swettenham with you.'

'I can't see how that will help,' said Davis.

'It might help us to prove he's a liar,' said Dobbs, who had already established, regretfully, that the man had no police record.

Chapter Twenty

A little after six, Bridget, Daisy and Billy arrived home from their jobs almost together. Fred was already there, in the kitchen, frying a large amount of lamb's liver and bacon.

''Ere, now what's goin' on?' demanded Bridget, as fulsome a figure of womanhood as ever was in Whitechapel.

'Good evening, Bridget,' said Fred, looking homely in his shirt, braces and trousers. 'Evening, Daisy and Billy. I thought I'd be a bit of a help instead of just a lodger, seein' you've all been out to work while I came off duty early. The potatoes are ready, margarined and mashed, and the lamb's liver and bacon won't be long, nor the tinned peas.'

'Fred, you're a bloke after me own 'eart,' said Billy.

'Yes, you're a dear, Fred,' said Daisy.

'No, he ain't,' said Bridget, 'he's comin' it.'

'But, Bridget, 'e's cookin' our supper,' said Daisy, 'and lamb's liver and all, and we only ever 'ave ox liver usually.'

'He's tryin' to make 'imself one of the fam'ly,' said Bridget. 'Yes, and where'd you get the bacon and lamb's liver from, might I ask, Fred Billings?'

'I sincerely 'ope you won't mind I contributed them,' said Fred.

'Well, I do mind,' said Bridget.

'I don't,' said Billy.

'Oh, and I don't, either, not really,' said Daisy.

'Any lodger that contributes and cooks a supper for us ought to be taken to the fam'ly bosom,' said Billy.

'Well, this partic'lar lodger ain't bein' taken to my bosom, nor Daisy's,' said Bridget.

'That just leaves mine,' said Billy, 'and I ain't really got one that you'd call noticeable. Still, a bloke can't 'ave ev'rything, can 'e?'

'Why don't you all take yer hats and coats off and sit down?' said Fred. 'Then I'll dish up. I've got the plates in the oven, and I've set the table.'

''Ere, what's yer game, Fred Billings?' asked Bridget.

'Well, I've been thinkin' a bit,' said Fred, 'and it occurred to me you've all suffered years of struggle without yer parents. So I said to meself it's time you 'ad someone to be a sort of Salvation Army comfort to yer.'

'Salvation Army whatter?' said Bridget. 'Daisy, 'e's gone off 'is rocker.'

'Still, it's a kind thought, and we ought to 'ave a bit of religion around,' said Daisy. 'Let's all take our 'ats and coats off and sit down.'

'Yes, that's right,' said Billy, 'then our bit of religion can dish up.'

Bridget uttered a strangled yell and rushed upstairs. Seconds later something clumped and bumped down the stairs to hit the passage floor. Billy darted to investigate.

'Billy, what's happened?' called Daisy.

299

'Bridget's chucked Fred's Sunday boots down the stairs,' called Billy.

'Oh, well, now she's done that she'll be all right in a minute,' said Daisy. 'Come and 'ave yer supper, Billy.'

'Bridget, you comin' down now to 'ave yer supper?' called Billy.

'Yes, I am, so tell that bit of religion to say 'is prayers!' yelled Bridget.

'Oh, all right,' called Billy.

But Bridget arrived without any aggravation showing and sat down with the others to a tasty supper.

'All right, are yer, Bridget?' asked Fred kindly.

'I'm watchin' you, Fred Billings, don't think I ain't,' she said. 'I know what your game is.'

'What game is that?' asked Billy.

'Gettin' as close as 'e can to me virtue,' said Bridget.

Daisy shrieked. Billy grinned.

'Well, I ain't goin' to stand in Fred's way,' he said.

Daisy shrieked again.

Bridget glowered.

Fred laid kind eyes on her virtuous bosom.

With Jane and William in their beds, Mrs Daphne Dobbs said to Charlie, 'You can talk about it now.'

'He's getting at me,' said Charlie.

'This man Oxberry?' said Daphne.

'I've got a peculiar feeling it's a personal battle just between him and me,' mused Charlie.

'Well, I suppose it would be,' said Daphne, knitting away. 'After all, he knows you're in charge of the investigation.'

'I think it's a bit more than that,' said Charlie.

'The saucy sod keeps calling me Dobbs.'

'What's he like exactly?'

'Cool, clever, handsome and impertinent,' said Charlie. 'He actually has been working for the men's outfitters in the Strand. George Davis checked. It's difficult to shake the swine. He makes all the proof we offer sound like circumstantial evidence. But he's been close to losing his temper a couple of times. It showed. He's got a scar on his left temple that turns livid, and his mouth shuts tight.'

The knitting needles stopped clicking, and Daphne stared at her husband.

'Did you say a scar, Charlie?'

'A small one, but very visible,' said Charlie.

'And it discolours when you feel he's getting angry?'

'It happened twice,' said Charlie.

'My God,' breathed Daphne.

'Something worrying you, Daffie?'

'The incredible,' said Daphne, body stiff. 'Charlie, fetch me our family album, there's a love.'

'Family album?'

'Just fetch it. It's in the bottom drawer of the bureau.'

Charlie fetched it and gave it to her. She opened it up, leafed through the first two pages and stared at a certain photograph. The family album was her labour of love, all photographs neatly inserted.

'You're making me curious,' said Charlie.

'Look at that,' said Daphne, and passed the open album to him. She leaned and put a finger on one of the photographs. He inspected it. It was a photograph of her parental family, of her

301

mother and father, her sister, her married brother and his wife and small boy, and of herself standing next to a tall good-looking man. 'That was taken before I married you,' said Daphne, 'and I kept it because it's the only one I had of all my family together, not because Edward is in it.'

'Edward?' said Charlie.

'Edward Vincent,' said Daphne.

'Your old flame?' said Charlie. 'I'd forgotten his name.' He took a more clinical look at the photograph. 'Well, I'm damned,' he said, 'now I know why I had a feeling I'd seen Oxberry before. It wasn't in person, it was in this photograph. I took a good look at it the first time I saw it, because I knew then the bloke had been my rival.'

'Charlie, do you think the man Oxberry could be Edward Vincent?' asked Daphne, slightly short of breath. 'Edward had that scar when I knew him, and I saw it turn very livid once, when I had to tell him I was going to marry you.'

'I never met him,' said Charlie.

'No, I was never foolish enough to bring the two of you together,' said Daphne. 'He was a near neighbour and I'd known him for quite a while before you came into my life. His job was that of a floorwalker, as you know, and he always looked the part.' Daphne remembered how often he seemed to arrive silently at her side, and how courteous he was. 'I thought him very pleasant, polite and well-mannered until the moment when I had to let him know I was engaged to you. I never mentioned it to you, but he became horribly unpleasant, and I couldn't repeat some of the things he said, especially about you. But I can tell you he said that one day he'd make your life not worth living. His

302

scar was a vivid red, his expression so ugly. Charlie, is Oxberry's scar a little straight line of pink puckered skin?'

'Yes,' said Charlie.

'My God,' breathed Daphne, 'then he could be Edward Vincent. That photograph is fourteen years old, but can you recognize Oxberry in Edward?'

'Yes, it's him, Daffie. Our suspect and your floor-walker are one and the same, I'll lay the Bank of England on it. Strike my Sunday shirt-tails, d'you know what he's been up to?'

'You tell me, Charlie, I'm too shaken to make guesses.'

'Looks like it's even put you off your knitting,' said Charlie. 'Edward Vincent, alias Jarvis Oxberry, is playing Jack the Ripper at my expense and the expense of his victims. You could say he can only think about me and the Ripper, and he's giving me the headache of the century. Well, from what you've just said, he had some idea about making me look a failure, a very peculiar way of getting his own back for losing you to me. He's very sure of himself, and probably believed I wouldn't be up to tracking him down. All the senior officers on the Ripper case were classed as failures by the public, the newspapers and certain authorities. It broke some of them. Edward Vincent is probably hoping this case will break me. Jesus Christ, could anyone ever get into his kind of mind? Well, for God's sake, why didn't he simply make an attempt to murder me instead of taking the lives of two women who'd done him no harm at all? I suppose the answer is that the Ripper's ghost took hold of him, and that he enjoyed the feeling of power his knife gave him.'

'Charlie, how could he have known you'd be in charge of the investigation?' asked Daphne.

'It was almost certain I would,' said Charlie. 'I was the Yard's bright boy at the time Maureen Flanagan's body was found. Dalston police wanted me to investigate another case – a woman beaten to death – but the Yard sent another officer.'

'Charlie, you'll have a dramatic confrontation with your suspect in the morning,' said Daphne.

'I won't dress up for it,' said Charlie. 'By the way, I'll borrow this photograph for a bit if I may.'

'You can always borrow whatever you want from me,' said Daphne, 'and some things you don't have to borrow, they're yours for keeps.'

'Such as?' said Charlie, extracting the photograph.

'Me, William and Jane,' said Daphne.

He woke up with a start in the middle of the night. He might have woken Daphne, to ask a question of her, but he spared her that. He returned to his sleep, and put the question to her after the alarm went off.

'He was a floorwalker at the Stamford Hill stores when you knew him, Daffie?'

'Pardon?'

'Edward Vincent.'

'Oh. I see. You're already at the Yard. Yes, the Stamford Hill stores.'

'And where did he live? Can you remember?'

'Yes. Downs Park Road, south of Stamford Hill, and in a bachelor flat not far from my parents' house. Why'd you ask?'

'I've got a bee in my bonnet.'

'About Edward Vincent?'

'About him and his walking-stick, and if he still lives south of Stamford Hill, not far from Queensbridge Road, Dalston.'

At half-past nine the following morning, Chief Inspector Dobbs and Sergeant Ross were received by the general manager of the Stamford Hill stores. Agreeing to help them with their enquiries, he informed them that Mr Edward Vincent had been promoted from floorwalker to departmental manager in 1895, but left seven weeks ago. He also confided to the CID men that Mr Vincent had been acting peculiarly for months prior to giving notice.

'Peculiarly?' said Sergeant Ross.

'He referred to every matter as trivial, he referred to the store itself as trivial, and that he had more important things to do. We invited him to resign, and that was when he gave notice.'

'I'd be obliged if you'd let us have his address,' said Dobbs.

'Under the circumstances, I've no objection,' said the general manager, and gave the address as Flat two, nineteen Downs Park Road, Hackney Downs.

After a few more questions and answers, the Chief Inspector and Sergeant Ross took themselves off to the address. Flat two was empty. Ross went into action and sprang the lock of the door. They entered. The first thing of interest they came across was a collection of books on the case of Jack the Ripper. The next was a folded raincoat of water-proofed gaberdine in a small suitcase tightly lodged beneath a standing wardrobe. The coat was badly bloodstained, and it reeked.

'Bloody 'orrible,' said Ross.

'Quite correct, my lad, bloody 'orrible, and smells like it too,' said Dobbs. 'But I think we can now say we know why that walking-stick looks battered and bruised. We'll call in at the Dalston police station on our way back to the Yard.'

Since the case of the woman beaten to death had not yet been solved, the Dalston police received Chief Inspector Dobbs and all that he had to tell them with evident relief. While reminding him that one of his Yard colleagues, Inspector Duggan, was in charge of the case, they allowed him to retain the raincoat. That is, he refrained from parting with it for the time being.

'Good God,' said the Chief Superintendent of Scotland Yard. 'Oxberry is a man called Edward Vincent, once known to your wife and employed by the Stamford Hill stores up to seven weeks ago?'

'I'm certain of it,' said Dobbs.

'Hold on, Charlie, you mean you haven't established it as fact yet?'

'Not yet,' said Dobbs. 'He's a bachelor, lives by himself near Hackney Downs usually, and Mr Harold Newcombe, general manager of the Stamford Hill stores, will be arriving at the Yard early this afternoon to say hello to him.'

'You suspect him now of the Dalston murder?'

'I suspect there's a nasty reason for the blood-stains on a raincoat of his. It was found in his flat and has his name on an inside label.'

'D'you think you can break him today?'

'I'll know when I have.'

'When he offers a confession?'

'More like when his scar turns livid and he asks for the help of a solicitor.'

'I'll leave him to you, Charlie.'

Jarvis Oxberry, demanding civilized treatment, had been shaved by a barber. Accordingly, when he was brought up from his cell, he looked smooth-chinned and self-satisfied. His manner was that of a seemingly unworried man, and he said good afternoon to Chief Inspector Dobbs and Inspector Davis. Sergeant Ross sat to one side, ready to continue taking notes.

''Ad a good night, sir?' asked Inspector Davis.

'As good as that fellow, I daresay,' said Oxberry, nodding at the Chief Inspector. 'Do you intend to carry on with this farce?'

'We don't have any alternative,' said Dobbs. 'Let's see now, where were you living before you took rented rooms with the Pritchards?'

'Oh, here and there, in various lodgings.'

'And what was your last address before you moved in with the Pritchards?'

'I've no idea. I've used so many addresses that I can pin-point none, except my present one: Scotland Yard. Oh, and the Pritchards' house, of course. When can I expect to be released?'

'As soon as we've eliminated you from our enquiries,' said Dobbs, looking friendly. 'Now, sir, regarding a capital crime committed in early October in Queensbridge Road, Dalston, I wonder if you can help us with that. A woman was beaten to death late at night. A witness—'

'Sod you, Dobbs.' The interruptive oath arrived crushingly. 'You jump about like a flea-ridden kangaroo. I'm not in the least interested in what might have happened in Dalston, and even if I were, you'd get no help from me.'

'I've a feeling you don't like me very much,' said Dobbs.

'Does anybody?' Oxberry was caustic again.

'Well,' said Dobbs on a cheerful note, 'there's my wife, Mrs Daphne Dobbs, who lets me know on my birthdays that she's still fairly fond of me.'

The mouth shut tight, and the pink scar flushed. Dobbs knew he'd struck a telling blow. At least, he sensed he had.

'Really?' There were vibrations in the voice. 'You surprise me.'

'It's sometimes a surprise to me,' said Dobbs affably, 'but it's always comforting. Where was I? Yes, there's a witness, a young man, who passed a couple misbehaving themselves in a shop doorway just off Queensbridge Road. It—'

'Don't go on, you tiresome man.'

'It won't take long,' said Dobbs. 'The time was about eleven, the night dark, but the young man saw what was going on with the help of a little light from a street lamp. He noted the woman had red hair. He also noted they'd been seen by another man, who'd been walking ahead of him. The woman—'

'Damn the woman and you too,' said Oxberry bitingly.

'She was found dead at two in the morning in Queensbridge Road by a constable on night beat. She was a widow of thirty-three, who was known to – um – ply her trade in the area. A Mrs Amelia Fairbanks. The man—'

'Give it a rest,' said Oxberry.

'The man who'd been seen with her in the shop

doorway, and was naturally under suspicion, came forward the following evening to clear himself of her murder. She was brutally beaten to death, her skull cracked in two places, her face and neck gashed, and up to now her murderer hasn't been found.'

'Your incompetence is your own affair,' said Oxberry, 'and I repeat, I'm not in the least interested in the matter. I'm not even interested in why you're telling me about it. Can we get down to the fact that you're unable to charge me with any offences, since you have no real proof in each of the cases you've mentioned?'

'That's a reasonable request, and I won't say it isn't,' said Dobbs. 'But first, let me say in regard to the Queensbridge Road murder that we now think the man who preceded the witness stopped at some point and tucked himself away. We think he waited until the man and woman in the shop doorway had parted, and that he then followed the woman until he was able to attack her in Queensbridge Road, stunning her with the first blow of his walking-stick, and then finishing her off.'

Oxberry looked at Inspector Davis.

'Can't you arrange for this man Dobbs to be taken away and put in a straitjacket?' he asked. 'He's quite mad.'

'Well, the point is, sir, is his madness useful to the Yard or not?' said Davis. 'There's this small suitcase, y'see, and what's in it.' He shifted a mackintosh that was lying over the seat of a chair. The removal of the mackintosh uncovered the suitcase, which he picked up and placed on the table. He opened it, showing it contained a folded raincoat. He took it up and shook it out. The garment was thick with dried blood, its condition vile, its smell noxious. 'Look at that, sir, don't you call that ruddy awful?'

Oxberry, who had regarded the disclosure of the suitcase and the raincoat tight-lipped, did not falter.

'I call it disgusting,' he said. 'Who owns it? Dobbs? I'd burn it.'

'Yes, why didn't you do that?' asked Dobbs. 'Was it because it would have made a Godalmighty stink?'

'You really are mad,' said Oxberry.

'Well, that's not as bad as being a calculating executioner of harmless women,' said Dobbs. 'I've not met many like you, Mr Edward Vincent.'

Oxberry grew rigid.

'You stupid fellow,' he said, 'you suffer from the imagination of a raving idiot.'

'Well, we think this is your raincoat, sir,' said Inspector Davis. 'It was found at your flat in Downs Park Road, south of Stamford Hill.'

'I'm entirely detached from Downs Park Road, wherever it is.'

Inspector Davis exposed the inside of the coat and a sewn label.

'There you are, sir. E. J. Vincent is the name on the label. For the interest of dry cleaners, I presume?'

'Ask Mr E. J. Vincent, whoever he is. My name is Oxberry. Take that relic away. Its smell is disgusting.'

'There's something else,' said Dobbs, and the walking-stick appeared. He placed it on the table. 'That's yours, sir, found in your lodgings. Bruised and battered, you might say. It takes a lot to put dents in ebony, and the silver handle's had a hard time too. What's made the stick look so sorry for itself?'

'Wear and tear, you brainless sod,' hissed the suspect, red flushing his scar.

'Well, sir,' said Davis, 'the fact is – wait, hold on a tick, there's someone at the door.' He moved and opened the door. The waiting Mr Harold Newcombe, general manager of the Stamford Hill stores, stepped in. He glanced at the man seated at the table, and affected surprise.

'Good Lord, what are you doing here, Mr Vincent?'

'Damn you, Dobbs, you bloody creep!' shouted Edward Vincent.

'Sorry, Mr Newcombe,' said Dobbs, 'but would you mind leaving us for a while?'

'Of course,' said Mr Newcombe, and left. Inspector Davis closed the door. He turned and saw the suspect glaring at Chief Inspector Dobbs, his scar an angry crimson.

'Feelin' a bit upset, are you, sir?' he said.

'Damn you too,' hissed Vincent.

'I suppose you're slightly embarrassed,' said Dobbs. 'Well, it can't be helped sometimes. And I'm probably going to make things worse by suggesting you were the man the witness saw ahead of him, that you'd seen the red-haired woman earning a street-walker's fee in the shop doorway, and that you subsequently made your first killing. Because she was a prostitute, you saw yourself as a second Ripper and used a knife on your other victims. Is that right, Mr Vincent?'

'Go to hell,' said Vincent, 'you can't prove a thing, you can't even prove my name's not

Oxberry.' He seemed in control of himself again, but his scar was still a tell-tale red.

'Oh, I think you're Edward Vincent all right,' said Dobbs. 'Your former employer, Mr Harold Newcombe, recognized you. And let's see, you once knew my wife, didn't you? When she was Miss Daphne Wells?'

'Now you're gibbering.' The words were forced through tight lips.

'You didn't come to the wedding,' said Dobbs. 'Sorry about that, you missed seeing Daphne looking – well, I'd say radiant. Oh, here's a photograph of her and her family.' He placed it on the table. 'And you're in it yourself. You were younger then, of course. So was Daphne. But she's still a lovely woman, and we've two lovely kids, a boy and a girl. Recognize yourself, Mr Vincent?'

The scar flamed to a livid purple, the mouth shut rigidly tight, and then ferocious breath escaped. Vincent leapt to his feet, seized the photograph, ripped it to pieces and flung them at Dobbs.

'You bastard, you stole that woman from me, and may you freeze in hell for it! And may she rot, as she will if I can get my knife at her neck!'

'Tell us about your knife and the books about the case of Jack the Ripper,' said Dobbs.

'I will, believe me I will! I—' Vincent stopped and pulled at his jacket, his noisy breathing subsiding. It took him some time to regain control of himself, then he regarded the Chief Inspector with cold hatred before turning to Inspector Davis. 'I can't stand this fellow Dobbs,' he said, 'and would prefer to put a request to you, Inspector. Would you arrange for me to see my solicitor?'

'Would that be first thing tomorrow, sir?' asked Davis.

'Now.' Temper leapt again. 'Now, damn you, now!'

'Have we got him or not, guv?' asked Sergeant Ross later.

'I think you can say so, my lad,' said Dobbs.

'There's still a lot of circumstantial evidence,' said Ross, 'and his counsel will jump on it.'

'They can jump all they like,' said Dobbs, 'but not on that overcoat, stiff with the blood of his first victim, you can lay to it.'

'It'll make you happy, will it, guv, just to get him for the Dalston murder?'

'I'll get him for the lot, sunshine,' said Dobbs. 'We'll release Archie Binns and let Fleet Street know of these new and final developments. I say final with confidence, since I'll show Edward Vincent a photograph of Mrs Dobbs on her wedding day when we interview him tomorrow morning with his solicitor. I'm in the photograph myself this time. He'll explode, you mark my words, and that's when we'll get him for the lot.'

'I'll have a quid on you, guv, even if I can only get odds of two to one,' said Ross.

'Give Archie Binns five bob to buy himself hot meat pies and mash twice a day for a week,' said Dobbs, 'and thank him for being our guest. Then take the rest of the day off. Pop round and see Nurse Cartright at her hospital. Take her a bunch of flowers.'

'Well, guv—'

'At my expense. And while you're doing your

313

stuff, treat her as well to a Scotch joke. A funny one, if you can manage it.'

'Don't think I can,' said Ross, 'except three Scotsmen once went to church. Just before the collection plate reached them, one fainted and the other two carried him out. Any good, guv?'

'Not very, and it'll upset Scotland,' said Dobbs. 'Try an Irish one.'

'I'll make do with the bunch of flowers,' said Ross.

The following morning, in the presence of his solicitor, Edward Vincent, after parrying a series of questions with controlled answers of an oblique kind, went suddenly berserk. Chief Inspector Dobbs had thrust a wedding photograph under his nose.

He condemned himself then out of a raging mouth, despite all warnings from his solicitor.

The woman in Dalston had asked for it, plying her filthy trade in public. The Ripper himself would have been delighted to execute her. As for Maureen Flanagan, that Irish tart had had the brazen effrontery to regard him as a friend merely because of one or two conversations he had had with her about the green lushness of Ireland. It had been the easiest thing in the world to follow her out one evening and discover she was a West End streetwalker. When she accepted an invitation to spend a discreet hour with him on the evening of her row with Pritchard, she also accepted an offer of ten pounds to go to bed with him, providing extreme discretion was exercised. He executed her from behind as soon as she removed her coat. She bled disgustingly, and i

314

took him a damned long time to clean everything up, using her own clothes and underwear. He dressed her in clean apparel he found in her wardrobe and took her corpse to Tooley Street sometime after midnight.

Poppy Simpson? Another obscene specimen, well deserving of the knife, well deserving of the Ripper himself.

All this came out of the raging mouth accompanied by froth and spittle, and ended with an attempt to throttle Chief Inspector Dobbs, who brought his knee up into the man's stomach and laid him low and gasping.

He was then charged with three murders and an attempted murder.

Charlie Dobbs, resurgent with well-being that night, made overtures to Daphne.

'Heavens, Charlie, what's brought this on?'

'Don't you know, Daffie? All work and no play makes me a dull old codger.'

'Well, I'm not sure what the Queen would say to that kind of levity within the more sacred realms of marriage, Charlie, but as I don't intend to ask her, play up and play the game, then.'

Having obtained the key from the landlord on Saturday, Bridget took Daisy and Billy across the river on Sunday to see the house in Pocock Street.

It was in good order, and Daisy liked the condition of the kitchen wallpaper. Billy liked the back yard, much larger than their present one. Bridget liked the fact that all the rooms, three up, three down, were larger. And they all liked the front bay window and the railed gate.

'We could 'ave an aspidistra in the parlour,' said Daisy.

'I could still do me grocery job,' said Billy. 'I could get up earlier till I got taken on by a Blackfriars grocer behind the counter.'

'Er, what about—' Daisy paused. 'Well, I mean, what about Fred?'

'Who?' asked Bridget darkly.

'Him that's our present lodger,' said Daisy bravely.

'Constable Fred,' said Billy.

'Who's he?' asked Bridget.

'It's him, like Daisy just mentioned,' said Billy.

'Oh, 'im,' said Bridget.

'We ought to ask 'im if he'd like to move wiv us,' said Billy.

'Well, I ain't askin' him meself,' said Bridget, 'he's still a copper and it's against me principles to ask any copper.'

'Oh, it ain't against my principles,' said Daisy.

'I know what's goin' to 'appen,' said Bridget. 'You and Billy will sneak 'im in behind me back, like you did before. Oh, well, I can't wear meself out arguin' with you, I'll 'ave to put up with it. And I suppose 'e could be a bit useful, he's actu'lly not a bad cook, and he can take a turn at doin' the washin' and ironing.'

'Bridget, you can't ask Fred to do washin' and ironing,' protested Daisy.

'I ain't goin' to ask 'im,' said Bridget, 'I'm goin' to tell 'im, and if 'e gets contradict'ry, I'll down 'im. I'll put up with 'im being a copper, but not with 'im gettin' my goat and chuckin' 'is weight about. I won't stand for a lot of that. Lord only knows what might 'appen if I let 'im get on top of me.'

316

Daisy yelled with laughter. Billy grinned all over his face.

'Bridget,' he said, 'wouldn't Fred 'ave to marry you first?'

It was a pity he said that, for he was having to run for his life seconds later.

THE END

THE TRAP
by Mary Jane Staples

When James Blair, twenty-four, unemployed, and back from the trenches, took lodgings at Larcom Street in Walworth, he had no idea he was walking into a trap.

The house was owned by Henry Mullins, big, burly, and a hard drinker. Henry made life hell for his four step-children who looked half starved and frequently got bashed. Seventeen-year-old Kitty was the one Jamie felt most sorry for. She took the brunt of Henry Mullins' bad temper whilst trying to protect her sisters and brother.

When Mullins suddenly died – in somewhat suspicious circumstances – Kitty realised they could be in trouble. If she wasn't careful the authorities would take the younger children away – split the family up. She wasn't having that, not after all they'd gone through, and nice, kind Jamie Blair was the one to save them.

Too late Jamie found himself with a ready-made family and a stubborn and fiery young termagant called Kitty who was determined not to let him go.

0 552 14106 2

THE LAST SUMMER
by Mary Jane Staples

Job and Jemima Hardy weren't Londoners by birth. They had both lived in a Sussex village until lack of work had sent Job and the family to Walworth – to a house in Stead Street. They got it cheap because of the poltergeist but they were sensible folk and decided that eight shillings a week rent was a bargain and – well – if the floors and doors sometimes moved a bit, they could live with it. They settled quickly into London life – particularly Jonathan, the eldest. Jonathan got a job at Camberwell Green and it was there, in Lyons teashop, that he met Emma Somers, niece of Boots Adams. Over a long and hazy summer – the summer of 1939 – the two young people met, always at lunchtime, and never allowing their friendship to progress too far.

Then, as the clouds of war gathered over Europe, Jonathan got his call-up papers. And the first alarms of conflict began to affect the Adams family in other ways. Boots, on the Officer's reserve list, was called onto the staff of General Sir Henry Simms, and Polly Simms herself joined the Auxiliaries. Suddenly there was only a little time left for people to lead ordinary lives – and Jonathan Hardy and Emma Somers had to make decisions about their future.

Here again is the Adams family from *Down Lambeth Way*, *Our Emily*, *King of Camberwell*, *On Mother Brown's Doorstep*, *A Family Affair*, *Missing Person*, *Pride of Walworth*, *Echoes of Yesterday* and *The Camberwell Raid*.

0 552 14513 0

A SELECTED LIST OF FINE NOVELS
AVAILABLE FROM CORGI BOOKS

14049	X	THE JERICHO YEARS	Aileen Armitage	£4.99
13992	0	LIGHT ME THE MOON	Angela Arney	£4.99
14309	X	THE KERRY DANCE	Louise Brindley	£5.99
14097	X	SEA MISTRESS	Iris Gower	£5.99
14141	0	PARADISE LANE	Ruth Hamilton	£5.99
14297	2	ROSY SMITH	Janet Haslam	£4.99
14220	4	CAPEL BELLS	Joan Hessayon	£4.99
13910	6	BLUEBIRDS	Margaret Mayhew	£5.99
13904	1	VOICES OF SUMMER	Diane Pearson	£4.99
14123	2	THE LONDONERS	Margaret Pemberton	£4.99
14057	0	THE BRIGHT ONE	Elvi Rhodes	£4.99
14466	5	TOUCHED BY ANGELS	Susan Sallis	£5.99
13951	3	SERGEANT JOE	Mary Jane Staples	£3.99
13845	2	RISING SUMMER	Mary Jane Staples	£3.99
13299	3	DOWN LAMBETH WAY	Mary Jane Staples	£4.99
13573	9	KING OF CAMBERWELL	Mary Jane Staples	£4.99
13730	8	THE LODGER	Mary Jane Staples	£4.99
13444	9	OUR EMILY	Mary Jane Staples	£4.99
13635	2	TWO FOR THREE FARTHINGS		
			Mary Jane Staples	£4.99
13856	8	THE PEARLY QUEEN	Mary Jane Staples	£4.99
13975	0	ON MOTHER BROWN'S DOORSTEP		
			Mary Jane Staples	£4.99
14106	2	THE TRAP	Mary Jane Staples	£4.99
14154	2	A FAMILY AFFAIR	Mary Jane Staples	£4.99
14230	1	MISSING PERSON	Mary Jane Staples	£4.99
14291	3	PRIDE OF WALWORTH	Mary Jane Staples	£4.99
14375	8	ECHOES OF YESTERDAY	Mary Jane Staples	£4.99
14418	5	THE YOUNG ONES	Mary Jane Staples	£4.99
14469	X	THE CAMBERWELL RAID	Mary Jane Staples	£4.99
14513	0	THE LAST SUMMER	Mary Jane Staples	£4.99
14118	6	THE HUNGRY TIDE	Valerie Wood	£4.99